Fangtooth

Shaun Jeffrey

Published in 2013

Edited by Stacey Turner

Cover by Karri Klawiter

.

For Brenda and Darren

Chapter 1

The trawler *Silver Queen* plunged through the relentless waves, plaything of the Gods. Wood creaked and squealed, crying like an animal in pain as the boat plummeted from the top of a swell.

"What the hell is it?" Howser asked.

Billy Trasker looked up from the echo sounder and shook his head. "It might be a large school of fish ... but to be honest, I'm not sure."

Howser frowned at the display. It was all do to him. His wife, Maureen, had only recently dragged him into the technological age of mobile phones. That's why he employed people. But sometimes, a man had to go with his feelings, and this was one of those times.

He picked up the microphone from the panel. "Blunt, secure that buoy," he shouted, his voice coming through the speaker outside and fighting to be heard above the cry of the force eight gale.

The men on deck hurried about their jobs, working with proficiency gained from years of toil at sea. The wind howled around their ears, but they seemed oblivious to its roar.

Billy scratched his unshaven chin. He indicated a large, jagged line on the colour LCD display. "I've never seen a school of fish produce a pattern like that before."

Howser glanced at the display, but it still didn't make any sense to him. Waves as high as double-decker buses crashed against the bow, making the vessel appear about to sink. Howser struggled to keep the boat on course. After months of finding no fish, he wasn't going to let a little bad weather and a technological blip stop him from landing what looked like the biggest haul the villagers back home in Mulberry would have seen in years.

Howser rang the alarm bell three times to alert the deck crew he was going to shoot the nets.

Seconds later the motors whined as the net descended into the icy depths, and Howser slowed the boat to two knots to compensate for the drag.

"We should get a better indication about what it is from the net recorder now that they're in the water," Billy said.

Howser nodded. He knew the basics of what the equipment did, and the net recorder worked alongside the colour echo sounder to give specific information on the net and the fish moving into it. Experienced skippers could tell not only how much fish they had, but also what kind they were catching. Again, Howser left that to the likes of Billy. All he wanted to know was when to haul it aboard.

"So what we looking at?"

Billy frowned and pressed a couple of buttons. He shook his head. "I haven't got a clue."

"Then what the hell do I pay you for?"

Before Billy could answer, a huge wave swept over the bow, knocking a man on deck off his feet.

Howser snatched up the microphone. "You okay, Blunt?"

The man struggled to his feet and gave a thumbs up.

Without warning, the boat lurched in the water, the net having caught on something. Howser ground his teeth. This was all he needed. The hydraulic clutch to the winches whined.

The wheelhouse door opened with a clatter and Blunt stepped into the room, his body moving in time to the waves, in tune with the rhythm of the sea.

"Skipper, we've got a problem. The starboard trawl wire's leading across the afterdeck to port and the spare net's blocking the freeing ports, so we're taking on water fast."

Howser was about to respond when the vessel lurched to port. He gripped the wheel as tight as he could.

Wave after wave crashed over the boat.

Despite the seriousness of the situation, Howser felt calm. He clenched his teeth. "See if you can help free the trawl wire."

Blunt nodded and staggered outside.

Another wave rolled across the boat, smashing down like a giant fist. Through the spray, Howser saw Blunt sliding across the deck, but there was someone beside him. Even with the wipers going, visibility through the windscreen was poor. *Who the fuck is that out there?* At a glance, the figure didn't look natural. Although hunched over, even from a distance it looked stocky; the spray distorted the scene further, made the figure look deformed.

Howser frowned and picked up the microphone. "Blunt," he shouted. "Who's that with you?"

Blunt turned.

Next minute, the figure beside Blunt lunged forwards. The hands on the end of its stubby looking arms latched onto Blunt and it opened its mouth impossibly wide and bit the deckhand's throat. Blood gushed out, turning pink as it spread across the deck.

Howser gagged. *What the hell is going on out there?*

In his fright, he let go of the wheel, allowing it to spin like something possessed, and the hull of the boat squealed as the sea contracted against it.

Regaining his composure, Howser strapped himself into the chair, reached out to grab the wheel and the boat listed violently. The vessel seemed to teeter on its side for a moment, then rolled over like a dog offering its hull to the malevolent Gods to scratch. Unsecured equipment rained down on the ceiling. Hanging upside down, Howser felt the blood rush to his head. The vessel's lights illuminated the turbulent sea, highlighting Blunt's face as it smashed against the glass. Scraps of skin flapped on the deckhand's cheeks like grotesque gills.

What the fuck has happened out there?

Next minute something sleek and black snatched Blunt's body away. Howser stared aghast at the swirl of bloody water beyond the glass.

He reached up to undo the harness securing him to the chair, and the glass around the wheelhouse shattered as gallons of water gushed in.

With the water came something else. Something that moved with ease through the swirling current.

The force of the water gushing through the broken windows pressed Howser into his chair. He felt as though he were in a washing machine filled with glass shards slicing his flesh. He tried to move, but the force of water pinned him more securely than shackles.

Something swam past his face, something that danced in the turbulent currents. Too afraid to close his eyes, he stared through the stinging water. Blood from cuts on his face swirled around his head, hampering visibility. His lungs felt about to burst. He needed to undo the harness and swim to the surface. No way was this captain going down with his boat.

With a final desperate attempt to move, he managed to raise his right hand and grab the buckle, but the last of his breath gushed out in a gargled scream of absolute terror as the thing that had entered the wheelhouse swam into view.

He gagged and saltwater filled his lungs, but death didn't come quick enough to relieve him of the horror of the creature closing in for the kill.

Chapter 2

"So what do you think, Jack?"

When he didn't receive a reply, Bruce Holden looked across at his son. He'd forgotten Jack had his earphones in, the volume on his mp3 player cranked up. He tapped him on the leg.

Jack pulled one of the earphones out, the tinny sound of The Prodigy filtering through. "What?" he snapped as he peered from beneath the brow of his baseball cap.

Bruce pointed at the view. "What do you think?"

"I think it's a crock of shit and I want to go home."

Despite his son's sharp rebuttal, Bruce held his tongue. He gazed down through the windscreen of his Ford Focus at the small fishing village. The whitewashed wooden houses looked like a picture postcard, and the array of fishing boats moored to the horseshoe shaped harbour looked almost toy-like from so high up. It had always been his dream to live by the sea; a dream he'd shared with Veronica until the cancer took the light from her eyes and the life from her body. Knowing she wasn't here to share it with him brought a sudden tear that he quickly wiped away.

The wedding ring on his finger glistened in the sunlight.

"It won't be that bad. Just think, you can meet new people; find new things to do, walk Shazam along the beach."

At the mention of her name, the black and white Border Collie barked and sat up in the back. She poked her head between the front seats, her tongue lolling.

Jack grimaced. "That sounds just great. It's alright for you. You're nearly an old man. You'll enjoy walking on the beach and shit like that. Look at it. There's nothing here."

"For your information, thirty-seven is not old, and if you say shit again, I'll—"

"What? Send me to my room? Hit me? I'm sixteen, old enough to do what I want."

9

Bruce sighed. *Sixteen going on sixty.* "You never know, you might like it."

"Like hell I will."

Bruce put the car in gear, eased off the clutch and started driving. The lucky horseshoe pendant hanging from the rearview mirror swung back and forth. He had removed it from Veronica's neck when she died; now it never came out of the car.

After three hours at the wheel, his shoulders ached, and he was eager to stretch his legs. He'd known Jack would find it hard moving, but after Veronica's death, and having found pot in his son's bedroom, he knew he had to get him away from London. Jack had gotten in with a bad crowd.

Then two months ago, Bruce noticed the ad for the house while redesigning an estate agent's website. It was like an omen, a sign from God. Next thing he knew, he'd made an offer, had it accepted, and now he was moving hundreds of miles across the country to a house he'd not yet stepped foot in. There were too many memories in the city, but they had turned sour, left a bitter taste in his mouth.

The road to the village of Mulberry snaked down the side of a mountain dotted with sheep. Cattle guards set in the road to stop the sheep straying made the car shudder, aggravating Bruce's aching shoulders and back.

He glanced at the field, saw the remains of a sheep that had been dragged through a barbed wire fence. A crow sat pecking at the remnants.

A few houses lined the road into the village, but the remainder clustered together behind the harbour.

He parked at the side of the road to consult the map the estate agent sent him. "Not far now."

"Great."

Bruce started driving again. He lowered the window a fraction, inhaled the briny air. Shazam poked her nose through the gap, dribbling saliva down the glass.

The road ran alongside the harbour where a couple of men sat fishing from the quay, and a couple of other men dragged lobster pots on board their boat. At the sound of the approaching car, the men looked up. Bruce nodded his head towards them as he drove past, but the men ignored him and returned to their tasks.

"Friendly bunch," Jack said.

"They're probably busy."

"Yeah, that *must* be what it was. Why don't you admit it? This place is s-h-i-t."

"Just stop, Jack. We're here now, and this is where we're going to stay."

A couple of shops stood on the main road. Buckets and spades decorated the outside of one, along with kites, beach balls, and a whole host of other holiday paraphernalia. Many of the items were faded—as though they had been on display for a long time.

A couple of narrow side streets snaked off the main road, but Bruce continued on for another quarter mile before taking a right turn onto a narrow, hedge lined lane opposite a small, sandy cove. The house sat a hundred yards further up the lane, recognisable by the 'for sale' sign hammered into the garden. No one had even bothered putting a sold sign across it. Of the moving van, there was no sign.

Bruce parked the car in the single drive and switched the ignition off. "Well, this is it." He crouched in his seat to look up at the detached house. It looked fantastic. The photographs hadn't done it justice. It needed work, the paint peeling and the wooden façade cracked in a couple of places, but what a bargain. "Isn't it great?"

Jack reinserted his earphones and turned the volume up.

Bruce clucked his tongue and exited the car. He stretched his arms and rotated his shoulders a couple of times.

A bark from the vehicle alerted him to Shazam, and he reached down and opened the back door. The dog bounded out and started sniffing around the ground before relieving herself.

A low hedge separated the house from the lane, which served to hide the weed riddled front garden from passersby. From his vantage point he could see the small cove, and in the distance, the harbour. The perfect scene quite literally

11

took his breath away. His only regret was that Veronica wasn't here to share it with them.

Sometimes when he looked at Jack, he saw Veronica looking back. He had the same brown eyes as his mother, the same cheeky grin, and the same lustrous, black hair, although Jack liked to keep his cut short. With so much of Veronica in Jack's features, Bruce felt there was no room left for any of his aspects. The only thing he thought his son inherited from him was his stubborn streak.

He quickly wiped his eyes and then turned his attention back to the house.

Bruce took the key from his pocket and tapped on the car window. When he remembered Jack had his earphones surgically inserted, he opened the door.

Jack looked up and removed his earphones. "What now?"

"I just wondered whether you'd like to open the door to our new home."

"Whoopee. I can hardly contain myself." He slid out of the car, snatched the key and loped towards the building.

Bruce smiled. Given time, Jack would grow to like it here. Hell, he might even appreciate it one day.

"The door's already open," Jack said, stepping into the house.

Bruce frowned. Talk about security. Anyone could have broken in. A moment later, he followed Jack inside. The first thing he noticed was the smell, an aroma of dampness and mildew.

Despite the price tag of his new home, he still had money in his pocket from the sale of his house in the city, which sold on the first day.

He stood in the hallway and ran his hand down the old-fashioned, flowery wallpaper. It felt damp, almost slimy. Old newspapers littered the bare wooden floorboards and junk mail had bred behind the door.

"You don't really expect us to sleep here?" Jack said.

"It won't be that bad."

"That's what you said about Tenerife, remember?"

Bruce couldn't forget. In an attempt to bond with his son, and to cheer them both up after Veronica's death, he had arranged a holiday. It had been an unmitigated disaster from start to finish. The flight had been delayed by a day, the hotel was next to a work site where the workers never seemed to put down their tools, and there was an all-night disco situated next door, out of which spilled a succession of drunken youths intent on making as much noise as possible. On top of that, the Spanish food upset Bruce's stomach and he was confined to bed for two days, leaving Jack to his own devices. He never did find out what that girl had been doing in their apartment at four in the morning.

Bruce waved his hand dismissively. "Well, this time I mean it."

A couple of doors lead off the hallway, and at the end, a staircase sat draped in shadows. Bright oblongs on the walls revealed where pictures had once hung. Bruce located the light switch, but when he flicked it, nothing happened. "They mustn't have turned the electricity on yet."

"Great. We haven't just moved to a village at the edge of the universe, but we've also gone back in time to the Stone Age."

"It's not that bad."

"Nothing ever is with you."

Ignoring the sarcasm in his son's voice, Bruce walked towards the first door when he heard a sharp bang that froze him in his tracks. The sound originated from the room to his right. He remembered the unlocked door. There was nothing worth stealing in the house, but what if some kids had broken in? His heart started beating faster.

"Who's there?" he shouted. Receiving no reply, he grabbed the door handle and braced himself.

"What was it, dad?"

Bruce held his hand up to indicate silence. Another bang reverberated from the room.

He imagined it might only be a bird or another animal that had taken up residence in the house, anything rather than thinking there was an intruder. He took a deep breath, exhaled and opened the door.

The room was empty. Bruce sighed with relief. He needed a drink. The bang rang out again, making him jump, and he looked across to see an unfastened window.

"It was just the window banging."

Watermarks and bits of underlay marred the bare floorboards. Someone had daubed black doodles on the blue painted walls. Upon closer inspection, the doodles became grotesque faces with elongated teeth. Bruce shivered. The sooner he started decorating, the better.

Bruce stepped into the room and a floorboard creaked underfoot. He had a sudden recollection of the film *The Money Pit*, and wondered whether he had bought a similar white elephant.

He turned to walk back out, when a figure stepped out from behind the door and grabbed his wrist.

Bruce's heart almost stopped. His eyes failed to adjust in time to identify his attacker, leaving the figure a blur of orange and green.

He gagged, raised his free arm to defend himself.

"So you're the one," a woman's harsh voice said.

"Who the hell's that?" Jack shouted as he ran into the room.

Bruce focused on his assailant. Saw a stick-thin, bitter faced woman aged anywhere between fifty and seventy. She was dressed in a pale orange dress, over which she wore a green cardigan that had seen better days. Two grey streaks marred her long black hair. Liver spots dotted the back of the clawed hand that gripped his wrist, the tendons standing proud as though steel rods had been inserted beneath her skin.

The woman's piercing grey eyes made Bruce think of storm clouds. Her thin, pursed lips created a gash in the vitriolic mask of her face.

Bruce found his voice. "What the hell are you doing here?"

He grabbed her wrist and tried to prise her fingers off, but despite her age and frail appearance, the woman's claws held tight.

"A nice catch," she hissed.

"Get your stinking hands off my dad," Jack screamed, his face reflecting his confusion.

The woman narrowed her eyes, snorted loudly, then released her grip. Bruce massaged his wrist where her fingers had stopped the flow of blood. "What are you doing in my house? Get the hell out," he said, trying to sound calmer than he felt.

The woman laughed, then turned and hurried away through the door. Bruce watched her go. His pulse raced and he could feel the blood had drained from his face.

"Shit. Are you okay, dad?"

Bruce nodded without conviction. The woman had shaken him more than he liked to admit.

Seconds later, Shazam came clicking along the hallway with her tongue lolling. "Some good you were," Bruce said.

Jack shook his head and reinserted his earphones. "Remember Tenerife."

Chapter 3

Waves crashed over the bow of the 70ft trawler *Storm Bringer*. Trent Zander steered the vessel head on into the wind, the harness strapping him into the chair digging in as the bow smashed through the water. In weather like this, a skipper had to put his trust in the engineer. Zander knew Brad was one of the best, and he would keep the ship's engines turning over no matter what. That's why he hired him. Shockwaves reverberated through the hull as the bow sliced through the waves, *Storm Bringer's* main stern searchlight illuminating a whiteout spray of swirling streaks of foam.

Zander pushed the throttle forward, the bow of the boat thumping monotonously against the surface of the water. Beyond the insulated wheelhouse, wind screamed around the boat.

The door crashed open, letting the banshee roar inside. "What do you reckon today?" Jim asked as he leaned into the wheelhouse, his lips hidden behind a bushy beard streaked with grey and his dark eyes as lifeless as those of the fish they hauled from the deep.

"We'll go around the head and try our luck."

Jim shook his head. "If it's luck you're after, I suggest playing the lottery. If it's fish you're after, I suggest going further out."

Zander scratched his stubbled chin, the bristles of which were only slightly shorter than the brown hair on his head. Jim had a lot more experience under his belt; had been fishing these waters for nearly forty years, which showed in the brown coarseness of his skin and the hardened blisters on his hands, but Zander didn't like to let his crew dictate, not when he was skipper. Thrusting his angular chin out and gritting his teeth, he said, "I'll make that decision."

Jim snorted loudly, turned aside and spat a wad of phlegm that stuck in his beard before the wind caught it and whisked it away. "You're the boss."

16

Zander watched him turn and leave. *You got that right.*

The screens for the echo sounders and all the other electrical equipment around the wheelhouse washed everything in a pale light. First Mate Nigel Muldoon's chubby cheeks looked sickly pale in the glow. But Zander knew that wasn't the only reason for his pallid appearance. Muldoon's brother-in-law, Dawson, had been on board the *Silver Queen* when she went down with all hands the other week, the painful loss still a raw wound to the family. When you die at sea, you're gone. Those left behind have nowhere to go to pay their respects.

He couldn't understand why a competent old sea dog like Howser hadn't radioed for help. It didn't make any sense. The *Silver Queen* was one-third of Mulberry's fishing fleet, and it had hit the tight knit community like a tsunami. He sensed all the men on board were feeling jittery, but if they didn't sail, then there was no chance of catching any fish. He had never known it to be so bad.

The boat pitched and yawed, and the eardrum-pounding noise from the engines below went up in tone.

Gannets wheeled overhead, brilliant white as they reflected the early morning sun.

Zander hoped and prayed they would catch something today, if only to lift everyone's spirits.

After nearly twenty hours at the wheel, Zander's face was red and blotchy, the skin on his nose peeling. The only time he let anyone else take the helm was when he needed the toilet. The boat and the men on board were his responsibility, and his alone, and he wouldn't pass that burden on to anyone else.

From his position in the wheelhouse, Zander had an unobstructed view of the stern. The controls for the winching equipment were laid out before him, and he worked them with an efficiency gained from years of practice.

Robinson, the youngest of the crew, his blond hair made to appear black as the spray matted it to his head, had one of the most dangerous jobs: securing the otter boards used to keep the mouth of the trawl net open. Any misunderstanding

17

between Robinson and Zander could be fatal. The massive rusted rectangular iron doors clattered against the derricks and Robinson quickly attached the restraining chains.

With the boards secured, Robinson clipped the winch warp into the bridles to take the load, allowing him to disconnect the backstrop linking the bridles to the otter boards.

Zander operated the controls, drawing the bridles onto the drum. Gannets and kittiwakes rode the waves at the side of the net, pecking at the mesh.

The boat laboured, pulling back, and Zander knew they had caught something. He watched the net slide out of the water, snaking in the swell, a green translucent line of mesh.

Lines of foam streaked towards the bow window. Down on deck, Robinson worked tirelessly, only feet away from where the excess water flowed overboard through the large scuppers, drains big enough to let a man slip through.

Zander continued to work the controls, but he sensed something wasn't right. The previous sense of drag had gone and he had to adjust the controls to compensate. He watched in anger and frustration as the net rose out of the water, the mesh tattered and shredded. He had seen plenty of nets torn before after being snagged on rocks or shipwrecks on the seabed, but this … this looked as though it had been cut, chewed even.

"Muldoon, take the wheel."

Zander flung open the door to the metal cabinet at his side and yanked out his shotgun. Then he stormed down onto the deck and opened fire at the waves, the act of shooting relieving some of the tension that knotted his muscles.

At his side, the net flapped in the wind, mocking him.

Chapter 4

The first thing Bruce planned to do was change the locks.

He'd solved the electricity problem when he found the fuse box underneath the stairs: the switches had been turned off. Probably a safety precaution.

He looked at his watch. The movers should have been here by now with the furniture. He took out his mobile phone and keyed in the number they had given him. The call was answered on the eighth ring.

"Mr. Holden. Yes, we're stuck in traffic. We'll probably be about another hour at the least."

Bruce's stomach rumbled, reminding him he hadn't eaten since starting out this morning. "No problem. It'll give us time to have dinner. Let me know when you're here." He disconnected the call and put the phone back in his jeans pocket. Hopefully he could find a shop in the village that might have a lock.

Jack squatted against the wall across the other side of the room. Bruce mimed taking the earphones out. "The movers are going to be a while yet. Do you want to see if we can find a bite to eat in the village?"

Jack shrugged. "Whatever." He stood up and walked out of the room without waiting. Bruce followed.

At the door, Bruce took the keys from Jack and ushered Shazam back inside. "You stay here, girl. There's some food and water in your bowls," he said as he locked the door. It might not do any good if someone already had a key, but it made him feel better to leave Shazam on guard.

Jack stood by the car.

"Let's walk instead," Bruce said.

Jack grimaced. "It's miles. I'll drive if you want."

"Not until you're old enough you won't. And it's not that far. The fresh air will do you good. You'll sleep better for it."

Jack rolled his eyes and kicked at the gravel, then started walking with his head bowed.

Bruce fell in step as they walked out of the drive. The cove was visible at the end of the lane and seagulls wheeled noisily overhead. Fluffy white clouds dotted the sky. It was certainly going to be better jogging around here than in the city where he got a mouthful of exhaust fumes every time he inhaled.

The small cove looked like it would be a real sun trap in the summer. High cliffs arched around it, and the sea lapped gently against the sand. A small outcrop of rock protruded from the sea about two hundred feet out. Bruce wasn't a bad swimmer, but he'd never liked swimming in the sea. Hopefully, living here, he could combat his fear. He decided to make the outcrop his target.

He placed a hand on his son's shoulder. "It won't be so bad here, Jack. Not if you give it a chance."

Jack shrugged him off. "Are you asking me or telling me?"

"It's for the best."

Jack dragged his heels. "Not for me it's not. What am I supposed to do out here?"

"There'll be plenty to do, you'll see."

The main road through the village followed the coastline. The village itself curved around the harbour, while a few houses higher up clung like barnacles to the hillside.

One thing that struck Bruce was the peace and quiet. It was like being in a vacuum.

The two anglers were still fishing from the harbour wall, but the boat the other men had been on had sailed. There were a couple of other boats moored up, yachts and rowing boats.

Bruce peered up the side streets they passed, but couldn't spot any shops. On the main road, there was a bar called The Sheet and Anchor, which looked in need of decorating. The sign swung in the slight breeze bidding welcome. A man rolled barrels of beer from the back of a lorry parked outside. The barrels clattered as they rolled along the road before disappearing through a hatch in the pavement outside the premises. Further along was a shop with holiday gifts and buckets and spades, then a small cafe and a hardware shop that also sold gifts.

Bruce headed for the hardware shop. A bell above the door jangled as he entered. Jack trudged in behind him. Just inside the door, racks stocked with chocolate, sweets, postcards and tacky souvenirs held Jack's attention. Beyond these were more shelves filled with household items. "You've picked a nice day for a visit," the man behind the counter said. Bruce smiled; usually it looked more like a grimace, but he could see by his reflection in a seashell-decorated mirror above the counter that this time, he looked genuinely happy.

"Actually, we've just bought the house on Millhouse Lane."

The man raised his eyebrows. "The old Johnson place?"

Bruce frowned. "Yes, that's the one."

"Great. I hope you'll be very happy. My name's Duncan. Duncan Roberts." He held his hand out and Bruce shook it. "Now is there anything in particular you're after?"

Putting Duncan's momentary surprised expression down to the state of the property, Bruce said, "I'm after a new lock for the house."

Duncan stood up from his stool and walked around the counter. He looked a jovial man with a balding grey pate, a round face and rosy cheeks. He carried himself as though well accustomed to his paunch, which didn't stop him squeezing between the shelves to the rear of the shop.

"Here you are. Household locks." He held up two locks in dusty plastic cases. "I've got your standard mortise lock, or there's the five lever deadlock."

"I take it you don't get much call for locks."

"Don't get much call for anything. It's like we've dropped off the map since the new resort opened up the road."

Bruce recalled the lively, arcade-strewn promenade a few miles back up the coast. "I'll take the deadlock, please."

Duncan put one of the locks back on the shelf, then motioned towards Jack. "Is it just the two of you?"

"Yes." He made a point not to mention that his wife had died as it usually elicited fake condolences. He could never understand why people said 'I'm sorry' about someone they never knew.

"You'll find it's quiet around here. Not much goes on, but we're a friendly bunch when you get to know us."

"I don't know about that. When we arrived here there was an old woman in my house ranting and raving."

Duncan's cheeks seemed to go slightly redder. "Did she have two grey streaks in her hair? Thin old woman?"

"Yes, that's her."

"I'd pay her no heed. That's just Lillian Brown. She's what you might call the local fruitcake. Some folk say she's a witch, but then some folk say I'm a Lothario." He winked. "I prefer to think of myself as someone who helps those in need, if you get my meaning. A man in his prime like me can get a lot of action around here."

Bruce couldn't help but smile. "Is there anywhere we can get a bite to eat?"

"We've only just met, so don't get fresh." He winked again. "The bar along the road does a nice meal."

"That sounds great. How much do I owe you for the lock?"

"It's pretty expensive, I'm afraid. £30.00."

"No problem."

They made their way back to the cash register. Jack was standing by the window staring at a bunch of teenagers over by the harbour.

Bruce took out his wallet. As he counted the money, he noticed the four-leafed clover he kept behind the see-through plastic pocket. It had turned dry and brittle, but he couldn't pluck up the courage to throw it away in case it brought bad luck. Next to the clover there was an I Ching coin decorated with Chinese symbols and a tiny silver lucky leprechaun that he'd found on the pavement a few years ago.

After paying for the lock, he thanked Duncan for his help and walked out of the shop with Jack in tow.

"You see, there are young people here too," Bruce said, indicating the small group by the harbour.

Jack screwed his face up.

"Why don't you go and introduce yourself?"

"Are you crazy? They'll think I'm a sad case."

Bruce shrugged. "Come on then, you can keep your old man company and get some dinner."

Jack pulled his cap down to shield his eyes and then followed Bruce to the Sheet and Anchor bar.

Bruce entered first. The interior was brighter and more appealing than the outside suggested. A real fire roared away in the hearth. The walls were freshly painted a pale straw colour and there were plenty of nautical whimsies on the walls, including sharks' jaws, a ship's wheel, an old diving helmet, netting, a harpoon, starfish and shells. The oblong tables had been covered with glass, underneath which were ancient sea charts and examples of how to tie knots.

The barman cleaning glasses behind the counter looked as though he had stepped right out of the pages of *Moby Dick* or *Treasure Island*. A black patch covered his left eye, and he had a thick black beard and bushy eyebrows. He wore a cream coloured fisherman's sweater and a shark's tooth dangled from a chain around his neck.

"And what can I do you for?" the barman asked.

"I'll have a beer. Jack, what would you like?"

"One for me too."

"Nice try. He'll have a Coke. And one for yourself."

"That's mighty generous of you. Are you on holiday, or just passing through?"

"Actually, we've just moved here."

"I see," the barman said. "Well, if you keep buying me drinks, you're welcome here any time." He laughed, a deep sound that reverberated around the empty room. "I'm always open to new neighbours. My name's Graham by the way."

"Bruce." He shook Graham's hand. "Is it always this quiet?"

"It picks up in the summer when we get the fair-weather sailors and the sightseers. 'Bout now's the quietest it's been in ages."

Bruce picked up a menu from on the bar and scanned down the page. Graham scratched his beard. "If you're after a meal, we have everything on there but the fish. Seems the boys have had trouble catching anything of late."

"Really?" Bruce arched his eyebrows. "I would have thought you'd be swimming in fish this close to the sea.

"It happens now and again. Perhaps there's some truth in this fishing story the government's been spouting–but don't let the locals know I said so. Fishing was the lifeblood of this village. Now even the few tourists we used to get are being poached by the new resort."

Bruce looked over the menu, finally deciding on chicken in a basket. Jack was going through a vegetarian phase, and he settled for the vegetable lasagne with fries.

After ordering, Bruce picked up his drink and walked across and sat at a table in the corner by the window where he had a view of the harbour. The aged map under the glass on the table was decorated with sea monsters and faces with puffed out cheeks blowing a gale. As Bruce set his glass down, he noticed that one of the sea monsters looked remarkably like the graffiti scrawled on the walls of his house, its long teeth in the process of taking a chunk out of a boat. He shivered.

Jack sat staring through the window at the teenagers by the harbour. Bruce remembered his own teenage years. He didn't think he'd been as surly as Jack, but then his father would cuff him around the ear if he showed any sign of being rude.

Bruce sipped his beer. He stared out the window, the top panes of which had circular indents like portholes. A small boat was heading into the harbour. Bruce watched it slice through the water. Eventually it disappeared from sight below the wall of the quay.

Not long after, he saw three figures climb onto the harbour and head towards the road. All three were dressed in thick black coats. They crossed the road and out of sight. Moments later, the door to the bar opened and the figures stepped inside, bringing with them a babble of chatter.

"Back again, I see. What can I get you?" Graham asked.

"Three pints of beer," a tall man with blond hair said as he shucked off his coat.

"That saltwater gives me a raging thirst," said a shorter man with brown hair. He slipped his circular glasses off and wiped them on his sleeve. He breathed on them, held them up for inspection and then wiped them again.

"Kev, just listening to you moan gives me a raging thirst," said the third person, a woman.

Bruce looked at the newcomers. The woman had her back to him and all he could see was that she had long, wavy red hair. He watched as she removed her coat to reveal a slim physique clothed in a blue jumper and black pants.

Feeling slightly voyeuristic, Bruce looked away, caught Jack staring at him with his lips pinched tight, and his eyes narrowed.

"What?" Bruce demanded.

Jack shook his head, sipped his Coke and turned to look back out the window.

"I don't suppose you have a light do you?"

Bruce looked up into the greenest eyes he'd ever seen. The woman smiled down at him with pale pink lips. Around her late twenties, she had a cream complexion and her forehead was speckled with faint freckles. Her face was narrow, her hair damp from the sea spray. She reminded him of John Everett Millais' painting of Ophelia. His pulse increased and he felt hot and clammy.

"Sorry, I don't smoke," Bruce said. His face felt flushed, and he hoped she thought it was through the heat of the fire and not his embarrassment.

"Here, I've got one." Jack thrust out a lighter.

Bruce scowled at his son. "We'll talk later."

"Thanks," she said. "I'll bring it back in a minute." She walked out the front door. Bruce watched through the window as she lit a cigarette and then left it smoking in the ashtray as she walked back inside. "Thanks." She passed the lighter across, her gaze fixed on Bruce.

Bruce took a long swallow from his pint in the hope it would cool his face.

Although he knew he should reprimand his son for carrying a lighter, Bruce took one look at Jack's angry expression and relented. For the first time since Veronica's death, Bruce had looked at another woman with something more than indifference and it was only when he looked down that he realised that he had purposely covered his wedding ring with his free hand.

Chapter 5

Bruce's mobile phone rang with an insistent shrill. Jack watched his dad rummage in his pocket, holding the phone up like a trophy before answering.

"You're here, great. I'll be there in a minute." He disconnected the call. "The furniture's arrived."

Jack shrugged. "And you're telling me because…?"

"Because I'd like you to help."

"What did your last slave die of?"

"Jack, I'm not asking."

"Give me a break. You can't expect me to help when I didn't want to move out here."

Bruce ground his teeth and sighed through his nose. "Okay, what if you have a look around and get to know the place, then you can show me around later. How's that sound?"

Jack pretended to consider the idea, then he eventually nodded. Not that he would be seen dead walking around later with his old man. Way uncool. But if it got him off his back by agreeing, he was game. He could make up an excuse later.

"Right, come on then. I'll head back to the house and you can get the lay of the land."

Jack stood and followed his dad towards the door. On the way, he noticed his dad surreptitiously stare at the woman who'd asked for a light and he felt a cold ache in his stomach. The woman stared back and smiled. Bruce blushed and fiddled with his wedding ring.

A lump lodged in Jack's throat.

Outside he took a deep breath; could smell the sea.

"Try not to stay out too long," Bruce said before turning and jogging away.

Jack didn't watch him go. He looked across at the harbour where the small group of teenagers huddled against the wall. He checked if his dad was out of sight, then he pulled the packet of cigarettes from the pocket of his hooded top and lit one up. He inhaled deeply. He had been dying for a cigarette after being stuck in the car for hours.

Cigarette in hand, he pulled his cap down lower to shield his eyes, and wandered across the road. It was embarrassing being a newcomer in the village, and he was damned if he was going to walk across and start talking to the group.

Disinterested, he skipped over the harbour wall and sat on the edge of the quay, pretending to look out to sea. He had chosen to sit close to the group of teenagers, but not too close. He dangled his feet over the edge, the water's surface below marred by a multicoloured pool of petrol. With the tide out, water dripped from some form of outlet pipe further along the wall.

Despite the usual blue depiction of the sea in postcards, here it was green. Small, choppy waves crested by white foam splashed against the harbour entrance, but within the harbour itself, the surface was virtually flat.

"Who told you you could sit there?"

Jack flicked ash into the sea. The speaker sounded like a teenager, but Jack didn't look up to see. He knew they would goad him, but he wasn't worried. He could handle himself. He had a green belt in Judo, though if anyone ever asked, it was black.

He took a drag on his cigarette.

"Hey, I'm talking to you."

Jack exhaled and turned to look at the speaker from under the brow of his cap. The boy standing beside him looked about sixteen. He had a spotty face and shoulder length hair that, by the look of it, only helped make his acne worse. He was dressed in green combat trousers and a sweatshirt bearing the Nike logo. On his feet, he wore a battered pair of Converse trainers.

"It's a free country," Jack said.

The lad spat on the floor. "Not here it isn't." He looked back at his companions, two teenage girls, as if for support.

Jack swung his legs away from the sea and jumped up. The boy took a step back. They were both about equal height at five nine, but the other boy probably outweighed him by about twenty pounds. He had learned never to underestimate an opponent, but he figured if it turned nasty, he could bowl the boy over. He let his body relax so he would be as supple as possible.

By the looks of them, the two girls weren't interested in starting any trouble, but he knew that if it came to the crunch, camaraderie would probably spur them to help.

"Well, I've finished sitting down now, so you're welcome to it."

The lad licked his lips. "Are you trying to be funny?"

"No, but if you want a laugh then look in the mirror." One of the girls chuckled.

The boy scowled. Jack saw him clench his fists and his heart started beating faster. He took a deep breath, tried to calm down.

"Come on Rocky, he's got every right to sit there," the girl that had laughed said as she wandered across. She had an orange and white striped beanie hat pulled down on her head; strands of short blonde hair jutted from underneath. Two dimples accentuated her rosy cheeks and she had pouting lips. She folded her arms across her chest, the sleeves of her blue top pulled down to cover her hands. She smiled at Jack, accentuating the dimples.

"Stay out of it, Jen. This is between him and me."

"Come on Rocky, leave it."

Jack couldn't help grinning. *Rocky*!

"You find something funny?" Rocky snarled.

Jack dropped his cigarette and stubbed it under the heel of his trainer. "Funny enough."

"Knock it off," Jen said as she placed herself between Jack and Rocky.

Rocky puffed his chest out. "I'll knock something off. His block."

Jen shook her head. "If you want to hit someone, hit me."

"Don't talk stupid."

"Well then, cut it out." She turned to Jack and fixed him with her clear blue eyes. "My name's Jen. Are you here on holiday?"

"Jack." He nodded his head in the direction of the house. "I've just moved here. House on Millhouse Lane."

Jen visibly blanched. "No way," she said, drawing out the words.

Jack pursed his lips and raised his eyebrows. "Something I don't know?"

"You mean you've never heard?"

"Heard what?"

"That house. The one you've bought. The last people who lived there disappeared. No one ever heard from them again."

"Right."

"No, really. Tell him, Rocky."

Rocky nodded. "She's right. It's been up for sale for years. Everyone says it's haunted. People around here call it the Mulberry Triangle. Rather you than me."

Jack chewed his lip. Were they being serious?

The other girl hurried across. "You're really living in the Triangle house," the girl said. She had brown hair tied in a ponytail and a pert little nose that twitched like an inquisitive rabbit's.

"Well, we haven't moved in yet. Only got here today."

"I can't believe you've never heard the story. It was in all the papers. A man and wife and their two kids." She fingered one of the many earrings in her ear as she spoke.

Rocky grinned. "Well it'll save me the job of kicking your ass when you disappear."

Jack shrugged. "Do I look bothered? So I'm moving into a derelict house, so what?" Nevertheless, inside he felt a knot in his stomach. They couldn't be serious, could they? But so what if they were. There was probably a good explanation.

"Well, it was nice meeting you," Rocky said. "Anything you want on your gravestone?"

Jen. Jack kept the thought to himself as he forced a laugh. "You're a real joker."

Rocky put his arm around Jen and pulled her in close to his side. Then he made a show of kissing her. Jen pushed him away.

"Quit mauling me," she said, wiping her mouth with the back of her hand.

Rocky narrowed his eyes and glared at Jack, and then he grinned like the cat that had gotten the cream.

Jack was disappointed Jen was Rocky's girlfriend. For a moment there, he'd thought living here wouldn't be so bad.

"Well, it's been fun," Jack said. "But I'm going to have to fly." He turned and started walking away.

Rocky shouted after him, "Don't you mean, die?"

It wasn't until Jack turned and gave him the finger that he realised his hands were shaking.

Chapter 6

Small pebbles lined the edge of the road. Jack kicked them as hard as he could back towards the sea. He hated this shit village. Sure it would be good to live near a beach, but if that's all there was here, then he would probably die of boredom. There hadn't always been that much to do in the city, but at least there had been shops to look around, fast-food restaurants, bowling and cinemas. The least he would have expected here was an amusement arcade.

God. Why had this happened? If his mum hadn't died, he wouldn't be here. Sure, his dad wanted to get away to escape the bad memories, but they could have moved somewhere else in the city. This was just ridiculous.

He wondered whether his dad knew the story about the house. Obviously he didn't. Rocky and the girls had to be making it up. Even Jen must have been in on it. But just suppose they were telling the truth …

Seagulls wheeled in the sky above. Their raucous din was starting to get on his nerves so he inserted his earphones and turned his mp3 player on. The *American Idiot* album assaulted his ears and he bobbed his head in time to the title track.

He dragged his feet through the pebbles, dried seaweed, shells, and sand that had accumulated at the edge of the road. When he drew close to the turning to Millhouse Lane, he took the packet of mints from his pocket to hide the smell of cigarettes. About to pop a mint into his mouth, he looked up and noticed a figure standing above the cove. He recognised her as the crazy woman from the house. And she was staring at him.

Jack flicked the mint into his mouth, trying to appear nonchalant. Then he looked back down at the road and increased his pace. The woman had scared him in the house, so he didn't want to stare at her now in case it upset her. Sure, he could deal with kids his own age, but an old woman was something else. For a start, it wouldn't feel right hitting her if she did attack.

He hurried into the lane and glanced quickly back over his shoulder, but the old woman was gone.

He didn't know whether to feel relieved or scared. Damn this place. Further along the lane he could see the removal van. Two men were making their way out of it, carrying the brown leather settee between them. Jack hated that settee. He had tried to convince his dad it was wrong to sit on the carcass of an innocent animal, but his dad was adamant he wasn't getting rid of it, not when it cost so much and there was nothing wrong with it. He remembered his dad saying, 'The cow won't mind', which was a lame thing to say. Of course the cow wouldn't mind. The cow was dead.

The movers stopped walking and dropped the settee. The older of the two raised his flat cap and mopped his brow with a handkerchief. He looked about fifty-five and was dressed conservatively in a shirt and trousers that had seen better days. His friend appeared about thirty-five and was as big as a bull. He looked as though he could carry the settee under one of his enormous arms without breaking a sweat.

Although Jack wasn't exactly skinny, he always envied people with big muscles. They had an air of confidence about them he imagined came from knowing most people wouldn't say boo to them.

As Jack walked up to the van, his dad emerged from the house and waved. Jack took his earphones out and nodded in response.

"That was quick," his dad said. "I thought you'd be gone hours."

Jack chewed his lip and looked at the house. The windows were dirty. Set back into the brickwork they failed to reflect any light; looked like skeletal eye sockets. He shivered involuntarily.

"What is it?" his dad asked.

"Is there anything about the house you haven't told me?"

His dad frowned.

"It's just … I heard …"

33

"Heard what?"

Jack shrugged. "It's probably nothing."

"Tell me then."

"Where do you want this settee?" the old man wheezed as he and his partner made their way up the path, carrying the settee between them.

"Just put it in the first room along with everything else. Until I decorate at least one room, everything will have to go in there."

The old man nodded and then continued towards the house.

"Now, you were saying?" his dad said.

"I met a couple of locals in the village. They told me the previous occupants of this house disappeared without a trace."

His dad shook his head. "They're pulling your leg."

Jack stared at his dad for a moment. He believed him when he said he didn't know the history of the house, but that didn't mean it wasn't true.

Chapter 7

Zander stood at the helm and steered his vessel into the inky black sea. The sound of the engines and the waves slapping against the bow carried easily on the night air.

Clouds masked most of the sky, and few stars were visible. A fine spray obscured the glass, and he switched the wipers on to clear it away. He preferred to see miles ahead of him, but when the sun went down it was hard to see anything.

He often thought being on a boat at night on the seas was one of the loneliest places in the world. Other than Brad toiling away in the engine room, he was alone. But he felt as though someone was watching him, which was ridiculous. He was four miles out, and there wasn't another vessel in sight. In rough weather, the radar sometimes showed little blips on the screen from the tops of waves, but today it was calm and yet there were still a couple of blips showing up. He looked outside, but couldn't see any running lights to indicate the presence of another vessel. Thinking it could be flotsam or there might be a problem with the radar, he altered its sensitivity to tune out the blips. Technology was a wonderful thing, but it wasn't infallible.

Once the blips disappeared, he recalled the incident with the shredded net. It had taken days to repair and had cost more than he could afford. That's why this trip was so important.

Satisfied no one was around to see, he flicked a switch and spotlights above the helm illuminated the sea, creating a glare that was almost blinding. Less than fifty yards off the starboard bow he spotted a red buoy that marked the lobster pot in the depths below. Easing back on the throttle, he headed towards the pot and dropped anchor.

The deck was slick with water, and he cautiously made his way to the starboard side. Using a hooked pole, he snared the buoy and dragged it on board. Then he started to haul the pot from the deep. The cold rope felt slimy in his hands, and he braced his feet against the side of the boat and pulled hand over hand. Weighed down with its contents and the pressure of the sea, the basket was heavy and it took all his strength to raise it.

Water sloshed against the deck and ran back out to the sea as the boat pitched in the waves.

Something banged against the hull and Zander jumped. The rope slipped through his fingers before he tightened his grip. He tied the rope onto the gunnel and peered over the side into the inky black depths where the spotlights failed to illuminate. There was always the danger at sea of hitting submerged objects, perhaps some of the flotsam he thought the radar detected, but he couldn't see anything. The hairs prickled at the nape of his neck. Something didn't feel right, and over the years he'd come to trust his feelings.

The sooner he was done, the sooner he could head home, so he returned to hauling up the lobster pot.

Eventually the pot broke the surface and he lifted it aboard. Inside he could see the sealed packets of cannabis, which had a value anywhere from fifteen to twenty thousand pounds. It was a lucrative sideline now the fishing grounds seemed to be drying up. Eager to finish, he removed the packets as quickly as he could and dropped them on the deck. When he was done, he threw the pot overboard and watched as the rope snaked back into the icy sea. When the pot was on the bottom, he threw the buoy back out and then picked up the packets and returned to the wheelhouse where he stowed the cannabis in a secret hatch in the boards beneath his feet.

When that was done, he raised the anchor and turned the spotlights off. Out of the corner of his eye, he saw a faint blip on the radar screen. When he looked, the blip disappeared. He gave the radar a quick tap, but nothing reappeared.

Then Zander opened up the throttle and sailed into the night.

Chapter 8

Shazam barked eagerly as she ran along the beach for the driftwood Bruce had thrown for her. He watched as she splashed into the surf, snapping at the small waves that broke against her legs.

A warm day; there was already a heat haze on the horizon and Bruce had built up a sweat with the three-mile jog he'd undertaken after breakfast.

Jack had still been in bed when he left–probably still annoyed at moving out here. With the house being in such a state, Bruce had erected camp beds for them to sleep on until they were sorted out. Jack had complained as usual.

A couple of kids were making sandcastles at the water's edge while their parents lay on beach towels. Bruce was surprised how quiet the village was considering it had such a wonderful little beach, but he supposed most people opted for the new resort further along the coast, where the kids could be more easily appeased with arcades and amusement parks.

From where he was, he had a good view of the harbour and the houses clinging to the hillside beyond it. There were a couple of small dinghies setting sail, and a couple of trawlers moored up. The tide was out, which literally grounded the big boats. Bruce couldn't imagine being controlled by the tides of the sea.

A dog howled somewhere in the village and the sound carried across the bay. Shazam cocked her ears and barked in response and the dog howled twice more then fell silent. Bruce remembered reading somewhere that if a dog howls three times; it signified someone was going to die. He guessed the thing with superstitions was they had to have had some basis in fact somewhere.

When he reached the end of the beach, Bruce walked onto the path at the side of the road. The sand to his right had given way to rocks, and now the tide was out, numerous rock pools remained.

Recalling Jack's comment about the house, he headed for the bar to ask Duncan about its history.

When he reached the harbour, he spied the woman Jack had given the light to in the bar. His heart did a little flutter at the sight of her, which made him feel guilty. Not that Veronica would have wanted him to become a recluse; she had made that perfectly clear on her deathbed. It had been eight months, but he felt almost as though he was being unfaithful. He realised he was unconsciously revolving the wedding band around his finger so he released it.

The woman was talking to a man on one of the trawlers. She laughed, and the sound carried across the harbour. Bruce felt his cheeks flush with colour and he clenched his fists.

This is stupid. I don't even know her, he thought.

Ordering Shazam to heel, he walked around the harbour. It wouldn't hurt to say hello.

When they drew close to the woman, Shazam barked.

The man on the boat and the woman both turned.

"Hello again," the woman said, smiling.

"Hi," Bruce said, looking from the woman down to the man.

The man on the boat nodded and continued unravelling the nets, stringing them across the deck like a web.

Shazam growled from the back of her throat. "Shush," Bruce said. "I don't know what's got into her." He shrugged apologetically. "Away. Go and lie over there if you can't behave." He pointed to a spot by the harbour wall about twenty feet away. Shazam whined softly and then licked Bruce's hand. "You won't get around me like that." Tail between her legs, Shazam walked away. "Lie down," Bruce said. Shazam obediently dropped to the ground, resting her head on her front paws, ears pricked as she watched her master.

The man on the boat looked at Shazam and chewed his gums. "Perhaps she doesn't like the smell of fish."

Bruce nodded. "Yes, that's probably it."

"What's the dog's name?" the woman asked.

"Shazam."

"Strange name."

"Long story."

"Perhaps you'll tell it to me sometime."

Bruce blushed again. He hoped she thought it was only the heat. "Yes, I'd like that."

"I didn't introduce myself the other day. My name's Erin McVey."

Bruce shook her hand. "Bruce Holden."

He looked down at the man on the boat, noticed what appeared to be a look of green-eyed rage that disappeared almost immediately.

"Trent Zander." He nodded curtly and returned his attention to his nets.

"I'm not interrupting, am I?" Bruce asked.

Erin laughed softly. "No, Captain Zander here was trying to convince me to go for a drink with him, that's all."

Bruce felt another flush of jealousy. Zander looked up, his blue eyes unreadable. Toughened by the elements, his skin looked like leather, and his stubbled chin and angular jaw gave him a rugged appearance. He reminded Bruce of a young Clint Eastwood, so he wouldn't be surprised if Erin accepted and went out with him.

"You on holiday?" Zander asked.

Bruce wondered whether he should post an ad in the local paper. "I've just moved here."

"Was that your son you were with yesterday?" Erin asked.

Bruce nodded.

"And Mrs. Holden?" Zander interrupted.

Bruce swallowed. He still felt raw having to explain. "She's dead."

He noticed Erin glance at the wedding band on his finger. Women always noticed these things.

When neither Zander nor Erin apologized or asked further questions, Bruce found himself explaining anyway.

"She died of cancer eight months ago. Since then, it's just been Jack and me." He looked at Erin and smiled sheepishly as though apologizing. He noticed Zander staring up at him venomously "What about you two? Do you live around here?"

Erin reached into the pocket of her baggy grey pants and withdrew a packet of cigarettes and a lighter, which she held up for inspection. "I came prepared today," she said as she lit a cigarette. She exhaled slowly. "I'm a marine biologist employed by a deep sea mining company to ascertain the ecological implications of their drilling, so I'm just a visitor."

Bruce raised his eyebrows. He was impressed, but it made his fear of the sea seem childish.

Zander paused mending his nets. "If I had my way she'd move here permanently. The village could always do with more pretty girls." He shot Bruce a glance and then winked at Erin.

Clive Dunn wiped sweat from his brow. It was damned hot today.

He pulled his sunglasses down from his forehead to shield his eyes and sat up on the beach towel. Sweat trickled down his chest, navigating a course through the sand that had stuck to the suntan lotion.

"You two be careful," he shouted to Ben and Jane as they splashed at the water's edge. Kids! They seemed to have no fear.

"Now that you've woken up, would you rub some oil on my back?" his wife Gaynor asked.

"What makes you think I was asleep?"

"Because you don't usually snore when you're awake."

"You got me there." He leaned across and picked up the bottle of oil. He opened it and squirted a liberal amount onto his palm. Gaynor held her blonde ponytail out of the way to allow him to rub the oil onto her back.

"You could have wiped your hands," she said. "It feels as though you're rubbing me with sandpaper."

When he looked down, he noticed the sensual act of applying the oil had given him an erection, and he was glad the kids were too far away to see. He ran his hands over the thin string holding the blue bikini together; knew it would be a cinch to undo the bow before Gaynor could complain. Testing his luck, he circled his hands to the edges of her back, and then quickly slid them forwards and underneath the cups of the bikini and squeezed her breasts.

Gaynor let out a little squeal, turned, and playfully slapped him on the arm.

"The kids might see," she said as she readjusted her top. Then she noticed his erection and she gave him a quick kiss. "What do they say, only mad dogs, Englishmen and horny middle-aged men go out in the midday sun?"

He winked.

Clive leaned back on his elbows. Since the new resort had opened, the village of Mulberry had dropped off people's radar. Having holidayed here for a number of years, he remembered when you couldn't move on the beach. Now it was deserted. Life didn't get much better.

The sun was at his back and the shadows of the cliffs to his right were thrown across the sand and into the sea like a fisherman's net. In the distance, he could see a tanker moving slowly towards the horizon. As a kid, he'd always dreamed of sailing around the world, visiting exotic locales. The dream persisted until he left school, but then he met Gaynor and the dream was put on hold. He settled down, got a job in the local branch of a chain of supermarkets, worked his way up and was now the youngest manager in the company.

Occasionally the wanderlust returned, only now it was going to have to wait until the kids had grown up and left home–which would be at least another eleven years. But as he'd waited this long, he could wait a while longer.

"So what do you want to do tonight?" Gaynor asked as she lay back down.

"Do you really need to ask?"

"Well, that takes care of three minutes, but what about the rest of the evening?"

"Very funny. I'll have you know I'm a sexual athlete."

"More like a sexual deviant." She chuckled.

Clive grinned. "We could take a drive to that restaurant we went to the other year. The one a few miles along the coast."

Gaynor frowned.

"You know, the one where we had sex in the parking lot before the kids were born."

"Oh, you mean the one that we hadn't noticed had security cameras."

Although he was wearing sunglasses, he couldn't help noticing his wife blush.

"As long as they don't remember us," she continued. "Probably have our pictures on the wall of shame."

"Great."

"Or perhaps the film made its way onto the internet. Look what happened to Paris Hilton and those other celebrity tapes."

"We're not celebrities."

"Perhaps we are now." She laughed, then pulled a T-shirt over her face. "Anyway, it's your turn to watch the kids while I snooze."

He looked up and saw Ben and Jane were building a sandcastle, letting the incoming sea fill the moat they had dug around it. Satisfied they were okay, he picked up his Richard Laymon novel and began to read.

After fifteen minutes, the words started to blur as sweat rolled into his eyes, stinging. He reached across and grabbed a towel from the top of the bag Gaynor had packed. After wiping his eyes, he took out the bottle of water. He unscrewed the top and took a sip. It was warm. He was going to have to invest in one of those cooler packs. He would kill for an ice cream right now. Then he remembered they sold them in the village shop.

Deciding to take the kids for a walk while Gaynor slept, he looked towards where the kids were playing and saw Jane was on her own. He quickly scanned the beach, but couldn't see Ben.

Panic flooded his body; felt like a cold icicle piercing his heart and flooding his veins with ice. He jumped up.

"Jane, where's your brother?" he shouted.

Jane looked up from where she knelt at the water's edge, a collection of seashells in her hand to adorn the sandcastle. She shook her head. "He was here a minute ago."

"Clive, what is it?" Gaynor asked as she sat up and pulled the T-shirt from her face.

Clive didn't answer as he jumped to his feet and scanned the beach. He cupped his hands around his mouth. "Ben," he shouted. He shielded his eyes and looked towards the cliffs, then towards the rock pools on the way to the village, but there was no sign of Ben. He wouldn't wander off without telling them … when he found him, Clive was going to give him such a smack. He shouted his son's name again.

He ran down the beach to Jane, the warm sand oozing between his toes. "You must know where he's gone," he said when he reached her, a tremor in his voice.

Jane shook her head.

"Where's Ben?" Gaynor asked as she arrived at his side.

Clive felt a lump in his throat. He looked out to sea. Thought he saw something floating about thirty feet out. Liquid nitrogen superseded the ice in his veins. Ben?

Without hesitating, he ran into the sea. Despite the heat of the sun, the water was cold and gooseflesh spread from his legs to his torso. Bits of seaweed floated around his legs. The further out he went, the colder the water became. The seabed sloped quickly and he was soon up to his waist. He started to swim, heading in the direction he had seen the object. Saltwater stung his eyes. Panic fuelled his strokes, and before he knew it, he reached the spot where he thought he had spied something, but there was nothing there. He trod water. Looked around. Small swells caused him to bob up and down.

Suppose Ben was underwater?

The thought chilled him even more. He took a deep breath and dived. Visibility underwater was difficult, like looking through Vaseline, the saltwater stinging his eyes. Using his arms, he searched the area like a blind man, probing into the depths. Something brushed past his leg,

43

making him squirm. He reached out and grabbed it, only to find it was a piece of seaweed.

He didn't know how deep he was, but he hadn't touched the bottom. He kicked with his legs, spinning in circles, a human whirlpool. He was going to have to head back up soon, but he had to find Ben.

His lungs felt as though they were burning. He needed to reach the surface, take another breath and then dive back down.

He kicked and groped at the water, forging a path back up. Bubbles burst from his nostrils as he started to exhale.

Seconds later his head broke the surface and he gulped in a deep breath. His breathing was rapid, his heart beating fast. He hadn't exerted himself this much since betting his best friend Alex that he could beat him in a race to the bar. He'd lost.

Saltwater stung his eyes, and he rubbed them with the backs of his hands.

"Clive."

He heard Gaynor shout and he looked back towards the beach; saw she was waving, and then she pointed down to Jane and Ben at her side.

Relief washed over Clive like a wave. He exhaled a long sigh and let his legs drift up, floating on his back to breathe as he circled his arms to stay afloat. I'm going to kill him, he thought. But really he knew he was going to hug him so tight that Ben would shout for him to let him go.

About to turn over and swim for shore, he felt something brush his back. His first thought was more seaweed. Then something grabbed him.

Clive gasped. Sharp pain erupted around his waist. He kicked out and thrashed with his arms. Seawater frothed around his torso like rabid foam. He reached down to prise off whatever had grabbed him, felt sharp teeth and bony skin. Fear unlike anything he'd ever felt rushed through his body.

Shark!

The creature pulled powerfully down, and Clive sank into the deep. Bubbles surged past his face, and the inky blackness turned red with blood.

Chapter 9

Shazam jumped to her feet and started barking. Thinking she was barking at Zander again, Bruce was about to admonish her when he heard the scream. It emanated from back along the road towards his house and was the worst thing he had ever heard in his life.

"What the hell's that?" Erin asked.

Zander jumped up from his boat and clambered onto the quay. He stared into the distance where the sound originated, then started running.

Bruce looked at Erin, pulled a quizzical expression, and then ran after Zander with Shazam running effortlessly at his side. Despite his regular jogs, Bruce found himself trailing behind Zander, which made him feel somewhat annoyed. The pavement underfoot was cracked and worn, and Bruce instinctively made sure he didn't step on any of the cracks. The last thing he needed was any bad luck.

Zander was out of breath when he reached the beach. He could hear Bruce's feet slapping the ground behind him, and he increased his pace and charged across the sand. He wasn't going to get beaten. No one ever beat him. At anything.

He saw a woman and two kids at the edge of the sea. She was gesticulating wildly and pointing towards the water.

"Clive. My husband. Something attacked him. Oh God. I think it was a shark," she said as Zander reached her.

Zander put his hands on her shoulders and felt the slick sheen of suntan oil. He couldn't help noticing how attractive she was in her blue bikini. For some reason, a woman in distress seemed highly erotic.

"Calm down," he said.

"What's going on?" Bruce asked as he reached them.

"My husband. A shark's attacked him."

Both children cried as they clung to their mother's legs.

Zander shook his head. "There are no man-eating sharks in these waters." He knew that the most dangerous species,

Tiger, Lemon, Hammerhead and Great Whites' didn't visit these shores, so he was pretty certain that the man hadn't been attacked by a shark.

"A shark," Bruce said with a look of fear as he looked out to sea.

Zander exhaled loudly. "I just said there are no killer sharks in these waters." He hated landlubbers with a predilection for melodrama with regard to anything about the sea. Jaws had a lot to answer for.

"I saw him get attacked," the woman squealed. "Please, you've got to help him."

Zander looked out to sea, but couldn't see anything. "You're sure he's out there?"

"Of course I'm sure."

The children started to cry louder as their mother raised her voice. This was crazy. Zander knew there was nothing out there. The only explanation was that a strong current had dragged him under, or he had a cramp and had been unable to swim. Whatever it was, there was no sign of him.

The woman's incessant crying was starting to jar on his nerves. Zander tugged off his jumper and T-shirt to reveal a physique sculpted by hard toil.

Bruce looked pensive. "I'll stay here and take care of the woman and her kids."

Zander clucked his tongue and removed his boots. Then he charged into the sea.

The water was colder than it looked, but Zander ignored it as he put his head under the surface and swam powerfully away from the shore. The saltwater reduced his vision, like looking through warped glass. The sandy bottom dropped away quickly and darkness resided below. Tangles of seaweed drifted by, but Zander couldn't see anyone. When he was far enough out, he dived down into the depths and swam around, trying his best to find the missing man, but as he didn't know where he had gone down, it seemed useless. With his breath almost spent, he struck out for the surface and trod water for a while to catch his breath. He looked back at the beach; saw he had swum quite a way out.

47

He bobbed up and down as the sea rolled. When he was at the top of one swell, he noticed what looked like a dark patch on the surface of the water about twenty feet away. With a couple of powerful strokes, he swam towards the area. As soon as he reached the spot, he recognised the dark patch, had seen plenty of examples when throwing the remains of gutted fish back into the sea: blood. He could literally taste it in the air.

He took a deep breath, then dived back into the depths. The blood made it even harder to see so he used his hands to sweep through the water, searching for the woman's husband.

A sudden movement caught his eye and he turned his head and tried to focus. Five feet below him, something dark surged through the water and disappeared. Without any concern for his own safety, he swam down, entering a world where there was virtually no light. Sweeping his arms back and forth, he searched the area, but couldn't feel anything. Pressure built inside his chest and his ears felt ready to pop. About to give up, he felt the water swirl around him as something swam close by, and for the first time, he realised that something really had attacked the woman's husband, and that now it was circling him.

Panic welled through his body, and his pulse increased. He could hear the throb of his heart pounding in his ears. With no idea how deep he had descended, he started his ascent, frantically scooping the water with his hands and kicking his feet as though the devil himself were after him.

He felt strange currents swirl around his naked torso; thought he felt something brush against his leg. He needed to breathe. Light permeated the depths. But it was a reddish light, filtered through the blood suspended in the water like a huge, undulating jellyfish. Uneasy, Zander swam through the blood and surged to the surface where he gulped in a deep breath. He wiped the saltwater from his eyes; saw a thin film of blood coating his skin.

Without hesitating, he made for shore, arms and legs aching by the time he was able to stand and wade onto the beach. He stood with his hands on his knees, gasping for breath.

"Where's Clive?" the woman shrieked.

Zander looked up, breathing fast. He shook his head.

The woman screamed, but Zander didn't pay her any attention. He stood up straight, put his hands on his hips, and turned and looked out to sea. If a killer shark prowled the waters, then it would explain the shortage of fish, and it might also explain the incident with the nets.

Now he had a job to do. It was time to go fishing.

Chapter 10

"So you didn't see anything?"

Bruce looked at the young police officer and shook his head. Shazam stood at his side, her hackles up and her ears cocked as she looked out to sea.

The officer made a couple of notes. "And you said Trent Zander went in search of …" he perused his notes, "Gaynor Dunn's husband, Clive?"

"Yes, he swam out and looked for him." Bruce stared across at Zander who stood at the edge of the water looking out to sea. "He came back a few minutes later."

"And he didn't find anything?"

"Nothing that he mentioned. But …"

"But what, Mr. Holden?"

"Well, when he came out the water, he was, I don't know, pale. It was like he'd seen a ghost or something."

The flashing lights of the ambulance washed over the sand to his side, and Bruce gazed across at Gaynor Dunn as the ambulance men helped her into their vehicle. She was in shock, which wasn't surprising. She had just lost her husband, and those poor children, a father.

He twisted the wedding band on his finger and stared up at the cliffs where the silhouette of Lillian Brown, the madwoman he had discovered in his house, was discernible against the blue sky. He shivered. What the hell was she staring at? Perhaps moving here hadn't been such a good idea after all.

He realised the police officer was speaking to him. "Sorry, could you say that again."

"I said, will you be able to come to the station to give a statement?"

Bruce nodded. "Yes, sure. No problem." An irrational fear struck him, fear for his son's safety. He had been in bed when Bruce left the house, but that had been a couple of hours ago. Unlike Bruce, Jack was at home in the water, and he had mentioned only the other night how he was going to go swimming at the first opportunity.

"If you'll excuse me, I've got to go," Bruce said.

The police officer looked at him for a couple of seconds and then nodded. "Just don't forget to call in at the station."

"Come on, Shazam." Bruce jogged quickly back up the beach to the road. Shazam bounded along at his side. He stared up at the cliffs, but Lillian Brown was no longer in sight. He didn't know whether her absence made him feel better or worse.

When he reached the house, he ran inside and called Jack's name. Upon receiving no reply, he ran upstairs to Jack's bedroom, only to find it deserted, the sheets tossed on the ground and the clothes he had been wearing the previous day missing.

Bruce knew it was taking a risk phoning Jack on his mobile, as the wrath of a son who feels he's being spied on wasn't worth thinking about, but Bruce felt anxious. The phone rang a number of times before the automated voice of the woman at the message centre cut in to tell him the person was unavailable. Bruce disconnected the call without leaving a message. He was just being paranoid.

But what if he wasn't? What if Jack had decided today of all days to go swimming?

Today when there was something ravenous swimming in the depths. Something with a taste for flesh.

Chapter 11

Erin McVey stood on the diving platform of the research vessel and donned her dry suit. A slight wind tussled her hair. She pulled her hood up. Her diving buddy, Kevin James, went through the safety checks on her equipment, then she reciprocated, making herself familiar with his releases, confirming that he had ample air for the dive, that the valves were open, and that the regulator and alternative air sources worked. On a final inspection, she checked for out of place equipment, dangling gauges and missing gear. Their lives depended on making sure everything was okay.

She had been diving here with Kev for the last three weeks, taking samples of the local sea life. What had surprised her was the lack of fish. Usually they flitted from the depths, bright shoals in the glare of the Dive Light, but since she had been here, she had spotted only a few solitary specimens.

She tested her regulator, which made her recall her first diving experience and the alien feel of breathing underwater. Unlike one person on her diving course, she hadn't panicked, but it still took a couple of days to get used to. Now it was second nature, and sometimes preferable to being on the surface.

Erin had fine-tuned her buoyancy after eighteen dives–for some people it took a lot longer. At depth, she had to add air to the suit to stop it becoming uncomfortably tight. The downside was it added buoyancy, so she'd had to learn to manage the air via an exhaust valve.

She strapped the five-inch titanium dive knife to her leg.

Satisfied all the safety checks were complete, she picked up her mask, gave a thumbs up to the crew on deck, then stepped back to the edge of the platform and dropped into the water.

Kev dropped in beside her. He'd chosen not to wear a hood and his black hair hung in the water around his face like tentacles.

"You ready?" Kev asked.

Erin smiled. "Always ready."

"What about willing and able?"

"Now that's something you'll never find out."

"Your loss."

She grinned. "I'll live." She spat in her mask and then swilled it in the water to stop it fogging up before donning it.

Finally ready, she inserted her regulator, gave Kev the thumbs up and dived.

She followed the guide rope leading down from the platform. The water was a murky green colour, and after less than 20 feet, she switched on her dive light, illuminating tiny plankton in the beam.

Erin and her team had been assigned to determine the effects of exploratory and development drilling, exploring the impact on the environment, especially which hazards and environmental issues had to be considered when planning to drill in a specific location.

Not all of her work took place out in the field, but it was where she was happiest. Being stuck in an office didn't suit her, and after a few days she would start to feel like a mermaid out of water.

When she reached the seabed, she spotted a brightly coloured sea slug rippling across the rocks and an alien looking spider crab skittering into a crevice. The sight of the various undersea denizens never failed to amaze her. She'd once read that although three-quarters of the earth is liquid, only one-tenth of one percent of the ocean had been explored, and every time she dived, she felt she was entering an uncharted realm.

Shining her light across the seabed, she marvelled at the various colours reflected back. She could see Kev at her side, specimen bag at the ready, and she indicated the direction they should swim.

Erin felt truly liberated underwater; felt it was the closest a person could come to flying.

Up ahead she knew there was a steep drop off. Swimming over it made her feel vertiginous and disorientated, as though she were over an abyss. The drop off was almost at the limits of how deep she could go, so she didn't intend going too close.

The seabed slowly shelved down, and the deeper Erin swam, the less visibility she had. Despite the layers of thermal clothing, she could still feel the cold permeating through to her bones. Within her suit, she shivered.

As she swam, her thoughts drifted. She recalled the man she had met a couple of hours ago, Bruce Holden, and a warm thrill swept through her body. Although he was older than she was, she had fancied him straight away. His charismatic look appealed to her. She had never dated anyone with kids before–had never had a maternal streak–but in Bruce's case, she could make an exception.

Remembering the woman's scream, she wondered whether they had found the reason behind it. Perhaps she should have gone to help, but work came first.

She made a gradual descent, adding air to her suit to combat the pressure of the water while also keeping an eye on the depth gauge. If she descended too fast, she would suffer the same kind of ear popping experienced going up in a plane, which could be painful. When she reached the depth she required, she wanted to be in a neutrally buoyant state. Achieving that state meant she would sink a little when she exhaled and float a little when she inhaled.

One thing she didn't want to do was contact any solid objects. Contacting the substrate would stir up sediment, reduce visibility and damage the organisms that lived on the surfaces.

Kev appeared at her side. He indicated to her that he was moving away to look at something. Erin acknowledged his signal and watched him swim into the inky blackness. Almost out of sight, she could see a dim corona of light from his dive lamp, almost ghostly in the depths like the bioluminescence emitted by a host of marine animals.

Movement caught her eye. Expecting to see a fish, she turned her head, but there was nothing there. She shone the light around, following the course of its beam, but couldn't see anything. About to shine her light back on the path she was taking, she saw something caught in the beam. Situated at the limits of the light's reach, it appeared to absorb the light. Erin frowned.

About to swim over and investigate, she saw a flash of light to her left. She recognised it as Kev's flashlight beam. But there was something strange about the way it was moving, as though it was being waved frantically.

A strange sense of panic swept over her. She could feel the beat of her heart increase, could feel a thin layer of sweat glaze her body. Something wasn't right.

She watched the beam of light zigzag through the ocean. Kev was heading towards the drop off. She could see that he was already much deeper than she was. *What the hell was he playing at?*

Fighting the sense of dread, she started to swim towards him. Something moved in the blackness to her right, creating currents of water that made the plankton swirl in the beam. She swept the light around–thought for a moment she saw something large dart away. It looked too large to have been one of the many fish supposed to swim these waters. But if it wasn't, then what was it? A porpoise perhaps? Or a seal?

She noticed Kev's light had stopped moving. Relieved, she started swimming towards him.

Erin glanced at her depth gauge. She was at the absolute safe limits of her dive. Kev was at least another ten feet lower. It wasn't like him to do something so hazardous. He knew the dangers of going too deep. At this depth, it could be fatal. If they stayed down too long and too deep, they risked the bends, a painful condition caused by nitrogen bubbles in the blood.

She swam closer to Kev, regulating the air in her suit as she went. From the look of it, he was on the lip of the drop off. The thought of the great depths below where he sat made her feel nauseous. Or was it something else making her feel ill? The pressure?

She shone her light towards him, trying to attract his attention. But he didn't respond. Still unable to see him clearly, she descended deeper. She looked at her depth gauge. *There had better be a damn good reason for this*, she thought.

Close enough now to see him clearly, she thought her eyes were playing tricks. He looked to be buried in the seabed. All she could see was one of his shoulders, his head, and one hand holding the light, the beam of which pointed down into the depths.

Strong currents rose from the drop off, making Kev's hair undulate like tentacles. Erin shuddered. Something wasn't right. The substrate had been disturbed. A pale cloud drifted around his torso. She swam closer; her beam of light illuminated a thin red veil wafting gently around his shoulder. She narrowed her eyes, trying to see clearly.

When she reached Kev, Erin reached out and tapped him on the shoulder. He didn't respond. Her mind whirled with questions. Fear circulated around her body. She grabbed his wrist and pulled.

And Kev's severed torso gently rose from the substrate, leaving behind a thin red cloud of blood that swirled in the currents rising from the depths.

Erin's eyes went wide. She gagged and the regulator flew from between her lips. Bubbles streamed from her mouth as she tried to scream in the water. She gurgled, almost choked. Frantic, she let go of Kev and searched for her regulator, sweeping her arm around in the growing gloom of blood and substrate.

Something moved in the darkness below the drop off. Erin gagged again. She floundered in the water. *Where was that damn regulator?* Her hands brushed against it, and she grabbed it and reinserted it between her lips; took a welcome breath.

She looked back at Kev's body. Ragged strips of flesh waved in the water from his severed torso.

She watched Kev's severed body fall over the edge of the drop off and descend into the depths. The beam of his lamp spiralled down, creating a macabre red swirling vortex as it illuminated the blood.

Crazy thoughts fought for dominance in her mind. How the hell had he died? What the fuck was down here that could bite a man in two? And more importantly, where was it now?

She spun around, pointing her light in all directions.

Erin felt totally alone. Panic swelled in her chest, aggravating her breathing. She willed her pulse to slow, fought not to lose control.

The beam illuminated something black that swam quickly out of sight. But from what she had seen, it had been big, very big. The blood froze in her veins.

Calm yourself girl, she thought. The surface is a long way up.

She considered an emergency ascent, but rising too quickly from such a great depth would result in the bends. So what else could she do?

She remembered the object she had seen at the limits of the light's beam before Kev had distracted her. It occurred to her that it was a vessel of some sort.

Although she needed to get to the surface, she wanted to gather her wits. If she could hide for a little while, then maybe whatever was circling would swim away. Swimming faster than she had ever swum before, Erin kicked out into the cold water.

Something flitted about to her left. She flashed the light at it, saw two huge malevolent quicksilver eyes reflected in the darkness. Her heart leaped into her throat, but before she could identify it, the creature vanished into the depths.

Panicked, Erin felt her strength ebbing away. Whatever it was down here, she was in its domain.

The sunken vessel she had seen briefly in the glare of the light appeared ahead. She felt a moment of relief. Then the beam illuminated a jagged maw of teeth almost as long as her forearm–teeth poised to take a chunk out of her torso.

Chapter 12

Erin's lungs felt ready to burst. She simultaneously hit out with the flashlight at the creature swimming towards her and withdrew the knife from the sheath on her leg.

In the swirling mass of bubbles and semi darkness of the deep, Erin couldn't make out what she was looking at. There was something vaguely familiar about the monster, but she didn't have time to consider it. Not when the creature was trying to kill her. Over four feet in length, it fixed her with its close-set eyes the colour of mercury. Its head was larger than Erin's, but narrower. Its dark skin resembled the pitted surface of an orange, and when it opened its mouth, the real terror erupted in Erin's brain. Lined with needle-sharp teeth, its jaws resembled a Venus flytrap. The bottom teeth too long to fit comfortably in its mouth, she could only assume that they slid into pockets in the roof of its mouth.

She stabbed out with the knife, slashing through the water in a demented, determined way. What the hell was that thing? The blade met resistance like steel. She had struck the beast, but it seemed to have little effect. Terrified, she shone the light at the creature, causing it to shy away. She watched it swim into the dark. The beam illuminated dark scales and spines along its back. In the moment before she lost sight of it, she thought she saw something even stranger about it. Something her brain couldn't rationalize…

She thought she had seen arms protruding from its sides.

But that was impossible. She must have imagined it. Fear and panic playing tricks with her brain.

Even though she could no longer see it, Erin knew the creature hadn't retreated. That it was waiting on the periphery of the beam. Waiting to attack.

Without wasting any more time, she swam towards the vessel she had seen. Fear propelled her along with the speed of a rocket. When close enough, she swept the beam across the object to discover it was a fishing boat. It sat on the ocean floor, stretched into the darkness beyond the beam of light, its tattered nets draped over the starboard side. *Silver Queen*. The boat that had gone missing a few weeks ago

With no other option, she swam towards the wheelhouse. Currents of water swirled at her side and she swept the light beam towards the source; saw a shape flash by in a terrifying blur of speed. The rate of its passing disturbed her swim pattern, threw her off course. She smashed into the side of the boat, jarring her skull. Momentarily disoriented, she shook her head to try to regain her equilibrium. Pure, unequivocal terror coursed through her veins, seeped through every pore of her body. She had to get inside the boat before it was too late.

Kicking furiously, she swam towards the wheelhouse. When she was within reach, she grabbed the sides and pulled herself in through a broken window.

Disturbed by her presence, pieces of debris drifted in the boat. A map floated by, followed by a small bag.

With no time to get her bearings, she swam towards what looked like a trapdoor in the far corner. She shone the light beam over it.

Sensing movement to her rear, she pointed the light back and almost choked as something rushed towards her face. Her heart stopped. She kicked out, realizing at the last minute that it was only a small fish come to seek shelter in the wreckage of the boat.

A cold sweat broke out across her body. She shivered. Her sudden movement moved the air around inside her suit, and like a marionette, her limbs moved in directions she did not intend them to go.

To regain control, she released some of the air through the valve in her arm. A geyser of bubbles gushed out and danced on the ceiling. A quick check of her air pressure revealed that she didn't have much time left. She needed to get to the surface–fast.

She looked back towards the broken window, and was horrified to see the creature, clawing its way in with spindly arms tipped by wicked claws. Its large baleful eyes looked towards her, and it opened its mouth to reveal long, vicious teeth.

Erin wondered whether she was dreaming, whether she was trapped in a nightmare, but she knew she wasn't. This was all too real.

The previous cold sweat intensified to freeze the very marrow in her bones. She needed to escape through the splintered trapdoor, but the displaced air in her suit still had control of her limbs, making movement difficult. She kicked furiously and scrambled with her hands, reaching for something, anything, to pull on to propel her forward.

There were now so many bubbles in the room, it looked as though the water was boiling. The creature was seconds away from her, its mouth open in anticipation of the bite it wanted to deliver. Unable to accept her fate, Erin's feet struck the ceiling. Without hesitating, she kicked out.

The motion was enough to propel her to the trapdoor, and she grabbed the frame and pulled herself through, feeling the displaced motion of water at her rear as the creature bit down where her foot had just been. The flashlight dangled from a strap on her wrist. The wildly swinging beam revealed she was in a short corridor, and using the narrow walls, she pulled herself along.

The beat of her heart thudded inside her ears, making hearing difficult. Although she wanted to look back to see where the creature was, she knew she couldn't. A second's hesitation could lead to her demise. A short flight of steps at the end of the corridor lead down. Erin followed them to another door. It was shut. She reached out and pulled, but the door didn't budge. It was probably the weight of the water holding it tight. Putting all her reserves of strength into it, she yanked the door open and a bulbous figure emerged, arms reaching towards her. Erin recoiled. Air rushed past her lips and streamed from around the regulator. The figure's face was blue and swollen, the eyes like golf balls in the fleshy remains of its eye sockets. Disgusted, Erin clawed past the figure, sending it floating along the corridor behind her. She risked a quick glance back, saw the creature bite down on the carcass, saw skin and bone severed as it ripped its way through the corpse, shaking its head in frenzy. Bits of shredded skin hung suspended in the water like paper at a tickertape parade. A sick feeling climbed Erin's throat. She fought it back down and swam on into the room. Once inside, she turned quickly and pushed the door shut. She was finding it hard to breathe, and a quick check of the gauges revealed that she was out of air, now running on what little remained in the tanks. Her vision was blurring, the edges of her sight going dark as though the world was shrinking.

There was no lock on the door, and when she turned to survey the room, she realised she was trapped in the boat's galley. There was nowhere else to go. The sick feeling returned. Drown, suffocate or be eaten alive. What a choice, she thought.

It reminded her of when she'd accidentally locked herself in the cupboard under the stairs as a kid. The same feeling of claustrophobia. The same feeling of panic. Only this time it was intensified a thousand times. She cast her diminishing gaze around and noticed a wrench on the ground. Thinking she could use it to barricade the door, she swam across and picked it up. As she straightened, she noticed a fire extinguisher on the wall. She grabbed it, hoping that she could utilize it to cloud the water to allow her to escape. Every action made her lungs burn as she eked out the last of the oxygen.

She needed to act quickly, but what was the point? She was going to die anyway. Exhausted, Erin put the fire extinguisher on the table and floated buoyantly in the water at its side. It seemed ironic that the sea she loved and tried to preserve would become her tomb.

Before she had time to ponder the situation further, the creature crashed through the door. Although incapable of expression, she was sure the creature was grinning. It opened its jaws, drawing its razor-sharp teeth from the sheath of its mouth like daggers.

Heart beating like a jackhammer, she picked up the wrench and held it ready, one last defiant act in the face of adversity. Time seemed to stretch out, seconds drawn painfully into minutes. The creature glided towards her, trailing its strange limbs as it thrust its grotesque head forward.

Then an idea sprang into her mind.

It was crazy, but she didn't have anything else.

She needed to time it perfectly as she only had one shot.

She waited …waited until the creature was five feet away, then she smashed the wrench down on the valve of the fire extinguisher with all her might and prayed to God that it would work. The valve shot away, and the fire extinguisher sped towards the creature like a torpedo, trailing white foam in its wake.

Blinded by the trail, Erin could only hope her plan had worked. She swam out into the milky depths, feeling her way. She expected any minute to feel the creature clamp its jaw down on her arm, and a cold dread nestled in the pit of her stomach. Her failing sight made the situation worse, and her burning lungs threatened to pump their last breath at any minute.

Up ahead, the water was clearer, and she could just make out the creature lying sprawled against the wall, the fire extinguisher at its side. Thinking it was dead, she swam across it towards the door, when the creature's mouth twitched.

She raised the knife in her hand, then stabbed it into the creature's eye. A milky liquid gushed out and the creature slashed out with one of its clawed appendages. Erin forced the knife as far as it would go; putting what remained of her strength into the thrust. Blood replaced the milky film. She watched it seep out and drift around her like a strange fog.

Exhausted and giddy with lack of oxygen, she swam out of the boat and started her ascent, going as fast as she dared, which didn't seem fast enough.

Despite knowing the creature was dead, she couldn't help feeling that something was out there in the inky blackness, watching her.

But before she could think about it further, the edges of her vision blurred and then darkness pervaded.

Chapter 13

"Why didn't you answer your phone?" Bruce asked.

"Chill, dad. It's not as if I could have gone far." Jack patted Shazam on the head, and the dog reciprocated by licking his hand.

"That's not the point."

"What's the big deal?"

"There was an accident earlier. A man was attacked in the sea. Some people think it was a shark."

"Cool."

"*Cool*? Jack, someone's died."

"Did you know him? Did I know him? No, then what's it matter? People die all the time." He could tell by his dad's face that he wasn't happy, but he didn't care. At least they were now both of the same frame of mind. He'd only come home because he was hungry, and now he had to listen to this.

"If your mother heard you speak like that, she'd—"

"She'd what? Turn in her grave?"

The slap came without warning, knocking his head back with the force. Jack rubbed his smarting cheek. Shazam barked and then turned and padded away into the corner where she slumped to the ground, watching with puzzlement.

"Jack, I'm sorry. I didn't mean to do that."

Jack fought to keep the tears from flowing. "Tell it to someone who cares. I wish it was you that had died. I hate you." He didn't mean it, but he could see that his words had hurt his dad more than any physical blow.

Bruce bowed his head, turned and started to walk out of the room. "I'm really sorry, Jack. I'm doing my best." Then he was gone.

Jack stood rubbing his cheek for a while longer. It was typical of his dad to make him feel guilty. This was shit with a capital S.

Well fuck him.

Jack picked up his jacket. "Come on Shazam, let's go."

Shazam barked eagerly and followed Jack out of the house. In a village where nothing much happened, Jack assumed a shark attack was probably big news.

There was a crowd of people on the beach, looking out to sea. Jack couldn't see much from where he was, but there didn't seem to be anything happening, so he continued towards the harbour.

Shazam ran on ahead. Before the high street, she sat down and waited, looking back with her tongue lolling as though saying hurry up.

Jack took his cigarettes out of his pocket and lit one. When he reached Shazam, he indicated she could cross, and then followed behind.

There were a couple of boats in the harbour. On board *Storm Bringer*, men were busy mopping down the deck. Jack sat on the harbour wall and watched them. At his side, Shazam sniffed the air, muzzle pointed towards the boat and her hackles slightly raised.

"What's the matter, girl?"

Shazam barked once, then sat down and used her hind leg to scratch behind her ear before settling on the pavement. She looked up at Jack with big, sad eyes. Jack wished he knew what she was thinking.

He exhaled a cloud of smoke and stared at the trawler. Rusty streaks ran down the sides of the pilothouse, above which antennas protruded like sea anemone tentacles. Large booms protruded from the deck.

"Hey, you haven't disappeared yet then?"

Jack turned to see Jen standing behind him on the road. A hot flush spread across his cheeks. Dressed in a pink crop top with the words *Sexy Beast* emblazoned across her chest, and three-quarter length green pants, she looked cuter than ever. Even the way she chewed her gum looked sensual.

"No, I'm still here. The house hasn't gobbled me up yet. No boyfriend around today?" he asked, peering surreptitiously along the road to see if he could spot him.

"Nah. I'm a free agent today. So what are you doing?"

"Heard something about someone being attacked in the sea, so thought I'd come see what's going on."

"Yeah, I heard about that. Someone on their holiday. News travels fast in the village. One whiff of scandal and the local gossips spring into action faster than the Marines. You've never lived till you've seen eighty-six year old Mavis Bench with a bee in her bonnet. Quicker than a fuel-injected rocket. Something about a shark, I heard. It's the first time I've heard of one attacking anyone in this country, never mind around here before." She shrugged, and Jack couldn't help staring at her chest which jiggled slightly. "So you're a voyeur?"

"What, sorry, I didn't mean ..." He looked up and blushed.

Jen grinned. "I mean about the attack. You know, like one of them people that slow down to look at car crashes on the motorway. What did you think I meant?"

"Nothing. That's what I thought you meant."

"Sure." She giggled.

Jack felt stupid. "So what are you up to?"

"Same as you. Thought I'd see what was going on."

Jack nodded. "Smoke?" He offered her the packet.

Jen shook her head. "Nah, them things'll kill ya."

"If the house or the sharks don't get me first you mean."

Jen laughed. "The shark would probably give you a miss for someone with more meat on their bones."

Jack tried not to show it, but her comment hurt, drilling home the insecurity about his weight.

"I don't mean you're skinny," Jen said as though she had read his mind. "I just mean there's probably plenty more people they would like to eat first."

"Like Rocky, you mean?"

Jen wrinkled her nose. "That's not very nice."

"I'm sorry. Just don't know what you see in him."

"I should hope you wouldn't, not unless you were, you know."

"Hey, I'm straight as a gun barrel."

66

"I don't doubt it. You want to get something to eat?"

Jack cocked his head to the side. "That a dig at my size again?"

"Nah, I'm just hungry. But if you don't want to..."

"I didn't say I wasn't interested."

"Good. Come on then."

"Is it okay if my dog comes too?"

Jen peered over the harbour wall. "Sure. At least then there'll be someone intelligent to talk to."

As if in agreement, Shazam barked.

"See what I mean." She leaned over the wall to stroke Shazam's head. Jack reluctantly looked away, embarrassed that he might get more of an eyeful.

"So where we going?"

"Well, you might have noticed the village isn't awash with McDonalds or Burger King, so we can grab a bite at my house."

Jack nodded. "Sounds great." As they started to walk away, he said, "That boat, *Storm Bringer*. You know much about it?"

"That's Trent Zander's boat. Local nutcase. Every town and village has one, but I think we've got more than our fair share."

"Nutcase. How?"

"He's just someone you wouldn't want to mess with."

Jen lived in a house just off the high street. Her parents were both at work and her grandmother was out, for which Jack was grateful. He hated meeting people's parents. Especially a girl's parents. A girl's father had that way of looking at you as if to say, 'if you hurt my princess, I'll cut you into little pieces'.

They sat at a small rectangular wooden table in the kitchen cum dining room. The large front window looked out to sea.

"Nice house," Jack said.

Jen shrugged. "It's okay, I guess. What would you like to eat?" She opened the fridge and pulled out a plate. "Ham sandwich?"

"Ah, I didn't tell you did I?"

"Tell me what?"

"I'm vegetarian. Sorry."

"No problem. You eat cheese?"

Jack nodded.

"Cheese and onion sandwiches okay then?"

"That would be great." Shazam whined softly from under the kitchen table and licked her lips. "I don't suppose you could give my dog some of that meat. Unlike me, she's a carnivore."

"No problem." She started to place some of the ham onto a separate plate. "Oh sod it. You can have the lot." She piled the ham back on the original plate and placed it on the floor. "There you go. Enjoy."

Shazam slinked out from under the table and stood over the food, her tongue lolling from the corner of her mouth. She looked up at Jen and then back at Jack.

"It's okay, you can eat it," Jack said.

Without further encouragement, Shazam started to gobble down the meal.

"She's well trained," Jen said as she sliced the cheese.

"House trained, just like me."

Jen giggled.

To accompany the sandwiches, Jen poured two glasses of Coke and filled a bowl of water for Shazam, who noisily lapped it up. They ate the sandwiches in silence. Knowing she had a boyfriend made Jack feel awkward, and whenever he looked at Jen, his eyes inadvertently strayed to her bosom. He couldn't see what the hell she saw in Rocky, but he sure saw what he saw in Jen.

The sound of a siren filled the silence. Jack and Jen looked at each other across the table. Then they turned and stared out the window. Jack could see a small boat speeding towards the harbour, where an ambulance was just pulling in.

"Looks like it's all go today. You want to see what's going on?" Jen asked.

Jack swallowed the bite of sandwich he had been chewing. "And to think I thought this was a sleepy village."

They left the house and quickly made their way back down to the harbour. The ambulance waited with its lights flashing, the paramedics standing beside it looking out to sea. A small crowd had already gathered, and among them, Jack noticed Rocky. When Rocky saw Jen approaching he waved and grinned. Then he saw Jack at her side, and his grin became a scowl.

"What the hell you doin' with him?" Rocky growled.

"We were just talking," Jen said, stepping between them and kissing Rocky on the cheek.

Shazam stood at Jack's side. A low growl emanated from her and she bared her teeth.

"You better hope that mutt don't come near me, otherwise it'll be dog meat."

"It's okay, girl," Jack said, patting the dog on the head. He stared at Rocky. "I know there's a bad smell around here, but I'm sure it'll be gone soon."

Rocky clenched his fists. He looked ready to start trouble.

"Cut it out you two," Jen said. "So what's going on here?" she asked Rocky, pointing towards the fast approaching boat.

Rocky held eye contact with Jack for a moment longer then turned to Jen. "I dunno. Did you hear about that man this morning?"

Jen nodded. "Yeah, it's awful."

"You can say that again. It got the wrong person." He glared at Jack.

For Jen's sake, Jack decided not to rise to the bait. He watched the boat as it sped into the harbour. There were two men in it from what he could see. When they reached the quay, one of them jumped out and moored the vessel up, while the other crouched down in the back.

The paramedics rushed down to meet the boat, carrying a stretcher. They boarded the boat, and moments later, they hurried back to the ambulance carrying someone between them. Jack peered through the crowd. He caught sight of the person on the stretcher; recognised her as the girl that he had given a light to in the bar. She wasn't moving.

"Do you think she's dead?" Jen whispered.

Jack bit his lip. If she wasn't dead, then she was sure as hell as close as she was going to get.

"Well I'm out of here," Jack said.

Jen turned and looked at him. "You don't have to leave. Stay." Rocky's expression said otherwise.

"Nah, guess it's time to head home."

Jen lowered her gaze. She kicked at the floor and then nodded. As he walked away, Jack couldn't help thinking that he had seen something in her expression. Something that said she really wanted him to stay. He smiled. Perhaps there was hope yet.

Chapter 14

"Are you sure it was her?" Bruce asked, putting down the paintbrush he'd been using to paint the window. White paint splattered the front of his blue shirt and speckled his cheeks and hair.

Jack nodded. "I don't know what happened to her, but she looked real bad."

Bruce shook his head. "My god. I was only talking to her this morning. What a day this is turning out to be."

Jack recognised something more than regular sympathy in his dad's voice. He saw concern; wished now he hadn't mentioned anything. The previous altercation with his dad seemed to have been forgotten, which was better than having to listen to another lecture.

"Perhaps I should go see how she is," Bruce said.

"Why? You don't know her."

"I know, but it seems the right thing to do. I think I'll go and have a wash. Do you know where they took her?"

Jack shook his head.

"Well, there's probably a hospital nearby. I'm sure someone in the village will know. And Jack, thanks for the milk."

Jack shrugged his shoulders. "It's no big deal."

Bruce ruffled Jack's hair. "Still, thanks anyway." He smiled and then left the room, leaving Jack feeling glad his good deed hadn't gone unnoticed, but resentful that his dad was going to see another woman.

Bruce parked the car opposite the harbour and then walked into the hardware shop. Duncan Roberts was sitting behind the counter reading a book.

"Hello again," Duncan said, smiling amiably. "It's Bruce, isn't it?"

"That's right. I don't know if you heard about the woman that had the diving accident earlier—"

Duncan nodded his head. "Terrible business. What with the attack this morning. Never seen anything like it in all the years I've lived here."

"Well I was just wondering if you could tell me where they might have taken her."

"Probably to the hospital in town."

"Is it far?"

"No, you passed through it on the way here. The one with the new resort."

"Thanks."

Duncan clucked his tongue. "Mind how you go now. You know what they say, bad luck has a way of travelling in threes."

Bruce subconsciously fingered his wallet with the good luck charms inside.

"If you'd like a drink later, get to know a few people, I'll be in the bar about eight," Duncan said.

"What … yes, thanks. I might just take you up on that."

Outside the shop, Bruce stared across the harbour and saw Zander standing on the bow of his boat, staring back at him. Bruce held his hand up in acknowledgement. Zander spat into the sea, turned and disappeared below decks.

Bruce didn't like animosity, but he didn't think Zander was going to be on his Christmas card list anytime soon.

Once in the car, he took out his phone and rang Jack, who answered on the sixth ring.

"Yeah?"

"I'm going to drive to the hospital. Don't know what time I'll be back. There's some money on the table in the kitchen. If I'm not back in time, buy yourself something to eat."

"Buy something where?"

"There's a cafe in town isn't there? Oh, and can you feed Shazam too?"

"Whatever."

"Thanks. See you later. Be good."

Bruce disconnected the call and started the car. He drove out of the village at a leisurely pace. With so much work to do on the house, he felt guilty leaving it. But he knew he was

72

going to have to get back to his real job of website designing eventually when they connected his phone line and set up his internet account. Some of the tasks, like the rotten bedroom window and the dodgy plumbing, were best left to the professionals. This reminded him to ask Duncan if he could recommend anyone; better not to upset the local tradesmen if he could help it by getting in outsiders to do the work. One person off his Christmas card list in a small village was already one too many.

The new resort was bustling. Families were playing on the beach, and kids were paddling in the sea and running through the arcades. Bruce wondered whether news of the attack had filtered through yet. Looking at the kids in the sea, he doubted it. Perhaps the attack was an isolated incident, but then what had happened to Erin? He assured himself it was probably unconnected, and followed the signs to the hospital.

He parked in the car park and made his way to the reception. The hospital was a modern building with a large glass front. The automatic doors glided open and Bruce walked inside. He basked in the cool interior, took a moment to waft the neck of his T-shirt. He'd tried to dress casually in new black jeans and a T-shirt, but now he wondered if it was appropriate attire for visiting someone in hospital. That's if they let him see her.

The woman seated at reception looked up and stared at Bruce over the top of her glasses. She had a studious expression, her black hair tied back in a severe ponytail that only accentuated the sharp angles of her face.

"Yes?" she said.

"Erm, I wonder if you can help me. There was a woman brought in earlier."

"Name?"

"Erin."

The receptionist stared at him as though he were stupid. "Erin who?"

Bruce leaned forward. He knew all too well that hospitals had strict visiting procedures. "McVey. She's my sister."

The receptionist tapped a pencil against her teeth.

Bruce gave her what he hoped was his best smile. After another moment, the woman ran her finger down a list on her desk.

"Well, visiting hours aren't for another hour."

"How is she?"

"I wouldn't know."

"Well, couldn't I just pop in and see how she is?"

After another embarrassingly long silence and prolonged staring match, she said, "Second floor. Ward four. Tell the duty nurse I said it was all right."

"Thank you." Anxious to be out of her sight, Bruce turned and followed the signs to the second floor. On the way, he passed a small kiosk selling flowers, and he bought a bunch. Probably the least green-fingered person he knew, he hoped the flowers didn't die before he reached the room.

Bruce followed the signs to the ward until he found himself standing outside the double doors. Small squares of glass in each door allowed him to peer through before entering. He couldn't spot Erin, although there was one bed with the curtains drawn around it. He realised his palms were sweating, and he felt slightly nauseous. What the hell was the matter with him? He was only paying a visit in the hospital. But he knew that wasn't all there was to it. He swallowed to dislodge the lump in his throat, then he took a deep breath, pushed open the door and stepped into the room. A small woman wearing round glasses sat at a desk inside the ward. She looked up at Bruce, and he quickly explained the reason for his visit.

The duty nurse pointed along the ward. "She's resting. Bed at the end with the curtain drawn around it." With that, she returned her attention to the paperwork on her desk.

As in the rest of the hospital, there was an antiseptic aroma in the air, but there was also the undeniable faint smell of blood and human waste that almost made him turn around and head back out.

The few patients who weren't drowsing looked at him for a moment then turned away. The television at the end of the room was on, but with the sound turned down low the muffled exchange of views between the host and guests on a daytime chat show sounded as though it was coming from another room.

The patients were all female, and seeing them in their nightgowns and pyjamas made Bruce blush. The ages of the patients ranged from late teens to late life. Some sat in chairs, but most reclined in bed.

He quickly made his way down the middle of the room, towards the curtained bed at the end. When he reached it, he coughed to clear his throat. Butterflies danced in his stomach, and he chastised himself. He wasn't a goddamn teenager.

"Erin? Erin McVey?"

When no one answered, he timidly peeked through a gap in the curtain. The woman lying in the bed was asleep, but he instantly recognised her. She looked pale, her breathing laboured. There was a tube in her arm, and a clear liquid dripped through at regular intervals. Bruce felt his heart miss a beat. Christ, what had happened to her?

He slipped through the curtain, shaking his head despondently. Not wanting to disturb her, he placed the flowers on the bedside cabinet, and turned to leave.

"I've got to get out of here."

Bruce jumped. He spun around and saw Erin struggling to sit up. She coughed, the action making her cringe in pain.

"Here, let me help you." He reached down to assist, but she held her hand up.

"I can manage," she snapped. After a moment's struggle, she sat up. "What are you doing here?"

Bruce stared at her, unsure what to say next. He nodded. "Yes, I … um, I—"

"Well, I don't know what you're doing here, but I've got to get out. I've got to warn them." She started to swing her legs out of bed. The tube in her arm pulled tight, almost toppling the stand it was attached to.

Bruce grabbed it before it fell. "Take it easy."

"Don't tell me what to do."

Bruce sighed and his shoulders slumped. This wasn't going how he had imagined. "I'm sorry. I'll leave you alone."

"Wait a minute. What did you come here for anyway?"

"I … Well, I heard about your accident–I don't know what I came for really." He shrugged, could feel his face burning up.

Erin exhaled noisily. "Look, I'm sorry. I didn't mean to snap at you."

"That's okay. You look like you've been through the mill."

"That's not the half of it." With surprising speed and strength, she reached out and grabbed Bruce's arm. "You've got to listen to me. They're saying it was lack of oxygen, but I know it wasn't. You've got to believe me. There's something out there. In the water. Something unnatural."

"Yes, I already know about it."

"You do?" Her hold relaxed.

"Yes, a shark I heard."

Erin shook her head and squeezed tighter. "Not a shark. It was something else. Something, I don't know … something monstrous."

Bruce patted her hand. "You're safe now. Nothing can hurt you here."

Erin sank back onto the bed. "I don't think any of us are safe," she said before sleep engulfed her.

Chapter 15

Jack was bored. He was also hungry again. A quick inspection of the fridge revealed milk, a tub of margarine, a couple of eggs, and a half empty can of beans.

He took a swallow from the milk to sate his appetite, then replaced it on the shelf and closed the fridge.

His dad had left ten pounds on the kitchen table, so he picked the money up, and with Shazam in tow, he left the house and headed back to the village.

Hopefully, Rocky would have gone by now, and if he was really lucky, Jen might still be around.

On the coast road, he stared out to sea. The great expanse of water stretched before him, and he wondered whether there really was a man-eating shark prowling beneath the waves. If there was, then he could see a scene straight out of 'Jaws' might ensue, and a flotilla of boats would set out to destroy it. Not that he would support that. The shark was only doing what came naturally to it. How the hell was it supposed to know that mankind was not on the menu?

When he reached the harbour, he noticed Trent Zander's boat had set sail. A couple of seagulls sat preening themselves on the harbour wall. Shazam barked at them and the birds cocked their heads and looked across at her before squawking loudly. They flapped their wings, then settled down.

The aroma of brine was heavy in the air. It stuck to the back of Jack's throat, making him feel a little sick.

Across the road at the cafe, *Bites*, there were still a couple of tables and chairs outside, but no one sat in them. Jack wandered across. A faded blue canopy shaded the front of the shop.

A chalkboard nailed to the wall listed the food available.

"I'll have to leave you out here," Jack said to Shazam, who stared up at him with her tongue lolling from the side of her jaw. "It's no good giving me your sad face. You see that sign, it says no dogs allowed." Although she was generally well behaved, he attached Shazam to her lead and tied her to a drain pipe. Then he quickly scratched her behind the ear and entered the shop.

After the smell of brine, the aroma of freshly baked food was wonderful. Jack breathed deeply to fill his lungs with the fragrance, and his stomach rumbled in response.

Inside the shop, a glass-fronted cabinet held a few cakes. Jack salivated at the sight of the chocolate éclairs. A big black potato oven sat behind the counter, along with a cash register, a microwave, and a rack of bread.

There was no one in the shop, so Jack knocked on the counter and a moment later, a stout, ruddy faced girl appeared from the back room. A small white cap covered her hair, and she wiped her hands on her blue apron. Jack guessed she was about twenty.

"Hello. What can I get you?" she asked, smiling to reveal large teeth. Jack settled on a cheese and pickle sandwich and soup.

While the girl prepared the order, Jack peered out of the window at the harbour, hoping to spot Jen.

"You on holiday?" the girl asked.

"No, just moved here."

"Oh yes, where to?"

"A house on Millhouse Lane."

The girl stopped in the middle of ladling soup into a bowl.

"You okay?" Jack asked.

"Is that the Johnson place?" Her previously ruddy complexion seemed to have blanched.

"That's the one. And yeah, I already heard the previous family was supposed to have disappeared."

The girl resumed ladling and a dollop of tomato soup splashed the counter like blood.

"They seemed like such a nice family. Hadn't been here that long either. Just plain disappeared. Some people say the house had something to do with it, others say the father was in debt and that the collectors found him, others say they ran away in the night."

"And what do you think?"

The girl turned and stared at him. She shrugged. "Don't really know what I think. Just that it was a shame, that's all."

When Jack had his food, he took it outside and sat at one of the two tables. Shazam looked up longingly. "Sorry, girl, but this is all mine." The dog whined softly, and Jack relented, broke some of the bread off, and tossed it to her.

A few white clouds gathered on the horizon. Jack stared at them as he ate. A boat came into view. He watched it make its way towards the harbour; saw Zander step on deck and moor the boat up.

Jack heard a car door open, and turned to see a short squat man exiting from a black BMW. The man lit a cigarette, hunched his shoulders and walked towards the harbour. Zander stood on the deck of his boat and nodded in acknowledgment as the man approached.

Zander looked around quickly, then threw down a white package, which the man deftly caught. Without saying a word, the man reached into his pocket, withdrew a small packet of his own, and tossed it up to Zander. Then the man turned and started walking away.

Now that he was walking back to the car, Jack had his first proper look at the man. Short and squat, he had a round face, short hair and deep-set eyes overshadowed by thick brows. He smoked his cigarette from the corner of his mouth, lips curled around it to exhale. For a brief instant, the man's gaze met Jack's and they stared at one another. Jack looked away first. He didn't know why, but the man scared him.

When he looked back at the boat, he saw Zander clambering down onto the quay with a battered duffel bag thrown over his shoulder. The sudden sound of the BMW's engine disturbed the relative silence. Jack kept his eyes averted as it drove by, but he thought he could feel the driver's eyes burrowing into him. He looked back up in time to see Zander disappearing inside a small wooden outbuilding on the edge of the harbour.

He had seen enough in the city to know there was something fishy going on that probably didn't actually involve fish.

Jack wolfed the remainder of his food, untied Shazam and then hurried across the road to the harbour. The building Zander had entered was a faded red painted structure that bore testament to the harsh weather with its buckling walls. Shazam sniffed around the bottom of the door, her ears cocked. Thinking she might alert Zander to their presence, Jack pulled her away. Around the side of the building, he tiptoed towards a small window. Caked with years of dirt, the glass was an impenetrable screen. Using the tips of his fingers, Jack carefully scraped away a small viewing area, and then he cupped his hands around his eyes and peered inside.

He could just make out a figure crouched on the ground prizing up a floorboard.

"Hey, what do you think you're doin'?"

Startled, Jack spun around to see Rocky standing not twenty feet away. His pulse went up.

Great. This was all he needed.

"If it isn't my girl you're sniffing around, it's other people's business," Rocky said.

Shazam stood with her hackles raised. "I'm just getting acquainted with the area."

"Acquainted. Mr. Lardy Da Big Shot from the city is getting acquainted. What say I acquaint you with my fists?"

"Try that and my dog will take a chunk out of your leg."

"You think I'm scared of a dog."

Shazam growled softly.

Rocky coughed and took a step back. "You'd better not let that mutt anywhere near me, otherwise—"

"Otherwise what?" Jack asked, enjoying seeing Rocky backpedal.

"Otherwise I'll make both of you pay."

"Whatever. Come on Shazam, let's go."

"Shazam. What a fucking stupid name," Rocky said as he guffawed into his hand.

"That from someone called Rocky. You're priceless, you know that." He knew he was treading dangerously, but he couldn't back down. Not now. He had to make a stand from the start, otherwise Rocky and his sort would think they could do what they wanted with him. Although he practiced Judo, it meant 'the gentle way', as the translation of the name implied, and was more self-defence than kick-ass.

Heart pumping fast, Jack walked towards Rocky. For a moment, it didn't look as though he was going to move, but then Shazam took the lead and he begrudgingly stepped aside.

Back out on the main road, Jack breathed a sigh of relief. Without looking back, he walked along the side of the harbour, intending to head home.

What happened next took him completely by surprise. He didn't even have time to react. One moment he was walking along, the next someone pushed him from behind. He instinctively let go of Shazam's lead and flailed his arms to maintain his balance, but it was no good. Pushed too far, gravity took over. Where a moment ago there had been solid ground beneath his feet, now there was only empty air. With his heart in his throat, Jack fell over the edge of the harbour, and down towards the cold water below.

He closed his eyes and landed with a loud splash. Although the water yielded, searing pain shot up his back. The water was as cold as it looked and he descended into its depths. He kicked out and his left leg struck something submerged beneath the surface. This pain was more acute, more centralized – it felt like someone had poured acid onto his skin. Bubbles spurted from his mouth as he gagged. When he opened his eyes, the saltwater stung; everything was blurred. Disorientated, he kicked and clawed out, striving to escape the fluid embrace. When he surfaced, he sucked in a deep lungful of air and trod water for a moment to compose himself. Up on the quay, Shazam barked loudly, her head visible as she looked down at him.

The pain from his leg was becoming unbearable. He lifted it in the water to caress the afflicted area and flinched at the resultant sting. His jeans were ripped where he had cut himself on something. Blood trailed away from his leg like a ribbon, wafted on the ebb and flow. Then he remembered the supposed shark attack, and with it came the thought that sharks were attracted to blood, could sniff it out from miles away. And here he was, sending out a personal invitation.

Panicked, he looked around the harbour walls for a way out, but he couldn't see anything, no ladder, no launching ramp, nothing. A line of green plankton and barnacles on the harbour wall indicated where the usual high tide mark was; he was about three foot lower in the water. The bricks looked too slimy to climb. Then he remembered Zander's boat. He turned and looked at it, the only apparent way he could see to haul himself out of the water. He swam towards the vessel, leaving a murky red trail in his wake. His clothes billowed around him, making progress difficult.

While swimming, he kept glancing around, terrified of seeing a fin break the surface. His heart beat like a drum in his chest, furthering his panic as he wondered if the sound was amplified in the water, another distress beacon to attract a hungry predator.

He swept his right hand into the water and something clammy brushed against his fingers. The panic he felt before was magnified a hundredfold.

Shark!

Terrified of losing his hand, Jack lifted it out of the water – to find there was something attached to it. In a fit of panic, he flung it away, but it was only a piece of seaweed. He couldn't be sure, but he thought he heard someone laughing.

Desperate to get out of the water, he continued towards the boat and hauled himself up using the tyres that hung from the sides of the boat. The weight of his soaked clothes made it difficult, but eventually he clambered over the side and lay on the deck, breathing hard.

The deck smelled slightly of fish. He didn't know how anyone could stomach working with such a stench all day and he quickly stood up. The thought of all those helpless fish slopping around underfoot made him angry.

A quick glance at the harbour revealed no sign of Rocky. Shazam stood at the edge of the quay, looking back with her tail wagging and her tongue lolling.

It must have been Rocky that pushed him, but Jack was surprised he hadn't hung around to gloat. He berated himself for not hearing him come up behind him. Even Shazam had apparently not heard anything, otherwise she would have alerted him with one of her ear-piercing barks.

The wet clothes made him feel uncomfortable, and he shook himself to try to shake some of the water off. As he passed the wheelhouse, he glanced inside and caught sight of a small package on a table, similar to the one Zander had thrown down to the man on the dock, but far smaller.

He stared quickly at the outbuilding Zander had entered. Satisfied no one was around to see, Jack tested the door. It was unlocked. With his pulse pounding in his ears, he opened the door and slipped inside the room. He had never broken in anywhere before, and he felt both guilty and exhilarated. Shazam barked loudly, and he silently urged her to be quiet in case she alerted Zander to his presence.

All manner of electrical devices filled the wheelhouse. Jack recognised sonar screens and a transmitter, but nothing else. With glass windows all around, he felt vulnerable, and not wanting to waste any time, he picked the small package up and immediately smelt the familiar aroma of cannabis. He opened a corner and pressed his finger into the brown substance beneath the wrapper. It felt soft, which meant it was fresh cannabis resin. He didn't know how, but Zander was smuggling drugs.

Although it was tough to break, he managed to tear a chunk off before wrapping the package back up.

With the cannabis safely in his pocket, Jack scurried out of the wheelhouse, ran across the boat, and scrambled up onto the quay. Shazam bounded across to meet him and licked his hand.

Satisfied no one had seen, Jack turned, intending to find somewhere quiet to roll a joint, only to find Lillian Brown standing before him. Before he could react, the old woman grabbed his arm and squeezed until he squealed.

Chapter 16

"You little bastard," Lillian Brown snarled as she squeezed Jack's arm. A wild look sparkled in her eyes. Shazam barked loudly.

"Let go of me, you crazy bitch," Jack screamed.

Lillian squeezed tighter. Jack wanted to punch her, but he couldn't hit a woman, not even one as mad as this bitch. He grabbed her hand to try to prise her fingers apart, but her grip was too strong.

The two grey streaks in Lillian's hair accentuated her piercing grey eyes. Her lips curled back, and when she spoke, spittle flew out and struck Jack's cheek.

"It's all your fault," she said. "You and your kind come down here and bring all the bad luck with you.

"Just let me go you stupid cow," Jack said, trying to remain calm. "You're coming with me," Lillian said as she started to drag him towards the road.

Jack tried to resist, but despite Lillian's thin stature, she seemed to possess the strength of the damned.

Shazam ran around the pair of them, barking wildly, seeming unsure what to do.

"What's all the commotion?" Zander asked as he appeared from the outbuilding.

"You'll see. You'll see," Lillian screeched. "Come with me, you'll see."

"Tell this crazy cow to let me go," Jack said.

"You look wet kid. Been swimming with your clothes on?" Zander replied, ignoring Jack's plea.

Jack tried to brace his feet on the pavement, but it was no good. Pain radiated from his injured leg.

Rather than intervene, Zander followed.

Lillian pushed Jack into the Sheet and Anchor bar. Jack counted at least fifteen people inside the room.

"Here he is," Lillian screeched.

Everyone turned to look. Graham stopped cleaning glasses on the bar and leaned forward. "What's all this about?"

Lillian pushed Jack into the middle of the room. "Ever since this lad and his father arrived, there's been nothing but bad luck."

A man with ginger hair stood up from his seat at the bar and raised his hands. Jack recognised him as the man from the shop, Duncan someone or other.

"Come on now, Lillian. Let the lad go."

"She's right," Zander said as he walked into the bar. "I've never had it so bad. It's as though the fish have all disappeared."

"Yes, what about the *Silver Queen*?" Lillian snapped.

"I don't know what the hell you're talking about," Jack said, his cheeks starting to burn.

"The *Silver Queen* was a boat that disappeared just before you arrived. Went missing with all hands," Lillian said.

"That's nothing to do with me."

"Of course it's to do with you. You've brought bad luck to the village. I told everyone it would happen. Didn't I tell you? When you start letting outsiders buy up the houses, it creates bad karma."

"Leave the boy alone," someone said.

"No, let her speak," a man with short hair and leather hardened skin said.

"She's got a point," piped up a middle-aged woman with her black hair tied back in a ponytail. A few of the other patrons nodded in agreement.

"And then there was that attack," Lillian said. More patrons nodded.

"And there was that woman, pulled from the sea like she'd seen a ghost," someone said.

Graham held his hand up. "There'll be a logical explanation."

"We don't need an explanation. We know what's happened. We need to get rid of the newcomers," Lillian said.

Jack trembled. He couldn't believe they were talking this way. The animosity directed towards him filled the air. He fought back tears. Didn't want to show any sign of weakness.

"So what, you want to chase them out of town, is that what you're saying?" Graham asked.

"Something like that," Lillian replied.

"Hey now hold on," Jack said, finally finding his voice. "We didn't come here looking for trouble." Rather than appear timid, he held his head up and maintained eye contact with Lillian. Judo had taught him that predators choose victims who appear unaware, timid or lost, and this was no time to be any of those.

"Then what did you come here for?" Lillian spat back.

"To make a fresh start." All eyes turned towards the door, where Jack's father stood. "Now can someone tell me what the hell's going on?"

Lillian released her grip.

Relieved to see his dad, Jack hurried across and stood next to him. Lillian shook her head in disgust. "You outsiders are all the same. All you do is bring misfortune."

Bruce grimaced. "What are you talking about? Surely you people aren't going to listen to this madwoman."

Graham puffed out his chest. "You can't come here and tell us not to listen to one of our own." The crowd made grunts of agreement.

"Everybody needs to just calm down," Duncan said as he stood up and placed himself between the two factions. "This is no way to treat newcomers. It's bad enough we've lost business to the new resort down the coast without trying to run people out of town."

"Yes, they were newcomers too," Lillian said, grinning maniacally as she sprung on Duncan's argument. "They put most of you out of business. Came from the city with their big plans, and now look what it's done to us."

"You can't blame everything on outsiders," Duncan said. "Where would we have been for all those years if people hadn't come here on holiday?"

87

Lillian cackled. "Yes, they built us up all right, just so they could knock us down."

"Can someone tell me what this is about? I'm sure we can straighten it out." Bruce said.

Jack shook his head. "They're trying to blame us for the lack of fish and for the recent incidents."

"That's crazy."

"Look, look, he's calling us crazy," Lillian shouted.

Bruce shook his head. "That's not what I said. You're trying to twist my words around."

"Will everyone just calm down," Duncan said. His permanently red cheeks looked overly flushed.

"How can we calm down, Duncan?" a large man wearing a hat and sporting a well-worn suit shouted. "As if it's not bad enough these people have left us with nothing, now we can't even make a living. Do you know how much money I earned last year? Less than twelve thousand pounds. It's not right. A man should be able to support his family."

"Aye, John's right," Zander said. "We don't need outsiders coming here disrupting our way of life."

"What way of life?" Bruce said. "By the looks of it, you need all the outsiders you can get to bring money back into the village."

"We'll manage," Zander replied.

Bruce grabbed Jack's arm. "Come on, we're going."

Not wanting to argue, Jack followed his dad out of the bar. Shazam was sitting outside. Her tail started wagging when she saw Jack and Bruce.

"Some good you were," Jack said, scratching the dog's head.

As they walked away, Jack glanced back, worried they might be followed. When he didn't see anyone, he relaxed a little.

"So much for a peaceful life in the country," Bruce said.

Jack could see his dad clenching his jaw. "I told you it was a mistake moving here. Remember Tenerife?"

Bruce didn't reply, but Jack could see by his expression that he was inclined to agree.

When his dad did eventually speak, he said, "So how come you're all wet? And where did you get those cuts? Did that madwoman do it?"

"I tripped and fell in the sea."

Bruce visibly blanched. He stopped walking and grabbed Jack by both arms. Jack grimaced.

"Take it easy," Jack said.

"You've been in the sea? Promise me you won't go in again."

"Hey, chill. It's no big deal.

"Jack, promise me." He squeezed tighter.

"Jesus, don't blow a fuse. Okay, I promise."

Bruce let out a breath then released Jack. "I'm sorry, but there's something going on out there." He pointed to the sea, lips pursed.

"I know. The shark, remember."

"Yes … the shark." He had a faraway, wistful look about him before he turned and started walking again.

Jack fell in step beside him. He gazed out to sea as he walked. Wished he was anywhere rather than here, even back in Tenerife.

Chapter 17

The night swept in across the sea. Jack sat in the living room, looking out the window. He had changed out of the wet clothes when he arrived home, quickly transferring the cannabis to his new jeans in case his dad found it.

The reflection of the full moon rippled on the surface of the sea like mercury. Lights flickered on the horizon from a passing ship.

Jack could see his dad's reflection in the glass. "So did you get to see that woman at the hospital?"

Bruce looked up from his newspaper. He licked his lips, then nodded.

"Well?"

"Yes, she's okay."

"So what happened to her?"

"She had an accident, that's all."

Something in the way his dad spoke made Jack think he wasn't telling him the truth, or at least not the whole story. When he turned around to look at him, his dad had buried his nose back in the newspaper.

"So what are we going to do about living here, you know, with what happened earlier?"

Bruce looked up again. "They'll get over it. They're just looking for a scapegoat, and unfortunately, as newcomers, we're it."

"So what are you saying, that we just accept it? That madwoman grabbed me and marched me into the bar for Christ's sake."

"A lot of these people have lost their livelihoods. They're upset. Give them time. Eventually they'll accept us."

Jack wasn't convinced. "I'm going out," he said.

"It's dark, and after what happened today, I think you'd better stay in."

"No way."

"Jack, I'm not asking you. This isn't open for debate. You're staying in."

Rather than argue, Jack stood up, said, "It's not fair," and stormed out of the room, banging the door behind him for good effect. He made sure his dad heard him thunder up the stairs and into his bedroom. Once inside, he fashioned a pile of clothes into a vaguely human shape on the bed and threw the covers over it. Then he went across to the window, opened it, and slipped outside onto the porch roof, shutting the window behind him. He'd known the porch would come in handy, which was why he'd chosen the bedroom at the front. From there it was a simple exercise to drop the eight feet to the ground, hanging by his arms onto the edge of the tiles to lessen the height.

A quick glance back at the house, then he ran down onto the road and started walking towards the village.

Lights blazed in many of the houses, but drawn curtains diminished their radiance. If it hadn't been for the full moon, he would have had difficulty navigating a path. In the distance, lights illuminated the harbour, and Jack saw Zander's boat bobbing gently against the quay. He wondered whether Zander would notice any of his cannabis was missing. Not that it mattered if he did. He wouldn't know who had taken it.

In need of a quiet place to roll his joint, Jack skipped over the harbour wall and settled down on the ground as he prepared his cigarette before lighting it.

The first hit tickled the back of his throat, and he held the smoke in his lungs for as long as possible before exhaling. Through the resultant pale cloud, he viewed the sea, chuckling to himself when he remembered how scared he had been when someone pushed him in earlier. The whole situation now seemed ridiculous. Of course a shark wasn't going to get him. There probably wasn't even one out there, just the result of someone's overactive imagination. But now that he thought about it, and far from making people stay away, stories of a man-eating shark would probably help the local economy. There were probably lots of people who would pay to see the killer from the deep.

91

Jack took another hit. He wondered whether someone local had made the whole thing up to make a little money. The thought made him giggle and he snorted and coughed out a cloud of smoke. Not as backward as they appeared, the villagers were the real sharks.

When the joint was smoked down to the end, Jack tossed it into the sea. He thought he heard it sizzle as it hit the water, but he couldn't be sure.

He stood up. His mouth was dry, and he swallowed in an attempt to produce saliva. The rippling water far out to sea was almost hypnotic. Jack stood transfixed for a while, listening to the gentle susurrations of the waves as they slapped against the harbour wall. Time became irrelevant.

The door to the Sheet and Anchor opened and a rush of chatter bubbled out. Jack snapped out of his daze, ducked down and peered over the wall to watch a man stagger from the bar. He giggled at the sight. The bar door swung slowly shut, and silence descended.

At a higher elevation beyond the bar, he thought he could see Jen's house. A bedroom window was alight. He wondered whether it was Jen's bedroom. The thought accelerated his already fast beating heart. What was she doing with that twat, Rocky? Jesus, he would love to get it on with her – at least then living here would be bearable.

Spurred by the thought, he lit a cigarette and started to walk towards her house. The buildings along the side street muffled any sound from the sea; it felt almost surreal, as though everything was holding its breath.

Shadows bathed the streets. The hairs on the nape of his neck prickled as though someone were watching him. Jack spun around, but as far as he could see, there was no one there. He proceeded with caution. It would be just like Rocky to be lying in wait somewhere. Wet clothes he could endure, but a broken skull wasn't so easy.

A rapid staccato clicking sound filled the silence. Jack flinched and an involuntary shiver ran down his spine. He stared around, wide-eyed to trace the source of the noise, but he couldn't see anything.

Not wanting to hang around in the dark to see what it was, he stubbed the cigarette out and ran up the slight incline to where brightly lit windows and a couple of streetlights cast a welcoming net of light. The brief exertion left Jack breathing hard. He stood and stared back down towards the harbour. For a moment, he thought he saw something large scurry across the path he had just taken, but he couldn't be sure. Somewhere in the dark, a cat hissed and then screeched. Unable to see anything else, Jack turned and hurried on.

When he reached the house, he stood outside, unsure what to do next. He rocked from side to side and wrung his hands together. She had a boyfriend, so what did he expect to achieve? As he was about to turn and walk back home, a shadow crossed his path. The movement startled him and he looked up, only to see Jen in the bedroom window. Jack could see she was dressed for bed in a blue nightgown. She combed her hair, staring absently at the window as she did so. It was such a simple, everyday act, but Jack stood entranced. She was gorgeous.

"*Jen*," he said as loud as he dared.

When she didn't respond, he shouted a little louder and waved his arms. She probably wouldn't be able to see him, as he knew at night windows in brightly lit rooms acted more like dark mirrors, but he was eager to attract her attention. He looked around the ground, spotted a patch of gravel at the side of the path that led to the front door, and scooped a few stones up. He threw them towards the window, and the gravel skittered off the wall and into the flowerbed. Dismayed at his aim, he grabbed a few more of the small stones and threw them again. This time his aim was better and the stones tinkled against the glass.

Startled, Jen approached the window and cupped her hands over her eyes to peer out. Jack waved up and Jen frowned. After a moment, she opened the window and leaned out, smiling.

"Hey," she said.

Jack nodded. "Just thought I'd see what you were up to."

"Well, let me see." She tapped a finger against her lips. "I'm not wearing any makeup, and it's late, oh and look, I'm dressed for bed."

"Very funny. I meant, you know…?"

"Actually, no, I don't know. But I'm glad you called by. Gran's locked herself away and Mum and Dad were moaning about some stupid program on the telly. Anyone would think they thought it was real life. You know, I sometimes wonder who the kid is in this family."

"Yeah, I know what you mean. So you're not a fan of TV then?"

"Nah, not really. I prefer listening to music."

"Me too. So what do you like listening to?"

"Oh you know, Blink 182, Rasmus, a bit of Korn, System of a Down, that kind of stuff."

"Oh, I had you down for Will Young and The Backstreet Boys."

Jen laughed. "Do I look that analy retarded?"

"Well now that you mention it…"

"Hey, anymore of that and I'll come down and give you a slap."

"Promises, promises," Jack said beneath his breath.

"What was that?"

"Nothing, just thinkin' out loud."

"Now there's a surprise. You can think. Einstein must be turning in his grave."

"I don't have to stand here and take this abuse, you know."

"Really, you mean there's somewhere else you can go and get it from instead?" She chuckled.

"Very funny. And here I was being neighbourly."

"Sorry. So what are you doing out?"

"I was bored. You know how it is."

"So you thought you'd pay little old me a visit. That's sweet."

Not as sweet as you. "Yeah, somethin' like that."

"Well, much as I'd love to stand here with the window open in the cold and talk, I had better go and get my beauty sleep."

"Nah, you don't need it," Jack said, blushing. Had he really said that? Jesus, she must think he was a dork, but he wanted to keep her talking. She was the best thing about being here.

Jen smiled. "Thanks, but I really do need some sleep. Mum's got me helping her with the shopping tomorrow."

Jack racked his brain for something to say. "Did you know Zander sells drugs?"

Jen leaned further out the window. "What sort of drugs?"

"Cannabis. I found some on his boat, and I saw him selling a packet to some bloke."

"Cannabis. Really?"

Jack was glad she didn't ask what he was doing on Zander's boat, because then he would have to explain about being pushed in the sea. Granted he could tell her Rocky had pushed him, but he had no proof, and besides which, he thought it would make him look like a bozo. "Yeah. Seems he's got a nice little operation going on." Of course he didn't know much about it at all, but if it kept Jen talking, he could make Zander into the biggest drug baron in the world for all he cared.

"That toe rag."

"What, you don't like drugs, is that it?"

"I've never tried any. Then I've never been offered any either."

"I could, you know, let you try some of mine one day, you know, if you'd like."

Jen smiled. "Most men woo a girl with chocolates and flowers."

"I'm not, you know … not when you've got a boyfriend."

Jen's smile faded. "It's okay. Anyway, I've really got to go. It's been nice talking to you. See you later."

Before Jack could say anything, Jen closed the window and drew the curtains across. He didn't know what it was, but something in her voice and expression told him that all was not well with her and Rocky. *In other words, they were on rocky ground.* He giggled at his little joke, then turned and started for home with a lot more spring in his step than before.

Rocky pressed himself into the shadows of the doorway as Jack walked by. He had stood listening to the bastard chatting up his girlfriend, and the blood in his veins was close to boiling point. He opened and closed the blade of the small penknife in his hand, liking the feel of the sharp steel as it brushed through his fingers.

He could have jumped out and attacked the little shit then and there, but he didn't, not where Jen might see. No, he would wait and bide his time.

Jack was going to get what was coming to him when he least expected it. Rocky was going to make sure of that.

Chapter 18

The sky looked overcast, but the sea was calm as Zander piloted his vessel out of the harbour. McKenzie had paid him promptly for yesterday's drug delivery, but then he had telephoned in the middle of the night to tell Zander there was another pickup. Zander had been half asleep and slightly hung over at the time after spending some of his pay in the Sheet and Anchor, but even he knew things were getting out of hand. But he was in too deep to pull out now, besides which, he didn't think McKenzie would just let him walk away. Zander wasn't weak, but he wasn't stupid. Like it or not, he was in for the duration.

He made a quick call to Brad and met him at the boat before setting sail. He didn't like involving the engineer, but the boat was too big to pilot by himself, and the engines were temperamental at the best of times, and only Brad seemed able to soothe the savage beast.

The rhythmic slap of the boat as it ploughed through the waves was a relaxing sound. A smudge of light illuminated the clouds where the sun peeked over the horizon.

Zander felt as though saltwater flowed through his veins. Almost mystical at times, the sea had an allure unlike any other.

In the distance, Zander spotted the red buoy that marked the lobster pot and he eased back on the throttle. Just then, something banged against the hull. Unable to see anything from the wheelhouse, Zander cut the engine, stepped out onto the deck, and peered over the side. He couldn't spot anything in the murky water, but the sea was good at hiding its secrets. Assuming it was flotsam and jetsam, he proceeded to the starboard side to haul in the pot

He couldn't remember the last time they had brought home a decent haul. He had been through rough patches before, but never one that lasted this long–if it was a shark scaring the fish away, then he needed to track the bastard down, but so far after a thorough search, he hadn't spotted anything that lead him to believe one had taken up residence on their doorstep.

But if things didn't improve soon, he was going to have no choice but to lay his men off. Word had gotten back to him that people were already starting to talk, asking how he could make a living and pay his workers when they never caught anything. He could live off the drug money himself, and he could pay his men with it, but he couldn't risk further suspicion.

He grabbed the pole and hooked the line to the pot, instantly aware something was wrong as the rope came up too easily. A deep frown marred his brow as he eventually pulled the last of the rope aboard to find what remained of the lobster pot. Someone had smashed it to pieces. It took him a couple of seconds to remember the drugs. How could he explain to McKenzie that someone had stolen the drugs?

Back at the harbour, Brad jumped down onto the quay to moor the boat up. When the boat was secure, Zander cut the engine, stepped out on deck, waved and watched Brad saunter home.

"Hey Zander."

Zander turned and looked at the figure leaning against the harbour wall.

"Rocky. You can tell your mum she's out of luck. I haven't caught anything." That kid always made him a little nervous. There was something about him that wasn't right. If he hadn't been fucking the kid's mum, he wouldn't speak to him. Jean wasn't too hot in the looks department, but she certainly made up for it in bed, which is why he usually kept her sweet with the odd fish. Since her husband had left her over eight years ago, Jean had turned to alcohol and a need to feel loved. Not that Zander loved her. As far as he was concerned, it was purely physical.

"I'm not here for fish," Rocky said.

"Okay, so what are you here for?" He turned and started walking away before Rocky could answer. He had too many things on his mind to listen to whatever the kid wanted, and he only asked out of a grudging politeness.

"You wouldn't happen to be missing some drugs, would you?"

Zander stopped dead in his tracks. He clenched his jaw and spun around, grabbing Rocky by the scruff of his neck. "Something you want to tell me?"

Rocky's eyes went wide and he stood up straight and gestured towards the boat. "That new kid in the village. He was bragging yesterday how he'd stolen some."

New kid? Zander released his hold and scratched his chin, feeling the coarse brush of stubble.

Rocky rubbed his throat. "You know, moved into the old Johnson place with his old man."

Alarm bells went off in Zander's head. He remembered showing the kid's dad up the other day. He didn't know how, but they were probably in on it together. The bastards would end up getting him killed. "Come here kid, you and me have got a job to do."

Chapter 19

"So what are you up to today?" Bruce asked.

Jack shrugged. "You know." He continued to wolf down his breakfast of Cornflakes.

"Actually I don't, that's why I'm asking."

"What's with the Spanish Inquisition?" He wondered if his old man was being so curious because he knew that he had snuck out last night, but then instantly rejected the idea. If his dad knew about last night, he wouldn't be so calm.

"Can't I take an interest in what my son's up to?"

"You tell me what there is to do in this dump, and I'll let you know."

Bruce rolled his eyes. "Well if you're short of something to do, you can help me decorate."

"I'm bored, not desperate."

"Well it wouldn't hurt you to help anyway."

"Seriously, dad, I'll find something to keep me occupied."

"That's what I'm afraid of."

Jack and Bruce stared at each other for a moment. Jack didn't know if there was a hidden subtext to his dad's comment or whether he was just trying to be funny. After a moment, Jack looked away and continued eating.

Despite what he had just said, Jack knew exactly where he was going today. To see Jen. He couldn't get her out of his head. After yesterday, he knew there was at least a glimmer of a chance that she and Rocky wouldn't be together for much longer. If she was going to need a shoulder to cry on, his was ready, willing, and able.

When he had finished eating, Jack stood and headed towards the door. "I'm going out," he said as he picked up his baseball cap.

"Keep out of trouble. And Jack, don't go anywhere near the sea. Okay?"

"Yeah, whatever. See you later."

Once outside, Jack hurried towards the harbour. The overcast sky looked leaden this morning. Out to sea, he noticed a bank of fog rolling in.

When he was out of sight of the house, Jack lit a cigarette. As he slid the lighter back into his pocket, he became aware of the sensation of being watched. He gazed around surreptitiously, but couldn't see anyone.

In the village, Jack noticed the cafe was open, so he headed across. Although he had only just eaten breakfast, he was hungry. The ruddy faced girl stood behind the counter, wiping the surfaces down. She smiled at Jack as he entered.

"Glad to see you're still around," she said.

Jack wondered whether there was more to her words than she was letting on. "You can't get rid of me that easily."

The girl grinned. "So what can I get you?"

"Can I have a can of Coke and one of those chocolate éclairs?"

"Looks like we're in for a bad one," she said as she walked across to the fridge to get the can of Coke.

Jack looked out of the window and saw that the fog bank had crept closer, nearly obscuring the harbour and Zander's boat, making it look almost ethereal in the gloom.

When he had paid, Jack walked back outside. The morning chill had now turned into a refrigerator cold and he shivered and tugged his baseball cap down. The fog seemed to blur reality and muffle sound. He could just hear the soft creak of the boat in the harbour, the clink of metal from the many masts and the peal of a bell, made ominous in the murk.

The fog lapped at his feet, then drifted over him in a cold embrace. Jack breathed deeply, and the air chilled his nostrils and iced his lungs. He coughed.

With visibility down to less than twenty feet, Jack felt slightly wary. If someone was following him, he wouldn't see them now. Dressed in only a thin sweater and jeans, he wasn't prepared for the sudden change in weather, and he couldn't believe how quickly the fog had drifted in.

101

His original plan had been to call on Jen, and despite the fog and the cold, he saw no reason to change it now.

The mist made the streets seem surreal; caused him to lose his bearings after only a few feet. He'd have thought he couldn't get lost in such a small village, but the thick fog soon changed his opinion. He popped open the ring pull on the can of Coke and took a swallow.

He thought he heard footsteps but he couldn't be sure so he stopped to listen. He couldn't be sure of anything in the fog. His pulse increased and when he shivered this time, it wasn't due to the cold. Whatever it was, he couldn't hear it now and so he continued, his ears attuned for the slightest noise.

Being in the fog was like being wrapped in cold cotton wool. Visibility was now around ten feet, and Jack followed a low wall at the side of the road.

Then he heard the noise again, louder and closer than before, and he spun around, eyes wide and ears alert.

"Hello, is anyone there?" he whispered. No one replied.

Sudden movement caught his eye. "Who's there?"

The figure didn't answer and was soon lost in the fog. Jack's heart did a little drum roll and he breathed deep to draw much needed air into his lungs. His fingers tingled slightly, and his cheeks prickled with anxiety. He didn't know what he was afraid of, but he used his training to try to regulate his pulse, concentrating on each breath he took.

He considered using his phone to call his dad, but then thought how stupid he would sound, asking him to come and find him because he was scared of a little bit of mist. If he could just reach Jen's house, then everything would be fine.

He started walking again when he heard the sound of scuffling feet directly behind him. In his panic, Jack dropped his cake and can of Coke. The can hit the ground and pop fizzed into the air. He didn't see the raised arm with something clamped in the hand before it was too late.

Chapter 20

Bruce had known asking Jack to help him would have the desired effect and drive him away. He felt a little guilty, but now he could visit Erin again without having his motives questioned. He knew Jack wouldn't be happy about him having feelings for another woman, but until he knew those feelings were reciprocated by Erin, he wasn't going to mention anything.

As he drove out of the village, he saw a bank of fog rolling in off the sea. From his higher vantage point, there was a dreamlike beauty to the scene.

The ruckus in the bar had disturbed him more than he let on to Jack, and although he knew his son could take care of himself, he was slightly apprehensive about leaving him on his own. The villagers' despair and anger was only to be expected under the circumstances, but it wasn't right for them to pick on Jack and himself.

When he arrived at the hospital, he parked and headed towards the entrance only to see Erin walking through the door with a bag slung over her shoulder. Although he had been nervous the first time he visited, now he felt more at ease, the ice already broken by his previous visit.

"Erin. I was just coming to see you," he said, smiling.

Erin looked puzzled.

"I was just coming to see how you are, but I see you're well enough to leave."

"The doctors gave me the all clear. They kept me in for tests, that's all."

"That's great."

Erin looked at him for a moment, and Bruce fell into silence. He didn't know what to say now.

Eventually, Erin spoke, "Well thanks for the interest in my well-being, but I've got to go and call a taxi."

"Right, right, of course," Bruce said as he stepped aside to let her pass. Then as an afterthought, he said, "You don't have to phone for a taxi you know. I mean, I've got to drive back to the village, if that's where you're going."

"No, it's all right; I'll find my own way."

"Honestly, it's no problem. It just seems daft you using a taxi when I've got the car."

Erin stared at him apprehensively and bit her bottom lip.

"I'm quite safe to be around. Honest."

"I'm sure you are. I just don't really know you."

"Well, here's your chance." He gave her what he hoped was a disarming grin.

A moment later, Erin shrugged. "What the hell. After what I've been through, a ride in a car's not going to hurt."

Erin's comment reminded Bruce of her previous assertion that there was something other than a shark in the water, but he wasn't going to badger her for more information now.

"Here, let me carry your bag," he said.

"I can manage," she said sharply. Then she smiled. "But thanks for offering."

Bruce led the way to his car, making idle chitchat on the way.

He drove out of the car park and onto the main road. Erin stared out of the passenger window, her arms folded across her chest in a protective manner.

"I heard your diving partner is missing."

When she looked across at him, her expression was grim. "He's not missing. He's dead."

"Dead? How?"

"Something attacked him."

He recalled the man on holiday that had supposedly been attacked in the sea. "So what do you think it was?"

She bit her lip, thought for a moment. "I don't know. There was something familiar about it, something that I recognised ... but I'm not sure."

"Give it time, and it'll come to you. The brain's funny like that. Leave it to its own devices, and eventually the subconscious will work it out."

"Perhaps I'm better off not knowing," she said quietly.

To change the subject, Bruce said, "So where are you staying?"

"I live and sleep on board the research boat, so I'll have to contact them and have them come pick me up."

"Well, you could come and wait at my house if you want, you know." He would just have to take whatever his son threw at him.

Erin frowned. "I don't understand why you're taking such an interest in my welfare."

Bruce coughed to clear his throat. "If I'm being honest, it's because I like you." He kept his eyes fixed on the road ahead, too afraid to look at her in case she was laughing. He noticed the wedding band on his finger. It felt as though it constricted slightly on his finger.

After a moment, Erin said, "Oh."

Bruce didn't know what he thought his disclosure would produce, but 'oh' most certainly wasn't high up there on the list. Thinking he had embarrassed her, and that she wasn't interested, he could feel his cheeks glowing red. He had ruined his chances before even getting to know her.

"I'll only come to your house on one condition: that you tell me why you call your dog Shazam."

Bruce turned to look at Erin, delighted to see she was smiling. It was almost unbelievable she had remembered his dog's name. "Yes, right, of course," he said, unable to keep the grin from his face. "As a kid, I always read Captain Marvel comics, couldn't get enough of them. When I bought Shazam as a puppy, I couldn't really call her Captain Marvel, especially as she was a bitch, and my wife … I told you about my wife, didn't I?"

Erin nodded.

"Well, she said Captain Marvel would be a stupid name for a dog, so I called her by the name of the wizard who granted Billy Batson the ability to transform into Captain Marvel, Shazam."

"That's quite sweet in a way, naming a dog after something you remembered from your childhood."

"Some people might say sad."

"That all depends on who you tell the story to."

Bruce smiled. It was the first time since his wife had died that the expression felt genuine.

When they arrived back at the village, the fog was thicker than ever. Dense clouds of mist rolled across the road, and Bruce cruised along at a walking pace to avoid crashing. It took almost fifteen minutes before he reached the house, whereupon he exited the vehicle and stood in the fog for a moment, shivering as the mist embraced him. Just as he made his way around the vehicle to be gallant and open Erin's door, she stepped out.

"You always leave your door hanging like that?" Erin asked.

Bruce frowned, then looked to see the front door hanging off its hinges. "Oh my god," he said as he ran into the house. "Jack, Jack, are you in there?"

The place was a mess. Cupboards were open and drawers were pulled out, their contents tipped on the ground. The settee had been torn open like a gutted animal. A sudden bark from the dining room alerted him to Shazam, and he tore across the room to find the door barricaded with a chair beneath the handle. Bruce yanked the chair away and flung the door open. Shazam bounded out, barking loudly.

"Where's Jack?" he asked the dog. At the mention of Jack's name, Shazam barked even louder. Bruce wished he could interpret the sound. He took his phone from his pocket and called Jack's number. The phone rang a number of times, then voicemail cut in asking him if he wanted to leave a message.

"Jack, it's me. If you get this message, call me straight away." Sensing someone behind him, Bruce spun around to find Erin standing in the doorway, looking around the room in shock.

"Good god, what's happened?"

Bruce shook his head and put his phone back in his pocket. "I think we've been ransacked."

"You mean burgled?" she said.

"I only hope that's all it is," Bruce replied.

106

Erin frowned. "Is there something you're not telling me?"

"My son and I, we had a little run in with the locals. They were blaming us for the shortage of fish."

"That's crazy."

"Try telling them that."

"And you think this could be something to do with it?"

"I'm not a gambling man, but I'd put money on it."

"Even more reason to call the police then."

"I know. It's just … it's Jack."

"Jack? What's he got to do with this?"

"Nothing. At least that's what I'm hoping. I just need to find him first."

Erin scratched her chin. "You think he's missing?"

"I don't know but I'd better go look for him."

"Well what are we waiting for, let's go."

Bruce followed her out of the room with Shazam at his heel. If anything had happened to Jack, he wouldn't be able to live with himself.

Chapter 21

Jack never would have believed his head could hurt so much. A roaring sound bombarded his ears, and he gingerly opened his eyes to find himself bound hand and foot to a stake in rocks at the edge of the sea. A thick wall of fog billowed around him, clammy and cold.

He tried pulling his hands free, but the binding was too tight. A ringing sound caught his attention, and it took him a moment to realise it was the phone in his pocket.

He couldn't understand what he was doing there. His fingers felt numb, the rope or whatever was used to tie his hands, too tight. He tried prizing his wrists apart to relieve the pain, but whoever had tied him had done a thorough job.

The phone stopped ringing.

He couldn't see much through the fog, but there were small rock pools around his feet, and waves crashed into the rocks, spraying him with rabid foam. Cold and wet, he shivered and fought to hold back the tears.

Tenerife had nothing on this.

"Hello, is anyone there?" he shouted. The only reply came from the roar of the sea as waves crashed ashore. "Please, tell me what's going on. Why am I here?"

When no one answered, Jack struggled against his bindings, but all he succeeded in doing was inflicting pain on his wrists worse than any Chinese rope burn.

A shrill cry made him jump and he twisted his head to see a seagull on the rocks. The bird eyed him for a moment, then took flight and disappeared into the fog.

Jack couldn't understand what he was doing here. It was crazy. Saltwater stung his head, probably from a cut where his assailant had struck him. He ached to rub it, to make the pain go away.

Movement caught his eye and he looked down to see a large red crab scuttling across the rocks near his feet. It stopped and clicked its pincers a couple of times. Jack wanted to kick it away, but couldn't with his feet bound. If it wanted to nip him, there was no way he could stop it. He watched as it scuttled closer.

"Get away, shoo," he said, a slight tremor in his voice. "Go on, get away." He felt ridiculous trying to scare a crab away, but by the look of its large pincers, it could deal a wicked nip, which was the last thing he needed on top of his current predicament.

Desperate to escape, he lunged forward as far as he could, hoping the post might be rotten and would snap, but it held firm.

At his feet, the crab scuttled into a rock pool and disappeared below the surface of the water, where it sat, seemingly staring up at him with its stalk eyes. Molluscs' clung to the rocks in the shallow pool, along with trails of seaweed that drifted like a mermaid's hair.

Jack looked back out to sea and screamed as loud as he could, his cry cut off when a fresh wave of sea spray hit him in the face, making him cough and choke as it entered his mouth.

The saltwater stung his eyes and he blinked rapidly to try to clear his vision. When he looked back down at the rock pool, he noticed the level of the water was slightly higher than before. The tide was coming in.

He screamed again until his throat was raw, but no one answered. Breathless and exhausted, he slumped against the post. He wondered how high the water would come, then remembered rubbing his face against the molluscs, a marker for the high tide, which meant the water would rise above his head.

Panicked, he struggled against his bindings, but it was hopeless. There was no way he could break free.

Why had his dad moved them out here? Why couldn't they have stayed in the city where he was happy? If only his mum hadn't died …

He chastised himself that last thought. It wasn't her fault. Tears ran down his cheeks, blurring his vision. Unable to wipe them away, he blinked rapidly and shook his head to clear his sight.

109

The crab still sat in the rock pool, but there was something next to it, wedged into a crevice. Jack squinted to see more clearly but the incoming tide churned the water, further obscuring his view. He waited for the water to retreat, allowing the rock pool surface to calm.

And that's when he recognised what it was. Bones.

There were bones in the pool. Jack was no expert, but these weren't any old bones–by the looks of them, they were goddamn human.

Chapter 22

"Duncan," Bruce said as he entered the shop, "you haven't seen my son, Jack, have you?"

Duncan looked up from where he sat behind the counter and shook his head. "I'm sorry about that scene in the bar."

"I'm not worried about that. I need to find Jack."

"He hasn't been in here. Sorry."

Bruce scratched his head and ground his teeth. "Someone's gone and ransacked my house."

"Good god. Have you called the police?" Bruce shook his head.

"I told him he should," Erin said from the doorway where she stood holding Shazam on the lead.

"I don't know what the world's coming to," Duncan said. "It wasn't that long ago when people could leave their doors unlocked."

Bruce pursed his lips. Where the hell was his son? Raw panic coursed through his veins. "I've got to find him."

Duncan frowned. "What's the big problem?"

"I think something might have happened to Jack. It's too much of a coincidence after yesterday's trouble in the bar."

"Happened to him in what way?"

"I don't know. I just feel … he isn't answering his phone."

"What kid ever does answer his phone to his parents?" Erin said.

"I know, I know, but … it's just, I feel it. Something's happened to him."

"Then what are we waiting for? Let's call the police," Duncan said.

"They'll only tell me to wait twenty-four hours or whatever it is before reporting anything."

"But at least you'll have let them know; and with the break in, they might take it more seriously," Erin said.

Bruce nodded and made the call. As he suspected, they said he'd have to wait twenty-four hours before they could do anything for Jack, but when he reported the break in, they said they would send someone around to investigate. He disconnected the call.

"Right then, let's go find your son," Duncan said, striding around from the counter.

"You're going to help?" Bruce said.

"Of course. I know the area better than you do. Perhaps he's just wandered off. I'm sure we'll find him."

"I hope you're right."

Duncan smiled to offer encouragement. "By the looks of the weather, I'll be needing my coat." He grabbed a seemingly damp jacket from the wall at the side of the counter, and then ushered them out of the shop. He turned the sign to 'closed', locked the door, and then turned to face them. "We should start down at the harbour. That's where most kids like to hang out."

Bruce looked across the road. Normally the harbour would be visible, but the fog was too thick to see anything. He could hear the faint clink of metal and the soft creak of wood from that direction.

"Shutting up early, Duncan?" said a stout girl with buck teeth who was standing in the doorway of the cafe. "Can't say I blame you. Not much business in this weather. I'd shut up too, but you know mother, she wants me working here all hours no matter what."

"Hi Samantha. No, we're looking for someone. Bruce here, well his son's gone missing."

Samantha visibly blanched. "New boy, moved into the old Johnson place?"

Duncan nodded.

"I knew it," she gushed. "I told him, said to him only the other day that place was bad news."

"Have you seen him today?" Bruce asked.

The girl nodded. "He was in earlier. Warned him I did. Least I could do."

"Do you know where he went?" Bruce asked.

Samantha shook her head.

112

"Well if you see him, get him to call his dad. Come on, let's go," Duncan said, striding away.

Bruce and Erin followed. When they reached the other side of the road, Bruce shouted Jack's name, but as he'd feared, there was no reply.

"Let's ask at the bar," Duncan suggested, already striding away before Bruce could reply.

As Bruce was about to follow, Erin grabbed his hand. "Don't worry. We'll find him," she said, squeezing gently.

He found her touch comforting. Any other time, he would want to maintain the contact for as long as possible, but with today's events uppermost in his thoughts, he broke the contact, forced a feeble smile and said, "I hope so."

Erin nodded and they started across the road after Duncan, who was already becoming indistinct in the fog.

Bruce and Erin caught up to Duncan outside the bar, where he was talking to a cute teenage girl with short blonde hair who stood with her arms folded across her chest to keep warm.

"So you haven't seen him?" Duncan said.

The girl shook her head. She looked at Bruce and Erin, then down at Shazam.

"Didn't I see you talking to Jack the other day, by the harbour?" Bruce asked.

The girl nodded. "Yeah, I was with my friends." She stroked Shazam's head.

"And have you seen him since?"

The girl shook her head again. "Sorry. No."

Bruce let out a loud breath. He couldn't put his finger on it, but something in the way the girl looked at him suggested she was lying. "Well, if you do see him, please tell him to contact me. It's urgent."

"Why, what's the matter?" she asked.

"I'm just worried something has happened to him. He's gone missing." Shazam whined as though in sympathy.

The girls left eye twitched slightly. "If I see him, I'll be sure to let him know you're looking for him. Anyway, I have to go."

113

Bruce watched her walk quickly away, and any thought he had of following her was lost when she disappeared into the fog.

Jen looked over her shoulder and breathed a sigh of relief when she saw only shadows and fog at her rear. She had never been very good at lying. She hadn't done anything wrong, but she couldn't get the thought out of her head that perhaps Rocky had been involved, so the less she said, the better.

She knew she didn't love Rocky, but she still didn't want to see him get into trouble, especially if he wasn't involved. It did seem a little bit too much of a coincidence that Jack had disappeared after arguing with her boyfriend. She knew Rocky was hot-headed, but she couldn't believe he'd had anything to do with it. But what if he had? What if Jack was lying in a ditch somewhere? She would never forgive herself.

Unnerved by her thoughts, she headed towards Rocky's house to have it out with him.

The house where Rocky lived was on the outskirts of the village. Rocky's father used to be a trawler man, but his career had been cut short, even before the present problems with quotas and lack of fish, when he lost an arm during an accident at sea. Not long after that, he walked out on the family. Whether it was out of some misguided sense of loyalty or just dumb choice, Rocky wanted to become a trawler man too. Didn't even seem bothered that rowing boats made him feel seasick.

Even though she could probably find her way around the village blindfolded, the fog was testing her to the limit. She almost walked into a lamppost, then stumbled into a dustbin, grazing her leg.

Cursing under her breath, she rubbed her injury to alleviate the pain, and then continued on her way.

When she reached Rocky's house, she climbed the three steps, walked along the short path and rang the bell. The downstairs lights were on, creating indistinct blobs of luminescence in the haze.

She stamped her feet and blew into her cupped hands while she waited. The fog was freezing, and she knew the dampness must have made her hair look like rats' tails. She didn't like people seeing her at anything less than her best, but now she had no choice.

She rang the bell again, and knocked loudly. Moments later, she heard a voice shout, "I'm comin'," and then Rocky opened the door. He stared at Jen for a moment as though he didn't know who she was, then he nodded his head in greeting.

"Jen, what are you doin' here?"

"Tell me you haven't hurt him. Promise me, Rocky."

Rocky held his hands up. "Hey, what are you on about?"

"Jack. That new guy in the village, he's gone missing. Tell me you aren't involved."

Rocky looked down at the ground. He shrugged. "He's a twat. It's nothing to do with me."

"Look at me," she said.

Rocky looked up, shoulders hunched, and shoved his hands in his jeans' pockets.

"Tell me the truth," Jen said.

"I'm telling you the truth. Anyway, it should be me questioning you."

Jen frowned.

"The other night. I saw the two of you. He was outside your house. It was obvious he fancied you, and by the sounds of it, you were leading him on."

"Was not."

"That's what it sounded like to me. I should have had it out with the cunt then."

"Had what out? We were only talking. It's not a crime, you know."

Rocky grunted in response. "Whatever."

"Look, he came to see me. So what? Trouble is, now he's gone missing."

"Great. Serves the prick right."

115

Jen bit her lip and scowled. "Just tell me you're not involved."

"I've already told you. But so what if I was? You're my girlfriend, not his. You're not supposed to worry about other guys."

"That is so lame. I can be concerned about whoever I like. Now tell me, where is he?"

"I've told you, I don't know."

"But you do know something."

"Yeah, and so do you."

"What are you on about now?"

"You know, the drugs he stole from Zander. He told you about it, right?"

The revelation hit Jen like a brick. Zander. But Zander didn't know Jack had stolen his drugs, not unless …

"My god, you didn't tell him, did you?" she said.

Rocky shrugged. "So what if I did."

"Zander's a lunatic. He'd kill him."

"Save someone else the job then."

"Rocky, how could you?"

"It was only what he deserved."

"You prick."

"You can't talk to me like that."

"I just did. And as far as I'm concerned, we're through."

"Fine. I prefer a girl who'll put out anyway, not a frigid bitch like you."

Jen fought to control her temper. She had more important matters to deal with now. How could she tell Jack's dad what she knew without getting Jack into more trouble? Talk about being stuck in a difficult situation.

Without another word to Rocky, she spun and started walking away.

"If Zander hasn't finished the creep, you can bet I'll do the job properly," Rocky said before he slammed the door shut.

Jen shivered, and made her way quickly towards the harbour. She only hoped she wasn't too late.

Chapter 23

Although she searched around the harbour and looked in the bar, Jen couldn't find Zander anywhere. His vessel was moored up, and she shouted out his name, but no one answered, and the boat looked deserted.

It was hopeless trying to look by herself. Zander and Jack could be anywhere. She took out her mobile phone and called her best friend, Sara to help with the search.

When Sara arrived, she was chomping bubble gum. "Hey, what's up? Have you seen this weather? It's thicker than custard," she said as she jumped up on the harbour wall to sit next to Jen

"Yes, it's no wonder someone's gone missing in this."

Sara blew a pink bubble and nodded. When the bubble popped, she dragged the gum back into her mouth with her tongue. "Yeah, he's cute. 'Bout time we had some decent talent around here."

"He's all right."

"All right! I saw the way you looked at him. Eyes almost popped out of your head. You'd better not let Rocky see you looking at another guy like that."

"Rocky and me are finished."

Sara's nose twitched and she flicked her brown ponytail through the air in disbelief. "No way. So what about this new boy? Are you, you know …"

Jen blushed and shook her head. "No, nothing like that."

Sara grinned and blew another bubble.

"Honest, there's nothing going on."

"Whatever."

"There's not. But we've got to find him. He found some cannabis on Zander's boat—"

"No way," Sara said, almost dropping her gum.

"Listen, will you. Rocky heard Jack talking to me about it outside my house—"

"So Jack's been to your house. And I thought you said there was nothing going on," Sara said. "You dirty dog." She winked.

"Look, will you let me finish. Rocky heard Jack mention the drugs, and he went and told Zander."

"Oh shit. Do you think Zander's done something to him?" Sara asked.

"I don't know, but you know what Zander's like. Remember that man the other year, that tourist they said spilt a bit of beer on Zander. He ended up in the hospital with his ear bitten off."

"That was just a rumour," Sara said.

"So explain why after Rocky told Zander what Jack had done, Jack goes missing?"

Sara shrugged. "I don't know. Perhaps he's gone back to the city. Who in their right mind would want to stay here?"

"If that was the case, he would have told his dad. But he hasn't. He's looking for him."

"Have you looked in the bar for Zander? That's where he usually is."

Jen nodded. "I already checked there. And at his boat, and at his shed at the end of the harbour."

"Well how are we going to find him in this weather?"

Zander's boat creaked against the harbour wall, the sound like a groan. Jen took a deep breath, shivered as the fog chilled her nostrils. "We can check around the village for a start. Anywhere you think they might be. It's better than doing nothing."

"And what about Rocky?" Sara asked. "Does he know where they might be?"

"He says not, but then he's not likely to tell me. Can you go and look around the village, ask anyone you meet?"

"On my own? You've got to be joking."

"It's better if we split up. We can cover more ground."

Sara shook her head. "I'm not going in search of an ear-chomping madman on my own. No way!"

Jen sighed. "Okay, then come with me. Hurry, we've wasted enough time."

She jumped down from the wall and headed into the fog with Sara at her side. Although she didn't say it out loud, she was glad Sara was going with her. Whether the ear-biting story was true or not, the thought of tracking down Zander by herself wasn't appealing.

Chapter 24

The water lapped around Jack's waist. He shivered. Throat raw through screaming, he fought the instinct to scream again and kept his mouth closed as a fresh wave pummelled against him.

The fog and sea seemed to be as one. Both were cold and pervasive. Something tickled his fingers in the water. He hoped it was only seaweed. But what if it was a jellyfish, or … Jesus, what if it was that shark people had been talking about. The thought made him quake and he tried again to get free, but it was no good. He might as well be clapped in irons. He scanned the sea that frothed around him, hoping, praying not to see a fin break the surface.

Who in their right mind would have tied him up out here anyway? It was crazy. He hadn't done anything to anyone.

Another wave crashed into him, submerging his face as it passed over. He kept his eyes and mouth shut as tight as possible; thought the water was never going to settle. Goosebumps mottled his arms and legs.

When the sea smoothed out, he took a deep breath. The pungent smell of brine and seaweed invaded his nostrils.

He looked down. The water was up to his navel. At this rate, it wouldn't be much longer before it was up to his neck. Then up to his mouth, then … God, he was going to drown.

He didn't want to cry, but he couldn't stop himself. Tears welled behind his lids; combined with the saltwater, his eyes stung, but he kept them shut tight, too afraid to open them in case he saw something he wished he hadn't.

He thought about his dad. There were so many things he wanted to say to him. So many apologies he wanted to make for the things he had done wrong. Now he might never get the chance.

A final, desperate scream born of anger, fear and frustration burst from his mouth. When his anger was spent, he slumped against the post.

Then he heard it. A voice calling his name. "Jack?"

He couldn't believe it. Hope rushed through his veins. "I'm here. Help me," he cried.

Although it hurt, he twisted his head as far as possible to trace the source of the caller. He heard rocks skitter, heard a muffled yelp, then heard his name called again.

"Jack, is that you? Where are you?"

He recognised the voice, Jen. His heart soared. "I'm here. Hurry. Quick."

Movement caught his eye, and he squinted to make out Jen in the fog. He had never been so glad to see anyone in his life. Someone else appeared beside her who he identified as the girl that he had seen Jen with at the harbour.

"Thank god," he said, choking back tears.

Jen and the girl stood just beyond the water's reach. "Jack, what the hell's going on?"

"I don't know. Someone's tied me to this post and I can't get free."

"Jesus. Hold on, I'm coming."

"Be careful," the other girl said.

Jen slipped into the water and waded towards him, holding her arms aloft.

A fresh wave swept in, causing Jen to sway precariously. "Watch how you go," Jack said. "It's not as if I can rescue you."

Jen shook her head. "This is no time to be joking."

"Who's joking?"

The other girl stood back on the rocks and watched.

"That bastard Zander," Jen said. "I thought he might be angry, but this!"

Jack felt something tighten in his bowels. "Zander? What's he got to do with this?" he asked as Jen reached his side.

"When I heard you were missing, I went to see Rocky. That night outside my house, he heard what you said about the drugs, and he told Zander."

"Jesus. Great boyfriend."

"Ex-boyfriend."

121

"You broke up?" Despite his predicament, a warm feeling swept over him that even the cold, incessant waves couldn't dampen.

"Yeah, he's a jerk."

Jack grinned.

He felt Jen's hands trying to undo the ropes. She gritted her teeth at his side, her sweet breath washing over him.

"Jesus, these ropes are tight," she said.

"Get away from him."

Jack and Jen turned as one to see who had shouted. The fog had dissipated over time, and Jack could see a figure scurrying across the rocks at the base of the cliff. The previous warm feeling in his stomach evaporated, replaced with ice.

It was the madwoman, Lillian Brown.

She ran past Jen's friend, pushing her aside as she went.

"Gran? What's going on?" Jen said.

Jack frowned. "You know her?"

"Of course I know her, she's my grandmother."

"Jenny, get away from him. *Now*," Lillian screeched.

The water lapped across Jack's chest, and with each ebb of the sea, the tidemark rose higher and higher. He tried to stand on his tiptoes to rise above the water, but it was useless.

"Gran, someone's tied him to this post. I've got to get him free."

"You stupid girl, I did it. Now leave him be, and get away."

Jen scowled. "You? I don't understand."

"How else are we going to bring back the fish? The sea needs a sacrifice. Fresh blood."

"Sacrifice! You're crazy," Jack squealed.

"Gran, tell me what's going on."

Lillian waded into the sea, waving her arms. "Don't you realise how hard it was for us to drag him all the way out here? Now get away from him."

"This is crazy. You can't let him die."

122

"Why not? How else are we going to bring back the fish? Why do you think they came back last time? We can't keep taking without giving something back."

Jen frowned. "Last time?"

"Yes, look what happened then. I offered a whole family, and the fish returned."

"The Johnson's," Jack said, remembering the story of the family who had lived in the house previously. "You're fucking crazy."

"Tell me that's not true," Jen said. "You didn't do something to the Johnson's, did you?"

A wave buffeted Lillian back. "It worked, didn't it? It was the only way. It's still the only way."

Jack felt Jen frantically tearing at the knot. His heart felt as though it were about to explode. This was madness.

"Hurry up," he hissed as another wave rolled towards them.

"I'm going as fast as I can," Jen said.

Jack stared at Lillian, saw the madness in her eyes, the savage look of fury.

The wave washed over them, sending Jen flying. Submerged, Jack held his breath and waited for the water to recede … and waited, and waited.

But the water didn't recede. He tossed his head from side to side, yanked against the bindings, twisted his wrists, and then without warning, his hands were free. Relief surged through him. Then he realised his feet were still bound.

His lungs felt as though they were about to burst. Bubbles streamed from his mouth and nostrils as he started to exhale. Frantic, he bent over at the waist and pulled at the binding around his ankles. He started to feel dizzy. The strong flow of the water buffeted him from all sides. His fingers struggled with the knot, searching for some way to untie it. When he had a hold of what he thought was one end of the rope, he traced it back to the knot, felt for the ridge where it crossed over, then pulled with all his might.

The knot came free, and he wrenched his legs out and swam, gasping for breath to the surface, where he gulped in a deep lungful of air. Nothing had ever tasted sweeter.

"Jack, thank God," Jen said as she swam across. When she reached him, she flung her arms around his neck and kissed his cheek, then his lips. Jack rejoiced in her salty kiss, never wanted it to end.

When she finally released him, Jen said, "I'm sorry, Jack. If I'd known …"

"It's not your fault," Jack said. He tore his gaze away from Jen and looked back towards the shore where Lillian stood, the wind buffeting her hair and clothes while she stood immobile, staring past them. There was no sign of Jen's friend.

"You're too late," Lillian cackled, pointing a bony arm out to sea.

Jack and Jen looked where Lillian indicated. Less than twenty feet away, the water appeared to bubble and froth as something rose from the depths.

Next minute a large, black, shiny head as large as Jack's burst forth, spraying water in its wake. Jack stared wide-eyed. He had never seen anything like it. Two small, beady black eyes set high on the head looked back at Jack, sending a chill through his body. The surface of the creature's head appeared haggard, riddled with small cavities delineated by serrated edges. Scales that resembled thin plates adorned what he could see of the thing's skin. The creature opened its mouth, revealing fangs at least six inches long.

Whatever it was, this creature wasn't natural.

At his side, Jen squealed, turned and started to swim for shore. "Come on," she shouted, forcing Jack into action

He found it ironic that although he had given up eating meat, that didn't mean he wasn't on the menu. Well, this meal wasn't going to be served up without a fight. He started to swim, hearing the terrifying splash of water at his rear as the creature came after him.

With the tide coming in, it made it easier for Jack to swim for shore. Of course, it was also easier for the monster at his rear, too, which, as a denizen of the sea, was probably a more adept swimmer. But Jack and Jen were far enough away that he thought they had a chance.

He looked towards the shore to see how far he had to go, glimpsed Jen's grandmother standing on the rocks, watching impassively.

Whether it was a result of the hit on the head, being tied up, fear, or the cold, Jack felt himself flagging. His arms and legs felt leaden, and he struggled to claw his way through the water. He couldn't get the creature's face out of his mind, those big, long teeth like curved knives bearing down on his legs.

The thought spurred him on and he kicked out furiously and swept his arms through the water like a man possessed. Up ahead, Jen waded out of the water, and he was glad that at least she wouldn't become the creature's dessert.

Next minute, his fingers brushed against the rocks below, and he scrambled to his feet. The rocks were slimy with seaweed, and he felt his left foot slip, but he just managed to maintain his balance. Waves crashed against him, as though lending a helping hand to push him to shore, and he sighed with relief when he finally stepped out of the ocean.

He hurried up the rocks towards Jen, and then stood with his hands on his knees, gasping for breath. After a moment, he turned to face Jen's grandmother, who stood further back, glaring at him vindictively. The fog had now thinned considerably, and he could see a cliff face behind her.

"What the hell is that thing?" he asked. "And what the hell did you think you were doing, you crazy bitch? I'm going to call the police."

Lillian smiled sardonically. She raised a spindly arm and pointed out to sea. "I don't think you will," she said. "The sea still needs its sacrifice."

Jack turned and looked where she indicated. In the swell of the waves, he could see the creature's head, its eyes peering back at him. Next minute, the creature swam towards the rocky shore. Jack crouched down, picked up a rock and threw it at the creature, surprising himself with his good aim when the rock struck it on the head. He felt a sense of satisfaction, but the creature seemed unfazed.

Knowing that he was safe where he was, he spat out to sea. "Fuck off back to whatever rock you crawled out from under," he said.

But as he watched, the creature drew closer and closer, then when it was feet from the shore, it raised itself out of the water and stood up on reptilian squat legs to reveal a thick, black body. The creature raked web-interlocked claws in the air, opened its mouth and made a high-pitched wailing sound, then it advanced.

Jack stared open mouthed. "Oh, shit," he said.

Chapter 25

Bruce cupped his hands around his mouth. "Jack?" he shouted. At his side, Shazam barked. When his son didn't reply, Bruce bit his lip and continued along the road. He slipped a hand into his pocket, fingering the wallet with the lucky charms. If ever there was a time he needed their aid, it was now.

With Duncan and Erin's help, he had searched almost all the village, but there was no sign of Jack.

"He's got to be somewhere," Bruce said.

At his side, Erin nodded. "We will find him."

Bruce hoped she was right. The thick bank of fog had started to thin out, but now the light was fading. A solitary streetlight had already come on, throwing a pale orange sheen across the road.

Bruce stopped and turned to face Duncan. "What about that old madwoman? You know, the one who grabbed Jack and marched him into the bar." He couldn't believe he hadn't thought of her before.

Duncan scratched his nose. "You mean Lillian Brown? I suppose it's worth a try."

"At this point, I'd try anything."

"Follow me," Duncan said, turning tail and marching away.

Bruce and Erin followed with Shazam trotting alongside. Bruce looked down at the dog. "Some help you are. I thought dogs were meant to have a heightened sense of smell."

Shazam looked up, and for a moment, Bruce thought there was sadness in the dog's expression. "I'm sorry girl. I know you'd help if you could."

Duncan led them away from the high street to a house overlooking the harbour. He stepped up to the door and rang the bell. When no one answered, he knocked.

"Doesn't look as though anyone's in," he said.

Bruce stepped forward and started banging on the door. "Jack, are you in there?" he shouted.

Duncan grabbed his hand. "I don't think that'll do any good."

Bruce exhaled slowly, turned away from the house and walked to the road where he leaned against the wall at the front of the property, trying to gather his thoughts. After a moment, he took his phone out and tried ringing Jack again, but the voicemail cut in straight away.

The sound of footsteps caught his attention, and he looked back down the road to see a slim girl with brown hair tied back in a ponytail running towards them.

"Mr. Roberts," she wheezed, head bobbing up and down as she fought to catch her breath. "It's … Jen and that … new boy …"

Duncan started towards the girl. "Sara, what is it—"

"What? What's happened to them," Bruce said, grabbing the girl by the shoulders before Duncan reached her.

Sara looked at him, her brown eyes wide with something he recognised as fear.

"Jen's grandmother … she's tied that new boy up. It's … crazy. I think … she's lost her marbles."

"She's *what*? Where are they?" Bruce demanded. He wanted to shake her, couldn't believe what he heard.

"Calm down," Duncan said, prizing Bruce's hands from Sara's shoulders.

"I need to find my son," Bruce said, fighting to remain calm. He could feel his temples pound, could feel the throb of blood in the thick veins sticking out on his neck as he clenched his teeth.

"I understand," Duncan said, "but terrorizing Sara isn't going to help."

"I'm not terrorizing her. I just need to know where Jack is."

"They're down by the cliffs past the cove," Sara said.

"Then take me there," Bruce said.

Sara looked at Bruce, her expression alarmed. "I … I…"

"It's okay," Erin said to Sara. "We're here with you now." She smiled.

Bruce nodded encouragement. "Please. If they're in trouble, then I need to find them."

Sara closed her eyes and nodded.

"Then let's go," Bruce said.

Sara lead the way, but Bruce could tell by the way she walked that her heart wasn't in it. She had seen something or experienced something that she obviously didn't want to repeat.

They followed the main road out of the village, past the small beach, and continued further along the coast. The road went up an incline so they now had a view of the sea to their left. The fog had virtually dispersed, but darkness had fallen, bringing with it a mantle of stars and a gibbous moon. If anything had happened to Jack, he would never forgive himself for dragging his son away from the city.

A scream pierced the silence, chilling Bruce to the core. "What the hell was that?" he cried.

"It sounded like Jen," Sara said.

Before anyone could say anything else, Bruce started to run. Shazam ran alongside, her hackles up like a cat. Whatever was wrong, she sensed it too.

On one side of the road there were fields bordered by a low hedge. On the other, there was a drop to the sea, which he could hear crashing into the rocks far below.

The scream rang out again, louder and more insistent. With it came a shout for help that Bruce recognised as his son, spurring him to run faster.

Although dark, the light of the moon was enough to see by, and Bruce spotted a small trail leading towards the cliff edge. He followed it to a meandering path that wound down the cliff face. Without waiting for the others, he started down, using his hands to steady himself. Shazam accompanied him, jumping from rock to rock with the assuredness of a mountain goat.

The drop to his left was precarious to say the least, and he didn't look in case it turned his stomach to see the water churning below. The tide was at its highest, and he could hear the waves sloshing between rock formations, invading crevices and cracks.

"Jack," he shouted. "Where are you?"

A moment's silence, then a voice, "Dad, we're over here... But be careful. There's … something here. Some sort of creature…"

Creature? Bruce followed the sound. Jagged rocks pierced the flesh of his hands, but he ignored the pain. He had to reach his son. Nothing else mattered.

Two figures stood in what looked like a recess in the rock less than twenty feet away, but between them and Bruce was the sea.

Bruce looked at the expanse of water, the moons reflection glinting from the surface like a shoal of dancing fish.

"Jack, swim across," Bruce shouted. Shazam stood on a rock, growling.

Then Bruce noticed movement at the water's edge, saw something black and shiny that clung to the rocks. Moonlight glinted from its body, and despite the distance and the lack of light, Bruce felt a sudden ray of terror pierce his soul.

The creature opened its mouth, revealing large fanglike teeth, and emitted a keen wailing sound that chilled the marrow in his bones.

What the hell was that thing?

Shazam barked loudly, her tail between her legs as though in fear.

He watched Jack throw a rock at it, trying to drive it away. The rock missed, splashing harmlessly in the water beyond the creature. Jack threw another, which hit the creature on the head, but with no discernible effect.

Rocks skittered at his side, and the next moment, Erin stood beside him.

"What the hell is that thing?" Bruce asked as he looked at Erin.

She swallowed, her face ashen. "I knew I'd seen them somewhere before, but not like that. It's impossible …." She pursed her lips, shaking her head as if unable to believe what she was seeing. "*Anoplogaster cornuta*."

"Can you say that in fuckin' English?" Bruce snapped.

"Fangtooth."

Chapter 26

Erin squinted to see through the dark. It didn't seem possible, but there was no mistaking that pitted face, the hard ridges between the two beady eyes and the teeth … god those teeth, which looked like a steel-jawed mantrap in the chasm of its mouth.

"I don't understand," Bruce said. "What the hell is it?"

Erin rubbed her eyes, hoping the action would change the scene before her, but it didn't, of course it didn't.

"Well, if it's what I think it is, they normally only grow to about the size of your hand. But this …"

Bruce pointed at the creature. "My god, it's crawling out of the water. It's got arms and legs!"

Erin swallowed to hold in the bile as she remembered Kev's body bitten in half.

"I've got to get my son out of there," Bruce said. Before Erin could reply, he clambered down the rocks to the sea's edge.

Erin wanted to follow him down, but her legs were shaking and she found she couldn't move.

Shazam barked like something demented. The sound drilled into her ears, deafening.

She stared at the creature, almost too afraid to blink. Arms and legs! It wasn't possible. It was like something conjured in a nightmare. Almost close enough to reach out and touch already, she didn't want to get any closer. She thought she could smell it in the air, a pungent fishy aroma that made her feel sick.

"Hey, get away," Bruce said as he picked up a rock and threw it at the creature, striking it on the back.

The Fangtooth turned its head and looked at Bruce, then it raised its head higher and stared at Erin. Her legs turned to jelly. On the verge of collapsing, she tried to control her breathing, was hyperventilating.

Its black eyes seemed to bore into her, and it almost looked as though it were smiling. The spiky dorsal fins along its spine seemed to quiver, then it slowly slid back down into the water and disappeared below the surface.

"Can you climb along the rocks?" Bruce shouted.

Jack shook his head. "There's no way we can get across. We tried."

The creature's disappearance spurred Erin into action. With her legs functioning again, she scrambled down to Bruce. She was still breathing erratically, but at least she didn't feel as though she were about to collapse. She kept warily glancing at the sea, and was about to speak to Bruce when she saw movement in the water, and the creature's head broke the surface only feet from where she stood.

Erin staggered back in alarm as the creature started to swim towards them. When it reached the rocks, it scrambled ashore, and with nothing to stop its progress, it moved quickly up the slight incline towards where they stood. Shazam growled, baring her teeth.

Bruce picked up a large rock and threw it at the creature, hitting it square between the eyes, but the creature didn't even flinch.

"Come on you bastard." Bruce picked up a piece of sturdy driftwood as thick as his arm and smashed it across the creature's head. The wood shattered on impact with a loud crack, but the creature seemed unfazed. "What the …"

The Fangtooth opened its mouth, allowing Erin to see inside its cavernous, tubular throat. A rotten stench flowed out, like something dead, then the creature started to advance, using its arms and legs to move in a lizard-like fashion across the rocks.

"Bruce," she yelled, "Come on, we've got to get out of here."

"I can't leave Jack."

"They're safe where they are, but we're not. And you'll be no use to them dead."

With an almost imperceptible nod of his head, Bruce shouted, "Jack, stay where you are. We'll go and get help. Come on Shazam, we've got to go." He grabbed the dog's collar, turned tail and followed Erin back up the cliff.

On the way up, they saw Sara and Duncan making their way down. "Back," Erin shouted. "Get away. There's something down there."

Duncan frowned and shook his head, perplexed. "Are they down there? Did you find your son?"

"There's something coming after us," Bruce shouted. "A fucking monster of some sort. I don't know what it is, but run."

Sara threw her arms in the air. "Where's Jen? Is she all right?"

"Yes," Bruce said. "But we won't be if we don't run."

Erin heard rocks skittering behind them, propelling her to move faster. The incline made her breathing laboured and she gasped to draw breath.

Whether it was the look on their faces or the sincerity behind their words, Duncan and Sara turned tail and hurried back to the top of the cliff. When she reached the summit, Erin looked back down. She thought she saw movement in the jagged shadows of the rocks, but it was getting too dark to see, the moon's light unable to illuminate the path she had just taken.

"So what do we do now?" Bruce asked.

Without answering, Erin took out her phone and dialled 999. When the call went through, a female operator said, "Emergency, which service?"

"There's two teenagers trapped in the cliffs here at Mulberry."

"So you need the coastguard?"

"No, we need the fuckin' army."

"I don't understand. You said two teenagers are stuck."

"Not stuck really, more like trapped."

"I still think you require the coastguard in this situation."

"You don't understand."

"Calm down, and tell me again what the problem is."

"Okay, there are two teenagers trapped in the cliffs." She took a breath, couldn't think straight. "They're not really trapped … well they are—"

Before Erin had a chance to say anything else, Bruce grabbed the phone from her. "It's my son, goddamn it, and he's trapped by these monsters in the sea. Hello, of course I'm not joking. Do you think I'd joke about something …hello. Hello." He shook his head and closed his eyes. "She cut me off."

Erin took her phone back, "You should have left it to me."

"Can someone please tell me what's going on," Duncan said.

Erin pointed towards the village. "First I think we'd better get as far away from here as we can."

Bruce shook his head. "I can't leave my son down there."

"Where's Jen?" Sara piped up.

Erin felt like screaming. "Bruce, you've just seen what's down there. The tide's at its highest, so your son's safe for now where he is. So's Jen. But we're not."

Bruce looked pensive. "You're sure he'll be safe?"

"If the creature hasn't gotten him yet, then it's unlikely it will get him now. The rocks were too steep, and by the looks of it, the creature wasn't able to climb very well. Now come on, we've got to get out of here and get help."

"We'll pick up my car on the way. It'll be faster," Bruce said.

Without waiting to argue anymore, Erin started jogging back towards the village. After a moment, she heard the others following behind, and she breathed a sigh of relief. She didn't want to be on her own.

Erin burst through the doors of the bar. Graham looked up and scrutinized her with his one good eye. The next minute, Bruce, Duncan and Sara piled in behind her.

"Pour me … a stiff … brandy," Duncan said, wheezing for breath as he leaned against the bar, head down.

"You look like you've seen a ghost," Graham said to Erin. "Duncan, what's going on?"

Erin wiped sweat from her brow. "Not a ghost, a monster."

135

Graham scowled. "Duncan, what's this all about?"

Duncan looked up, his cheeks inflamed. He took the brandy and downed it in one. "I don't know. I really don't."

Erin looked back at Bruce. He seemed hardly winded by the exertion prior to driving into the village. Behind him, Sara collapsed in a chair by the door. There was no one else in the bar, which she found disconcerting. More people would have calmed her fears, providing security in numbers.

"We need to get help," Bruce said. "It's a waste of time calling the police again."

"Police!" Graham said. "Can someone please tell me what's happened?"

"It's my son—"

"And Jen," Sara said.

"They're trapped in the rocks by this ... this creature." Bruce held his hands up to ward off any questions. "I don't know what it is."

"I told you, it's an *Anoplogaster cornuta*," Erin said.

Duncan turned and scowled. "A what?"

"*Anoplogaster cornuta*. Otherwise known as Fangtooth. It's a deep sea creature."

"That's not like any deep sea creature I've ever seen," Bruce said.

Erin nodded. "They normally grow to the size of your hand, but something's made that one mutate."

"And what could do that?"

Erin shrugged. "There could be any number of reasons. Natural mutation, overfishing, chemicals being dumped into the ocean."

Bruce shook his head. "So why haven't they been spotted before?"

"I can't say exactly, but as they're a deep sea fish they could have gone unnoticed for years. We know more about space than we do about what's in the ocean. New species are being discovered all the time."

"So why have they come ashore now?" Duncan asked.

Erin looked at everyone in the room in turn. "I don't know. There always has to be a first time."

"Do you think it's an isolated incident?" Bruce asked.

Erin pursed her lips. "I highly doubt it. But one thing's for certain—"

Bruce swallowed.

"—we're no longer at the top of the food chain."

Chapter 27

Jen's bottom lip trembled and she shivered. "Where've they gone?" she whispered.

She was trying hard not to cry, but Jack could see that she was on the verge of breaking down. A monster had chased her, and she had discovered that her grandmother was a nutcase, so was it any wonder?

Jack noticed Lillian had scuttled away when his dad turned up. He wondered where she had gone; wondered where the monster had gone too. He hadn't seen it since it scurried into the rocks after his dad. He hoped his old man was all right.

He sat at the edge of the recess. Open to the elements, it was cold and sea spray kept soaking them whenever a wave rolled in, but it was a difficult climb, which kept the creature out.

Jen slouched in the rear of the recess, and Jack shuffled back and snuggled up next to her, trying to keep each other warm. The moon was bright enough to enable him to see down to the water, and he kept his eyes alert for any sign of the creature.

"They're going to leave us here, aren't they," Jen said.

Jack turned and shook his head. "Of course they're not. But you saw that thing, they had to get away."

Jen sniffled and wiped her eyes with the back of her hands. "We're going to die, and it's all my gran's fault. What was she thinking? I know she's a little batty at times, but this…"

Jack squeezed Jen's shoulder. "It's going to be okay, trust me."

Jen looked at him with big, moist eyes, and without even thinking what he was doing, Jack kissed her quickly on the lips. A jumble of thoughts ran through his head as he turned away, and he could feel his cheeks burning. What a dumb ass stupid thing to do. Why did he have to go and do that?

138

He felt Jen's hand touch his cheek, and he flinched, thought perhaps she was going to slap him or swear or something, so he wasn't prepared when she turned his head towards hers and kissed him back. The kiss didn't last long, but it was long enough to send a delicious shiver down his spine.

When their lips parted, there was an embarrassing silence, then Jack took Jen's hand in his and squeezed.

"I'm sure someone will come for us soon," he said.

Jen nodded and pursed her lips. "They'd better. I don't think my hair can take much more of this." She ran her hand through her sodden locks and smiled.

Jack grinned back.

Then he settled against the wall with his arm around her shoulder, offering the comfort of his embrace.

After a moment, a noise caught his attention, and he turned and stared across the expanse of water to see a boat approaching, its bow slicing through the waves like a cleaver leaving a foaming trail in its wake. Bright lights played across the surface of the water.

"Jen, look," he said, "someone's come to rescue us."

Jen sat up and a look of hope spread across her face. She smiled at Jack. "You were right."

"I always am."

She punched his arm playfully.

The boat drew closer, and Jack could see someone standing on deck. It took him a moment to realise that it was Rocky—and that the figure at the wheel was Zander.

"Oh shit," he said.

Jen frowned. "What is it?"

"Zander and Rocky."

"I don't care who it is as long as they're here to rescue us."

Jack wasn't so sure that that was what they were here for. He had a sinking feeling, as though his heart had taken an express elevator down to his stomach.

He heard Zander ease back on the throttle, and the boat came to a virtual standstill about fifty feet away.

Rocky cupped his hands around his mouth. "Well isn't this romantic," he shouted, rocking precariously as the boat pitched in the waves.

Even from a distance, Jack could see the sickly look on Rocky's face.

"Is he being sarcastic?" Jen said.

"I doubt he has enough brain cells to know what being sarcastic is."

"That asshole."

"I knew there was something going on between you," Rocky shouted. "Well, you're welcome to each other."

Zander stormed out of the wheelhouse and yanked Rocky out of the way to shut him up. "So where are my drugs?" he shouted.

"Jesus," Jack said to Jen. "Is he mad?"

"I did warn you."

"Look," Jack shouted back. "I took less than an eighth. It was no big deal. Now just fuckin' help get us out of here."

Zander shook his head. "It wasn't in your house, me and dickhead here looked."

Jack noticed Rocky grimace, and he felt a slight sense of glee at Rocky's discomfort. "I'm sorry. What else can I say?"

"I don't know how you found it all the way out there at sea, but where've you put it? And don't fuck me around, because I'm not in the mood."

"What's he on about?" Jen asked. "I thought you only took a bit."

"I did. He's lost it." He turned back to Zander. "Look, I don't know what you're on about, and I don't know how you found us, but can't you see we're stuck out here."

"Luckily for me, I was outside the bar when your old man was telling Graham where you were. Now tell me where my stuff is, otherwise I'm going to make you wish you'd never been born."

Jack shrugged.

"Goddamn it, where are my drugs?" Zander roared.

The sound sent a shiver down Jack's spine, and he was glad there was fifty feet of water between them. The man was crazy.

"Rocky," Jen called, "you've got to help us. There's something … something in the water."

Rocky scowled. "Don't you remember, we broke up. Or rather, you broke up with me. And now you want my help. Well you can go to hell, you bitch."

"Rocky, for God's sake, can't you see we're in trouble?

"Ask me if I care. I'm sure old Jacky boy there will help rescue you. Oh, I forgot, he's stuck too." Rocky laughed, then turned and lurched to the side of the boat where he was violently sick.

Zander turned towards Rocky and scowled. He said something that made Rocky shake his head in reply.

"Now, enough of the teenage tantrums and love sick kid bullshit," Zander roared. "Where the fuck are my drugs?"

Jack shook his head. "Fuck your fuckin' drugs. You've got to listen to me, there's something in the water, some sort of creature, a monster, I don't know." Jack knew he was rambling, but he didn't know what else to do. They couldn't stay where they were much longer. The creature would be back soon, he was sure of it.

Zander ran both hands through his short brown hair, his lips pursed. "Listen kid, give me back my stuff and I'll say no more about it."

"I've told you, I don't have anything."

Zander looked furious. Even from a distance, Jack could see the tendons in his neck protruding like thick cables, his ruddy cheeks aflame.

"Okay, I'll tell you where they are when you rescue us," Jack shouted.

Jen glared at him. "I thought you said you didn't take them."

"I didn't," Jack whispered, "but if the only chance of our being rescued was to say that I robbed Fort Knox, I'd fess up to that, too."

141

Zander nodded his head. "I'm glad to see you've seen sense. I'll bring the boat as close as I can, but then you're going to have to swim."

"*Swim!*" Jen shrieked. "No way. There's no way I'm going in that water."

"I know how you feel," Jack replied. He turned back to the boat and shouted, "Isn't there another way, you know, without going in the water?"

"Not without running aground. Now I'm going to bring the boat as close as I can." He turned and started back towards the wheelhouse.

"*We can't go in the water,*" Jen squealed.

Zander stopped and turned back. "Look, either you get in the goddamn water, or I come over there and drag you across."

"There's something in the water," Jen shouted.

"And there'll be something else in there in a minute, you pair. Now get a move on."

"Can't you throw us a line?" Jack hollered.

Zander rolled his massive shoulders and turned to Rocky, who was still leaning over the side of the boat. He said something, then grabbed Rocky by the scruff of his neck and hauled him to his feet. Then he pointed at something on the boat and said something else that Jack couldn't hear. Rocky shook his head, and Zander clipped him around the ear, which forced Rocky into action.

Rocky staggered across the deck, his face turning green. Every time the boat moved, he almost fell to his knees. Zander made his way back to the wheelhouse, moving as though man and boat were one.

Towards the front of the boat, Rocky bent down. When he stood up, he had a lifebuoy attached to a rope in his hand.

The sound of the engines grew louder as Zander brought the boat closer to shore. A moment later, his voice boomed out of a speaker.

"The lad here will throw you the lifebuoy," he roared above the noise of the engines, waves and wind. "You'll have to jump in the water, then we'll pull you aboard."

Jack felt Jen shivering at his side. "I know it's scary, but they'll be able to pull us aboard pretty fast."

Jen cupped her face in her hands. "I don't know whether I can do it."

"Well, I know you can." He smiled to offer encouragement. "If you go first, I'll keep an eye out, and if I see anything, well, you know, I'll …"

"What?"

Jack swallowed. "I'll jump in the water and distract it if I have to."

"Don't be stupid. I can't ask you to do that."

"You didn't ask. I'm volunteering."

Jen kissed him on the cheek.

Concerned that Rocky might have seen, Jack glanced across at the boat as it drew nearer to the rocks, but Rocky was leaning over the bow, shaking his head.

"Okay, that's as close as I dare come," Zander said through the speaker. "Kid, throw them that lifebuoy, and be quick about it."

The boat's engines revved as Zander fought to hold his position, and Rocky stood up and threw the lifebuoy as far as he could. The red and white striped float hit the water about fifteen feet from Jack and Jen's location.

"It's too far away," Jen said.

"It won't be that far when you're in the water. Come on, I'll help you down." Jack lowered himself from the ledge to the rocks below. A nervous tremor ran through him, but he tried to put on a brave face and despite his fear, he helped Jen down. The waves rolled across the rocks at his feet.

"I don't know whether I can do this," Jen said.

Jack put his hands on her shoulders. "Yes, you can. Rocky will pull you aboard before you know it." He looked across at the boat, which seemed to lurch closer towards the rocks with each fresh swell. "I'll keep an eye out, now go."

He ushered her towards the water, and despite her obvious fear, Jen complied. She waded out, and after only a couple of steps, the water was up to her neck. "Now swim for the lifebuoy," Jack said. "You can do it."

Jen started to swim and Jack kept his eyes peeled on the sea for any sign of the creature. When Jen reached the lifebuoy, she grabbed hold of it. "Okay, pull," she screamed.

Rocky didn't respond, and Jack could see he was leaning over the side of the boat again, fighting not to be sick.

"Rocky, goddamn it, pull Jen aboard," Jack shouted. He sensed Jen's fear as she bobbed in the water like the bait on the end of a line, and wished he could comfort her.

"Pull her in," Zander boomed through the speakers, "or God help me, I'll toss you overboard."

Spurred into action by Zander's voice, Rocky lurched to his feet and grabbed hold of the rope. He looked on the verge of being sick again as he started to pull, and Jack hoped he could hold it together long enough to haul Jen aboard.

The engines revved as Zander fought to hold position. Jack bit his lip and scanned the water. He glanced back towards Jen, saw something, and narrowed his eyes to see through the swells. There was something in the water twenty or so feet away from Jen. Jack tried to swallow, but his mouth was dry. The short hairs on the nape of his neck tingled.

"Pull," he shouted, but Rocky seemed to lack the strength to heave. Jen kicked with her legs to assist, but she wasn't moving very fast.

He hoped the shape in the water was just a piece of seaweed or driftwood, but when it moved counter to the waves, it dashed his hopes.

The creature was back.

In the beam of the boat's searchlight, the creature's head looked like a shiny black carapace and its two beady eyes glinted. It rose and fell in the waves, its attention fixed on Jen as she struggled to swim towards the boat.

Jack felt a pang of fear, but he had made Jen a promise, and he wasn't about to break it. "*Over here, you son of a bitch*," he screamed, waving his arms.

Whether it hadn't heard or wasn't interested, the creature continued towards Jen. She turned at the sound of Jack's voice, and her eyes grew wide as she saw the creature gliding towards her.

She screamed.

"Pull faster," Jack shouted, but Rocky was either oblivious or was feeling too sick to respond.

Seeing no other option, Jack plunged into the water. Despite being cold and wet already, the sea was freezing. He started to swim, fighting the overwhelming lethargy that invaded his body. The incessant waves rolled over him, submerging his head and he came up each time gasping for breath. White froth floated around him like the rabid salivations of the beast he was trying to attract.

What the hell was he doing out here, offering himself up as live bait? If the creature attacked, he knew he stood little to no chance of fighting it off. But he couldn't let Jen die. He had felt a connection between them, and that was enough. Besides, he couldn't stand by and let someone die while doing nothing to help.

Summoning all his strength, he ploughed through the waves, kicking furiously while his arms swept through the water. A powerful swimmer in the local pool, he found swimming fully clothed in the sea sapped his strength.

Caught in the swell, it was hard to see much, and he couldn't see the creature anywhere.

Jen was now about ten feet away, hanging onto the lifebuoy, and Rocky looked as though he had given up on pulling her anymore as he hung with his head over the side of the boat.

He heard the engines turning over, saw Zander in the wheelhouse struggling to maintain the boat's position – he knew Zander wasn't going to wait around forever.

When he reached Jen's side, Jack said, "You've got to swim."

Jen looked at him with wide, fear-filled eyes. "We're going to die," she wailed.

A wave washed over Jack, filling his mouth with saltwater. He coughed and choked; bone weary, he struggled to tread water. "Don't think like that. Just swim for the boat."

He looked around for the creature. Where was the blasted thing? He tried not to think it could be directly under him, in the dark expanse of water, but it was hard not to when his legs were dangling below the surface. Something buffeted his side; he thought it was the creature and panic washed through him. Even when he realised it was only a wave, he couldn't relax. They were sitting ducks out here – had to get aboard the boat as fast as they could.

"Rocky," Jack shouted, "goddamn it, pull, you son of a bitch."

Rocky raised his head, and despite his sickly demeanour, Jack could see his words had elicited a response, the set of his jaw now locked in anger. He looked about to respond, when his expression changed. His eyes grew wider, his jaw going slack, frown lines wrinkling his brow. He pointed, his hand shaking.

"There's something in the water," he shouted.

Jack didn't think Rocky would win medals any time soon. He grimaced and battled to keep his and Jen's heads above the rolling waves before turning to look where Rocky indicated. And there it was, less than eight feet away, its enormous jaw open to reveal the wicked curve of its long, pointed teeth. Water rolled from its head, following the course of the ridges that covered its surface. The light from the searchlight illuminated the creature; its dark shell gleamed in the light.

The next minute, the creature ducked below the surface. Absolute terror raced through Jack's veins. He scanned the water, but there was no sign of it. Any minute he expected to feel its teeth attach themselves to his legs, to bite through skin, muscle, flesh and bone as it dragged him down into the depths. Thinking he was drawing his last few breaths, he embraced Jen, using the lifebuoy to keep him afloat.

Then, without warning, he was moving through the water. He looked up to see Zander pulling on the rope. The tendons on the skipper's neck stood out, and the muscles in his

146

forearms flexed. He appeared to have braced himself against the side of the boat, and he gritted his teeth and pulled for all he was worth, hauling hand over hand.

Jack and Jen helped by kicking with their feet, but Jack didn't feel they were moving fast enough. He could see Zander was pulling as hard as he could, his face red with exertion, but he wasn't strong enough.

Rocky then appeared beside Zander and grabbed the rope. With a brief nod of his head towards Jack and Jen, he started to help.

At the back of his mind, Jack knew there was no one at the helm, and that the boat was floating towards the rocks, but he tried to dismiss the thought, the more pressing matter of the creature paramount.

With Rocky's help, they moved swiftly, slicing through the waves until they reached the boat. Water sluiced through wide gaps in the side of the boat, runoffs for the water on deck. The boat's masts and booms swayed as the boat lurched to one side. Jack felt a sick feeling in his stomach as he thought the boat was about to capsize. Next moment, the vessel righted itself, and Zander called out, "Heave."

But they were too heavy. He heard Zander cursing, but from his position in the water, he was unable to see him. Realizing if they were to stand any chance of surviving, he had to let go of the lifebuoy. Jack kissed Jen quickly on the cheek, tasting the saltwater on her skin, and then let go. He immediately sank down into the water, and without his added weight, he watched as Jen rose out of the sea.

Alone in the water, fear penetrated his body, and he wondered why the hell he had let go. It was crazy.

The cold water was making his body go numb, and he could no longer feel his fingers. He wondered if his mind would go the same way, numb to the pain that would surely follow, and he closed his eyes and waited.

"Grab hold, and be quick about it," Zander said.

Jack opened his eyes and looked up to see the lifebuoy hanging above his head. He reached out and grabbed it, and a sense of relief washed through him as he slipped one arm and his head through the hole in the centre.

He heard a splash in the water behind him, and his heart missed a beat. The creature was coming. He could feel his temples pound, his breath coming in rapid little bursts. Then he was out of the water, his free arm slamming into the side of the boat and sending a nerve-jarring pain up to his shoulder.

Ignoring the pain, he lifted his legs clear of the water and walked up the side of the vessel as the others pulled.

Seconds later, he lay on the deck, panting. Sodden through to the skin, he felt cold and miserable. But at least he was still alive.

Zander crouched down and grabbed Jack by the scruff of his neck. "What the blazes was that thing, kid?"

Jack struggled to breathe. "I don't know," he gasped.

"How many of them are there?"

"One, we've only seen one."

"Make that two," Jen said, pointing out to sea. Zander dropped Jack on the deck.

"I count … three," Rocky said as he fought not to be sick.

Jack jumped to his feet and stared out to sea. He counted quickly. "There's four, no five. Hold on, there's another one. Jesus, there are loads of them."

Zander bounded towards the wheelhouse.

Jack watched Zander disappear inside, saw him buckle himself into the chair, and then he heard the engines roar and the whole boat seemed to vibrate as they reversed away from the rocks.

Jack looked towards the shore, only then realizing how close they were. Jagged rocks protruded a few feet from the bow. He heard something scrape across the hull, felt the boat judder, the engines splutter. They were going to run aground.

Jack clenched his teeth. Jen grabbed his hand and he squeezed her fingers.

Loose buoys and rope slid across the deck as the boat pitched to one side. Jack stumbled, just managing to stop himself falling by grabbing hold of a winch arm. He held on tight to Jen, who still had a hold of his other hand, and stopped her from falling, too. Rocky wasn't so lucky. He rolled across the deck and collided with the side of the boat where he lay, unmoving.

The boat was still at a precarious angle, and a fresh wave washed over the side. Jack held on tight. For a brief moment, the wave was illuminated in the boat's lights, made almost glass like. And in that instant, Jack saw something dark contained within the wave, something that rode the swell aboard the boat.

Next minute, the boat righted itself, and the engines grumbled as Zander opened up the throttle, steering them out to deeper water, away from the rocks.

Jack let go of the winch and stared back towards the wheelhouse, and his jaw dropped open.

One of the creatures was on the boat. It scuttled across the deck, snapping its jaws, eyes glinting with malevolence.

A hunter stalking its prey, the creature advanced towards Jack and Jen.

Chapter 28

Jen squealed. Without even thinking, Jack grabbed her by the shoulder and pulled her out of the way so that all that lay between him and the creature was empty deck.

The creature bounded along on its stubby legs, its claw-tipped hands raking the air.

Jack knew he had to act quickly, so he crouched down and grabbed the nearest thing at hand, a small red buoy attached to a piece of rope. Standing up straight, he swung it around his head and released it at the creature. But he was no David, and this was no Goliath, and having misjudged the length of rope to let out, the buoy sailed past the creature. Jack cursed under his breath, but the buoy continued in a semi arc until the rope hit the creature's body, wrapping around the creature's torso, and entangling the beast in the rope.

A grin cracked Jack's face as the entangled creature stumbled and fell to the deck.

But his joy was short-lived as the monster severed the rope with its sharp claws. The buoy rolled away and clattered into the side of the boat, next to where Rocky lay motionless. The creature pushed itself back to its feet, opened its mouth and produced a deep-throated roar.

The sound sent a shiver down Jack's spine. He stood rooted to the spot, trembling. Was this nightmare never going to end?

Movement behind the creature caught Jack's eye, and he stared wide-eyed as Zander appeared, carrying a shotgun.

"This is my boat, and I didn't invite you on board," Zander growled through gritted teeth. The creature turned, but before it could respond, Zander opened fire, a flower of flame bursting from the barrel. Lead shot pierced the creature's abdomen, and it let out a high-pitched squeal that filled the air. It raked its claws in the air, and its feet skittered across the deck as it staggered back, tumbling over the side and into the water.

A door burst open beneath the wheelhouse and a giant ginger-haired man wearing blue overalls covered in oil rushed out onto the deck. "What's all the shooting about?" he shouted.

Zander turned towards the man. "Brad, you'd better take a look for yourself." He pointed towards the side of the boat.

Brad strode across, braced his hands on the rail and stared down. "Jesus H. Christ."

Jack followed and looked down at the sea, shocked to see the water bubble as a score of creatures attacked the fallen creature. Bloodstained froth floated on the surface, giving some indication of the ghastly feasting taking place.

"That's the freakiest shit I've ever seen," Brad said. "What the hell are they?"

Sickened, Jack turned to see Jen staggering towards him. He shook his head and ushered her away. "Believe me, you don't want to look," he said as he led her to the steps to the wheelhouse, where he sat her down.

He heard gunfire and looked back to see Zander standing with his feet planted, firing indiscriminately into the water. When Zander turned, his expression was resolute.

"I've seen hundreds of things dredged up from the depths in my time, but what the blazes was that?" he bellowed.

Jack swallowed to clear his throat. "God knows," he said, "but we should get out of here."

"It's the Devil's work," Brad said, making the sign of a cross across his broad chest.

Zander stood with the gun resting against his shoulder, seemingly oblivious to the movement of the boat. He glared at Jack. "And since when did you become skipper?"

Despite Zander's threatening presence, Jack didn't waver. "Didn't you see what those things just did? Jesus Christ, we can't stay here. There are hundreds of them in the water. We've got to warn people."

"Yes," Jen said, "we've got to get the hell out of here."

Zander narrowed his eyes. "I've never run from anything in my life."

"They have a point, Skipper," Brad said.

"We can't stay here," Jen squealed.

"Listen, just drop us off, then you can do anything you like," Jack said.

After a moment, Zander nodded. "Okay, but I think you'd better help him." He pointed at Rocky who sat rubbing his head, then made his way towards the wheelhouse with Brad shadowing him.

Zander opened up the throttle, turned the wheel and set a course for the harbour. He watched the kids on deck as they helped Rocky to his feet. He had to give it to that lad, Jack, he had balls standing up to him like that.

In the glare of the spotlights above the wheelhouse, he saw movement in the water, the residual splash of things diving below the surface to hide in the depths.

"Whatever the hell they are, there's loads of them," Brad said.

Zander nodded. Like he had said to the kid, he had seen many strange things brought up in the nets from the deep, things with names just as horrific, such as black dragonfish, humpback black devil and hammerjaw, but these, whatever they were, they were like nothing he had seen before.

The vessel travelled along at an average speed of fifteen knots, the quickest Zander dared push it. He followed the coast, spotting the odd house light in the distance on the shore and the cliffs above, the people in their homes unaware of the threat lurking in the waters near their property.

The door to the wheelhouse banged open and Jen staggered in, followed by Rocky and Jack.

"Take a seat, but just make sure you don't get in my way," Zander said. "And whatever you do, don't fucking touch anything!"

Although he felt sure of himself, Zander wasn't stupid. He knew this state of affairs was bigger than he could handle on his own. As he grabbed the microphone to radio in the situation, he could tell this was going to be a long night.

Chapter 29

"So he's safe," Bruce said to the police officer standing before him.

The officer whose nametag identified him as Powell nodded, then after a moment, the lashes above his brown eyes bristled with confusion and his boyish face took on a look of anxiety. "There's been a lot of strange reports coming from this area lately about things seen around the coast."

Bruce looked across at Erin, who was sitting staring through the bar window. "Do you want to start?" he said, knowing she had more knowledge of the situation than he did.

"Don't listen to them. It's all poppycock," Graham said before he took a swallow of his brandy.

"Miss?" Powell looked at Erin. "Do you have any information that might be relevant?"

Erin turned to face the officer. She rubbed her hands and folded her arms across her chest. "I can tell you what I believe, but whether *you* believe me is another matter."

"Go on."

Erin told Powell about the creatures, and her assumptions about over fishing, pollution and chemicals.

When she finished, Powell laughed.

"I told you," Graham said, grinning.

"You didn't see those things," Bruce spat. "If you had, then you might not be so quick to ridicule."

"I can see all the monsters I want on late night television," Graham said, chuckling.

"And I suppose you're an authority on sea beasties?" Powell asked Erin.

"Actually, yes. I'm a marine biologist."

Powell's smirk faded and he licked his lips. "Well, erm, can you substantiate your claims? I mean, fish can't breathe out of water."

153

"Actually, there are some fish that can breathe out of water for short periods. Like Mudskippers and Snakeheads."

Graham snorted and wiggled his hand to simulate downing an imaginary drink. "If you ask me, I think they've had one too many, officer."

Sara sat next to the bar, nursing a glass of orange juice. Next to her sat Duncan. Both of them remained quiet throughout the exchange. Neither of them had seen the Fangtooth, but at least they had the good sense to listen.

Erin seemed oblivious to Graham's ridicule. "I need to contact the research vessel I'm stationed on," she said. "There's equipment on there I might need, and I need to warn them of the situation."

Powell scratched his chin. "To be quite honest, miss, I don't know what to believe, but your story, well, it is a bit farfetched. Mutated fish!"

"Yeah, this isn't Sellafield, you know." Graham chortled.

"Believe me, I know how it sounds. But if you don't do something, radio it through, then it'll be too late."

"Too late? Why?"

"Because these creatures, whatever they are, they're hungry." She exhaled slowly, as though composing herself. "If they are a mutated form of Fangtooth, they'll live in small shoals. In the day, they stay in the depths, but at night, they rise to feed by starlight. They sense their prey by using contact chemoreception; basically they taste their prey in the water, relying on luck to bump into something edible. But I don't know how they react on the surface. Perhaps their eyesight has evolved, too, because the one we saw certainly didn't seem to have any problem locating us."

"That man on holiday, he was attacked in the day," Bruce said.

Erin nodded. "That's what concerns me. If they have mutated, it's not just in the physical sense, but in the—"

"I'm not going to listen to any more of this rubbish," Graham said.

"Just shut up," Duncan snapped.

Graham turned his one good eye on Duncan and scowled. "This is my bar, and I'll say what the hell I like. I'll certainly not have these outsiders come in here telling fanciful tales. It's hard enough getting customers in as it is. Since the fishing fleets have been disbanded, I hardly get anyone in. I never thought I'd miss those trawler men with all that cash to throw around after being paid, but I do. So I'll be damned if I'll lose what little livelihood I've got left.

"Officer, are you going to stand there and let them carry on this ridiculous conversation?" Graham asked. "Can't you do something before I throw the lot of them out?"

"And what would you have me do, sir? Arrest them?"

"That would be a start."

"On what grounds? Storytelling?"

"Ah, so at least you agree it's only a story." Graham grinned, an expression his one eye made appear sinister.

"I really don't know what to believe, but I'll call through to have someone check the coast out."

Graham rolled his eye and clucked loudly. "They'll have you believing in little green men next. I don't know what the world's coming to when a man of the law can be made a fool of."

Powell walked to the corner of the room and started talking into his walkie-talkie. Bruce went and sat next to Erin.

"Are you okay?" he asked.

Erin forced a smile. "I'm glad your son's safe."

Bruce couldn't help wondering for how long, though, if what Erin had said was true. "So am I. But these creatures, are they really coming ashore to eat?"

"That would be my guess, yes."

Bruce looked at the clock above the bar, which read 9:30. He had never been truly afraid before, had not known what real fear was, until he had seen Jack being terrorized by the creature. The feeling hadn't subsided. He needed to rescue his son, needed to wrap his arms around him and hold him tight.

Powell returned to the middle of the room. "Okay, the coast guard is going to send a patrol boat to check the area out."

"You'd be better sending the navy," Zander said as he stormed into the bar. "They have fuckin' big guns."

Jack walked in behind Zander, followed by Jen and another young lad with a cut on his forehead.

"*Jack!*" Bruce jumped up, ran across the room and embraced his son. Shazam jumped to her feet and bounded across the room, barking excitedly.

Jack returned the hug, and then said, "Okay, there's no need to suffocate me."

Bruce could see he was embarrassing Jack, but he didn't care. He was just glad that he was safe.

"I take it this is your son," the officer said.

Too choked to reply, Bruce nodded and squeezed his son harder.

"Daaaad," Jack wheezed.

Eventually, Bruce relaxed his hold. "I thought I was going to lose you," he said, his voice raw with emotion.

Jack stroked the dog's head. "You can't get rid of me that easy."

"And you are?" Powell asked Zander.

"Trent Zander, skipper of the *Storm Bringer*. Graham, pour us a double whisky." He stomped to the bar and leaned against the counter.

"Well, I'm going to have to ask you a few questions."

"I've only come to drop these kids off, so I haven't got time."

"Then you'll make time. I need to know what's going on. So either we do it here, or I take you down to the station."

Zander laughed. "It'll take more than one of you to stop me from leaving, and for your own good, I'd advise against trying."

Powell looked rankled, as though unfamiliar with disobedience. "Mr. Zander, that wasn't a request, it was an order."

156

"There's not a man alive who can order me to do anything," Zander said. He accepted the whisky as Graham handed it to him, and downed it.

"I need to know what's happening."

"I'll tell you what's happening. There's a fucking great shoal of killer fish out there, and by God, I'm going fishing."

Before Powell could stop him, Zander stood up straight, nodded at Jack, then ran out of the bar.

Chapter 30

On the way to his boat, Zander took out his phone and called his crew. He didn't tell them what it was about, just asked them to meet him at the boat, and to come armed. There was no way he was going to let them sail with him unless they knew the truth, but he couldn't explain over the phone.

The fog had all but dissipated, but the clouds made the darkness seem absolute. The globe shaped harbour lights provided the only illumination, their radiance broken up into fractal patterns on the water's surface. The wind made the wooden shutters on Zander's outbuilding clatter and the waves drove *Storm Bringer* repeatedly up against the dock, making her antennas, masts and winches jangle and clank.

He had left the engine running, leaving Brad down below to make sure everything ticked over. Once on board, he skipped down to the galley and made a pot of black coffee, a cup of which he took back up to the wheelhouse while he waited.

The first to arrive was the first mate, Muldoon, his brown hair sticking up all over the place and his chubby cheeks flushed. He jumped aboard and scurried up to where Zander sat waiting.

"You do realise I was just about to get down and dirty with Jill," Muldoon said as he dropped his duffel bag. "So you'd better have a good reason calling me out here in the middle of the goddamn night."

"Let's wait for everyone to arrive. I don't want to keep repeating myself. There's a brew on down below," Zander said. He ignored Muldoon's inquisitive glare and sipped the coffee, which was hotter than lava and just as thick.

A couple of minutes later, Jim arrived. He clambered aboard and stepped into the wheelhouse, muttering something about the weather. He had a habit of talking by hardly moving his lips, an act made worse by his facial hair.

"So what's the problem?" Jim mumbled.

158

Zander nodded. "Get yourself a coffee, and I'll explain."

Jim scratched his beard and scuttled away, muttering to himself.

About to take another gulp of coffee, Zander saw a car's headlights sweep into the harbour. He instantly recognised McKenzie's black BMW and he cursed under his breath. The drug dealer was the last thing he needed.

He watched as the car stopped, its engine cut out and its headlights extinguished. Next minute, McKenzie stepped out of the vehicle. A cigarette drooped from the corner of his mouth and he thrust his hands into the pockets of his black jacket. He walked towards Zander's boat, shoulders hunched and barrel chest thrust out.

When he reached the side of the boat, McKenzie motioned with his head that Zander should come down.

He really didn't need this shit, but he stood up and exited the wheelhouse to stand on deck with his foot on the railing.

"You're early," Zander said.

McKenzie spoke without removing his cigarette, "Don't fuck with me. Where's my stuff?"

"Slight problem," Zander replied.

"Problems are for Dear Abby. Do I look like fuckin' Dear Abby?"

This wasn't going to go down well, but Zander wasn't about to start lying. "You'd better come aboard. We're about to set sail, and if you come with us, then you'll see what the problem is."

"Do I look like I've come to go fishin'? You're wastin' my time. You know what happened to the last man who wasted my time? I took him fishin', fishin' without a fuckin' rod and with him as the bait, you know what I mean?"

"I understand. But you aren't going to believe me if I tell you, so you'd better come and see for yourself."

McKenzie exhaled a cloud of smoke. "You fuck with me and I'll introduce you to a world of pain you didn't know existed, you get me?"

Zander nodded. "Yeah, but just keep our business deal between us. Now come aboard and I'll show you what's happened." He hated kowtowing to this city punk, a man who was only a go-between, but he knew that if he didn't pacify him, then those who swam in the higher echelons would rain down with fire and brimstone. He really had gotten himself in too deep, and no amount of regret would help. Now that he'd had time to think about it, he knew that young lad, Jack, hadn't stolen his drugs. No, it was the creatures. Perhaps intrigued by the contents of the pot, they had torn it open. Now all he could do was show McKenzie what had happened–show him what was lurking in the ocean.

McKenzie narrowed his eyes and looked the boat up and down. "You sure that old tub's not going to sink?"

"Not while I'm at the helm it's not."

Looking less than convinced, McKenzie stepped warily aboard just as Muldoon stepped out of the wheelhouse and clambered down onto the deck. He looked at McKenzie with a challenging expression.

"You got a fuckin' problem," McKenzie snarled.

Zander saw Muldoon bunch his fist. "Hey, Muldoon, it's okay, he's with me." He knew Muldoon could handle himself, had fought beside him, but the likes of McKenzie were a different kettle of fish. People like McKenzie didn't just swim with sharks, they were the sharks. Suburban predators.

Muldoon gave Zander a look that said, 'you'd better have a good reason for not letting me hit this piece of shit', and then he skulked away to the stern to busy himself with preparing the boat.

Zander led the way to the wheelhouse, and when Jim reappeared, McKenzie had seated himself in a chair at the back of the room. Jim hardly glanced at him. The same couldn't be said of McKenzie.

"You sure these men know how to sail this piece of shit?" he said, looking Jim up and down with disdain.

Zander saw Jim bristle and mumble something under his beard, which McKenzie thankfully didn't notice or hear. He was taking a big enough risk allowing McKenzie on board–

apart from Brad, his crew didn't know about his sideline–but it was a chance he had to take. Now if only he could get the jerk to shut his trap.

Next aboard came Robinson, looking as though he had jumped straight out of bed as he rubbed his knuckles into his eyes, his blond hair uncombed.

Brad climbed up from the engine room, wiping his oil covered hands on a piece of dirty rag.

Brad smiled broadly, displaying a couple of missing teeth between his large lips. "Jim," he boomed, slapping him on the back.

Just then, Muldoon entered the wheelhouse. Saltwater dripped from his oilskins and he shook himself and nodded a greeting at Robinson and Brad.

"Good weather for it," Muldoon said.

Brad stared at McKenzie as though he were someone he had caught breaking into his house.

Zander looked at each of his crew in turn. "Okay, I'll not lie to you because we've been through a lot, but tonight, Brad and me, we saw something I've never seen before."

"A bit of pussy. Good for you," Muldoon said, laughing loudly. Everyone apart from McKenzie joined in.

Zander waited for the laughter to subside, fanning his hands to quieten the men down. "If only I was that lucky."

"Don't tell me, she were a large one," Muldoon said, shaking his head in amusement. "No trouble, I've had a few, but you'll get over it, hey boys. As long as there's grass on the playing field." He winked.

Zander exhaled loudly. "Listen, this is important. Tonight Brad and me, we saw something in the sea."

Brad wrung his hands, his face pale. "I've never seen anything like it."

McKenzie snorted loudly. "Are you going to get to the point? I'm a busy man, places to go, people to talk to, you know what I mean." He winked at Zander in a way that hinted at malice.

Unperturbed, Zander continued. "Well it was a fish, but not like any fish we've seen before."

"Come on," Muldoon said, "we've seen all kinds of fish."

"Not like these you haven't. You remember the other day, when the nets were torn, well not torn, fuckin' shredded—"

"What about it?" Jim mumbled.

"I think this creature did it. Now I don't know what it is or where it's come from; could even have escaped from a secret laboratory for all I know, but I'm telling you, this thing was at least four feet long, and it had arms and legs and the biggest damn teeth you ever saw."

McKenzie rolled his eyes. "What the fuck! You think I've got time to sit here and listen to this shit?"

Muldoon glared at him. "I've sailed with Trent Zander for more years than you've had baths, and if he says there's something in the water he's never seen before, I believe him."

"Then you're as cracked as he is. You sure you haven't been smoking the merchandise, Zander?" McKenzie asked.

Zander felt like grabbing him by the throat and strangling the life out of him. He looked at his crew. Faced with McKenzie's accusation, which virtually told the whole story, he didn't know what to say, and for the first time in his life, he was rendered speechless.

Fortunately, Brad spoke up. "Aye man, you don't think they didn't know what we were up to? Give the boys credit. We sail out all by ourselves in the dead of night. I wouldn't be surprised if there's anyone in the village who doesn't know what we were up to. Not that everyone agrees with it, but a man has to make a living, and the boys knew you were using drug money to pay their wages. In my book, that went above and beyond."

Robinson nodded, and Jim chortled behind his beard.

Zander smirked. How did he think he could ever lead a secret life in a village where there were no secrets? A village where everyone knew everyone, a village as tight knit as Mulberry.

"Well if you've all stopped licking each other's asses, perhaps you can tell me where my fuckin' drugs are," McKenzie said.

162

Zander rubbed his neck. "They're gone. The lobster pots were smashed and the drugs were gone."

McKenzie jumped to his feet. "You'd better be fuckin' jokin'."

Zander shook his head. "I wish I was."

"So who's got the drugs?"

"That's what I'm trying to tell you. No one's got 'em. I think these sea creatures were inquisitive and they smashed the pots to see what was inside."

"Bullshit. You're yanking my fuckin' chain. Fuckin' sea monsters."

Brad puffed his chest out. "You want to make something of it?"

Before anyone could react, McKenzie pulled a knife out of his jacket pocket and thrust it towards Brad's stomach.

Despite his size, Brad was quick on his feet. He easily dodged the blade and grabbed McKenzie's wrist. Next minute, Robinson and Jim pulled knives from their waistbands.

"Little boys shouldn't play with knives. You might get cut," Brad said, prizing the blade from McKenzie's fingers.

"You're going to regret that," McKenzie snarled. "Don't you fuckin' inbreeds know who I am?"

"Stop, you'll have me quaking in me boots," Brad replied.

"Let him go," Zander said. "I'll not have any fighting on board my boat."

Brad passed Zander the knife, and Robinson and Jim put their weapons away. The drug dealer straightened out his jacket and ran a hand through his short hair.

"When Monty hears about this, you lot will be fuckin' dog meat," he growled.

Monty was the big cheese, the head honcho, and Zander knew McKenzie wasn't making idle threats. These people wouldn't mess around. They had lost a consignment of drugs worth a lot of money, and someone was going to have to pay. The only chance he had now at redeeming himself, and

163

the lives of his crew, was to show McKenzie what lay beneath the waves.

"Okay men, I won't force any of you to come as this is going to be dangerous, but I'm guessing these creatures are the reason we've not caught any fish lately. I'm also guessing they had something to do with the sinking of the *Silver Queen*, and that's why I'm going to kill every last one of them. Now's your last chance to leave, because the tide's in, and I'm about to set sail."

McKenzie grimaced. "If you think I'm—"

"Shut your trap, McKenzie. You're coming whether you like it or not," Zander said. "I'm going to prove to you that no one stole your fucking drugs, and that there is something out there." To his relief, McKenzie didn't argue. He was not stupid enough to think he could take on five men.

Robinson nodded his head. "I'm in," he said. Brad agreed, as did Jim.

"Oh damn it, count me in too," Muldoon said.

Jim started towards the door, then stopped and turned back. "How do you expect to catch or kill these creatures? They chewed through the net last time."

Zander stared out to sea. "From what I've seen, these creatures want to come aboard to feed. So that's what I'm going to let them do. We're going to use ourselves as bait. And then we're going to kill the bastards."

Chapter 31

The atmosphere in the bar was chilly to say the least. Since Zander had stormed out, Powell had been talking to someone on his walkie-talkie. Jack sat at one of the tables, talking to Sara and Jen. The other lad, Rocky, sat in a corner, glaring at Jen and Jack. Duncan sat nursing a brandy. Graham sat behind the bar, from where he eyed everyone as though they were interlopers from another dimension. Erin stood by the bar smoking a cigarette, and Shazam sat at Bruce's feet, her head cocked as though she was trying to take it all in.

Bruce couldn't help but feel what a ragtag group they made.

He looked at Erin as she lit another cigarette from the butt of her last one. Despite her dishevelled appearance, she still looked radiant. He noticed her hand shake as she put the cigarette to her lips, and he walked across and stood beside her.

"I don't think Zander endeared himself to the police officer. What do you think he's going to do?" he asked.

Erin turned towards him and he saw a deep sadness in her eyes, but also something else, something that made her appear as a frightened child. "Who, Zander or Powell?"

"Zander. What do you think he's going to do?"

Erin shrugged and puffed on her cigarette. "I don't know. He's crazy enough to do anything."

"You look worried." He hoped her concern wasn't for Zander; that she didn't have feelings for him.

Erin emitted a nervous laugh. "Is it any wonder? You saw those things. God knows how many of them there are."

"Well I don't think there's anything to worry about. The army will take care of them."

"You think it will be that easy." It was not a question.

Bruce put his hands on the bar. "They've got guns and all manner of weapons. I don't think a few fish, no matter how big, will be a threat."

165

"You seem to be forgetting, these fish, although I don't think it's right to call them fish anymore, are now as at home on land as they are beneath the water. That gives them an advantage, a big advantage in my book."

"We've got one of the best armies in the world."

"And now we've got one of the most fearsome predators after us. We've only seen a few, but a population can't sustain itself without there being a lot more of them." The fear on Erin's face was evident.

Bruce saw Graham peering at him and he turned away.

Through the window, he could see the harbour lights. He had watched Zander set sail. So had Powell, but he hadn't intervened. Bruce wondered what would happen when he returned to port. Wasn't disobeying a police officer a crime? Having never broken the law, Bruce was unsure of the rules, but he didn't think running away from a questioning officer would go down too well. But then again, from Zander's expression, he didn't think the man could care less.

The darkness outside was intimidating. It allowed things to hide too easily. He shivered at the thought. The bright lights of the bar reflected off the glass, so it was hard to see out, but Bruce moved away from the window in case anything looked in and saw him

He anxiously fingered the wallet in his trouser pocket, hoping the influence of the lucky charms would pass through the leather. The way things were going, he needed all the good luck he could get.

A sudden noise made Bruce jump. It originated outside, sounded like a glass bottle kicked across the ground. All eyes turned to the window, then the lights went out.

Bruce heard a scream. He didn't know who it was, or whether it was male or female. Shazam barked once. The tip of Erin's cigarette shook in the dark.

"It's probably the fuse," Graham grumbled.

Bruce heard a chair scrape across the cold stone floor.

A light penetrated the dark, blinding Bruce as it swept across his face. "Is everyone okay?" Powell asked as he shone the flashlight around the room.

Despite his impaired vision, Bruce saw a few blurred heads nod in the glare of the torch, and heard grunts of ascension before he rubbed his eyes to clear his sight.

"Do you need a hand?" Powell asked as he shone the flashlight behind the bar. "Where's he gone?"

"Who?" Bruce asked.

"The barman, Graham."

"He was there a minute ago," Erin said.

"Well he's not now." He approached the counter and shone the torch around the bar. "Graham, are you there?"

No one answered.

"Dad, what's going on?" Jack asked.

"It's okay, Graham's just gone to check the fuses."

"Then why isn't he answering?"

Bruce wondered the same thing, but he didn't want to encourage the nervousness permeating the room. He heard a sob, hoped it wasn't Erin, but couldn't see her in the dark. At times like this, he felt useless. Didn't know what to do or say.

The torchlight illuminated an open door at the rear of the bar. Behind him, Bruce heard footsteps as the assembled crowd gathered around, close enough for him to hear their breathing.

He stared at the doorway.

"Graham?" Powell said.

A noise filtered through the door. Bruce heard those around him hold their breath in anticipation. Sudden movement at the edge of the doorway caught his eye. One of the young girls squealed. Bruce involuntarily clenched his fists; his eyes went wide, fearful. Then a face appeared.

The figure shielded its face. "Get that light out of my fuckin' eye," Graham said as Powell shone the torch at him.

The group released a collective breath. Bruce unclenched his fists. Powell lowered the torch. "Why didn't you answer when I called?"

"Didn't hear you. Thick walls."

"Was it the fuse?" Erin asked.

Graham shook his head. "They all look fine to me. Probably a power cut."

Bruce pointed to the window. "Then why aren't the harbour lights out?"

All eyes turned towards the window, beyond which the harbour lights glowed. A murmur filtered around the bar.

"What's going on?" Jen asked.

Powell waved his arms in the air, making the torchlight chase shadows around the room. "Now if everyone will just calm down. It's probably nothing to worry about."

"Of course it's nothing to worry about," Graham said

Bruce felt something brush against his leg. He looked down and saw Shazam, her head held high as she sniffed the air, ears cocked.

"What is it girl?"

Shazam looked up at him. In the near dark, her eyes glistened.

"What, you think you're Doctor Doolittle now," Graham said. "First monsters, now this. Jesus." He snorted loudly.

"I'd better go and check around outside," Powell said.

"First sensible thing you've said all night," Graham snapped.

Bruce thought he saw Powell sigh, but he wasn't sure as shadows played tricks with Powell's face.

"Be careful," Erin said.

Graham spat. "Let the man do his job."

Although not a violent man, Bruce felt like punching Graham.

He watched as Powell turned and walked towards the door; wondered whether he should offer to accompany him, but decided against it. Now that he had Jack back, he didn't want to let him out of his sight.

Once Powell walked outside, darkness descended upon the bar. Bruce felt something brush his hand, felt fingers intertwine with his own. He looked up, could just make out Erin in the gloom. He squeezed her hand, saw the reflection of her teeth as she smiled in return. Her aroma filled the air, a smell that excited him. He felt they were like school kids, sitting in the back row at the cinema, too shy to surrender to their feelings, but her presence was comforting.

His eyes slowly adapted to the lack of light, and he watched as Sara wandered over to the window and peered out. Beyond the glass, he could see torchlight flicker as Powell swept the area.

He saw Jack staring at him, realised he was still holding Erin's hand and let go. As though sensing the reason for his action, Erin gave him an encouraging look and then lit another cigarette.

"What's taking him so long?" Sara asked.

Rocky spoke for the first time, "Perhaps those things got him."

"Not you as well. I would have thought you had more sense," Graham said.

"You weren't there."

Graham poured himself a whisky and knocked it back.

Bruce saw movement in the doorway behind Graham, but before he had a chance to say anything, a figure rushed forward and struck Graham over the head. He dropped his glass. Bruce heard it shatter. Then Graham collapsed in a heap on the ground behind the bar.

Bruce was too stunned to move. His gaze travelled up the body of the new arrival until he saw her face: Lillian Brown.

By now, everyone had heard the commotion and Bruce heard a voice say, "Gran! My God, what are you doing?"

He turned to see Jen on her feet, shaking her head.

"Hush child," Lillian said. Her wild eyes surveyed the room before coming to rest on Bruce. He shivered.

Although the bar was between them, Bruce could make out a club of some sort in her hand, which he surmised she had used to hit Graham over the head.

Lillian held her free hand up. "I've not come this far to be stopped now."

"I don't understand," Jen said, her voice choked with tears.

"The sea needs sacrifices, child. That's why this is happening."

169

Bruce couldn't believe what he was hearing. "You're crazy. Duncan, help me out here."

He heard a bolt snap into place and turned to see Duncan standing with his back to the door.

"I'm sorry Bruce, but she's right."

Chapter 32

Zander saw McKenzie keep stealing glances his way, and he knew given the chance the drug dealer wouldn't balk at killing him. But he hadn't counted on a crew of trawler men who stared danger and death in the face every time they set sail, men who wouldn't flinch at McKenzie's threats.

The sea stretched before him, relentless. A shroud for the denizens of the deep. Zander steered a course for the rocks where he had picked up Jack and Jen. Despite his brave countenance, he felt nervous, his stomach bubbling with apprehension.

He didn't really know what he was going to do when he found his quarry, but find it he would.

The searchlights illuminated choppy waves, from the crests of which the wind whisked trails of foam. He had hoped to see McKenzie looking pale and sick, but he seemed to take the movements of the boat in his stride, his jaw never losing the clenched aspect that made his cheeks prominent.

Muldoon sat to the side, scanning the sonar screen. He glanced at Zander and nodded as though in encouragement, but Zander couldn't help wondering if the bravado that had fuelled this voyage wasn't running out. It had seemed like a good idea at the time. Not that he would dismiss it as foolhardy now, but out here, where the sea ruled, it made him take stock.

He looked to port where Robinson was busy on deck, and caught sight of his own reflection in the glass. He looked manic, wide-eyed, crazy from lack of sleep. It's no wonder McKenzie didn't argue, one look at Zander probably made him think twice.

The cliffs were visible at the fringes of the searchlights. Zander knew them well, and he could plot his position by those alone.

When they reached the location where he had seen the creatures, Zander eased off on the throttle.

Muldoon leaned closer to the sonar screen. "There's something down there, but the readings are strange."

Zander knew it wasn't only the readings that were strange. He sounded the alarm, and then lifted the microphone, his voice booming out of the speakers: "Right everyone, make sure you're armed and ready. These creatures are tough sons of bitches."

The men on deck signalled with thumbs up and Zander started lowering the nets, creating a ladder leading up from the ocean.

Brad patted the six cylinder, turbo diesel engine, pleased to hear it rumble contentedly. The rocker arms clacked up and down in quick succession. He checked the gauges and monitored dials, giving the oil pressure gauge a tap. Oil and grease marred his forehead and his hands were black with grime.

The metal walls of the engine room were rusty. Remnants of paint made up abstract patterns that if he stared at them for long enough, formed into pictures. Here a face, there a cat.

Tangles of wires and pipes filled the room, each pipe colour coded: blue, fresh water; green, seawater; red, diesel and yellow, oil. The belts running from the engine whined, but Brad liked it down here. The engine was his baby. He was at home changing fuel filters, bleeding the system, doing oil changes, tune-ups and cooling system maintenance. His mechanical expertise was second to none, and he figured he could get her up to speeds of twenty knots if he needed to.

The engine shuddered, and he tapped it with a spanner, which made her tick over contentedly again. Out here, a loss of engines could mean certain death.

He heard the alarm. Metal clanged against the hull, the sound reverberating around the engine room as Zander lowered the nets.

Brad picked up a dirty rag and mopped the sweat from his brow. Plainspoken, he wasn't afraid of calling a spade a spade, and he didn't like that McKenzie fellow one bit. If it were up to him, he'd toss him overboard as fish bait. None of the men on board would comment, or breathe a word about what happened. They were closer than a family, so perhaps if he had a chance, he'd do it for Zander anyway. He had never killed anyone before, but had thought about it plenty of times, especially his ex-wife, Maureen. He couldn't believe she wouldn't let him see their son, Sean. What did she think he was going to do? The bottled rage bubbled up, and he concentrated on the engines to quell the anger. Now was not the time to lose it.

A sudden noise against the hull caught his attention. He was used to hearing noises down here, but this sounded different – almost like someone tapping against the side. He cocked his head and listened, heard a sharp rat-a-tap-tap, then a protracted scratching sound, like sharp fingernails dragged across the metal. He remembered the creatures he had seen in the water. Not an easy man to scare, Brad was surprised to find he was holding his breath, and that goose bumps mottled his arms. He scanned the sides of the boat, trying to trace the sound, but it seemed to be moving, first one side and then the other. That's when he realised the sound originated in more than one place at once.

The engine seemed to cough and wheeze, bringing Brad's attention back to the task of keeping the boat running. He adjusted a couple of valves and the engine sputtered and then continued chugging smoothly.

He kept a small cassette player in the engine room, and he turned it on. The sound of Robert Wyatt's haunting voice drifted out with the *Sea Song*: You look different every time you come from the foam-crested brine.

He had always thought the song was about a mermaid, but listening to it now, he heard it in a new light.

Down in the engine room, Brad turned the music up loud to drown out the sound of scratching on the hull.

Now alone in the wheelhouse with Zander, McKenzie glanced at the knife. Zander had put it on a shelf where it was clearly visible and accessible. McKenzie wasn't stupid.

173

He knew Zander wouldn't have put it within reach if it wasn't for a reason, and that reason was probably to let him know that out here, if he did anything stupid, there was no way he could pilot the boat himself. But as soon as they reached land …

He stared out of the window at the nets descending into the deep. In the beam of the lights, the nets seemed to glisten. Flecks of foam coated the buoys and clogged some of the holes in the net itself. He heard the heavy clang of metal as something banged against the side of the boat. This was nothing like the fishing he used to do in the river with his dad when he was a lad. He remembered the day they caught an eel. The thing hadn't been that long, but it had wrapped itself around his arm and refused to budge, which made him understand where the term slippery as an eel came from. The hook was wedged firmly in its mouth, and his dad had struggled for ages to unhook it without being able to get a good grip. Eventually fed up of watching his dad try to unfasten it, McKenzie sliced the eel with a knife – the same knife Zander had put on the shelf – and the fish unwrapped itself and flopped aside. Yes, that knife had a history, and that was the first blood it had shed, but it certainly wasn't the last. While many of the local gangsters used guns, McKenzie preferred the personal touch associated with a knife. There was nothing like standing next to your victim and being able to see the look of horror and pain on their face as the blade penetrated their flesh.

He had been questioned about various crimes, but there was never enough evidence to make a conviction stick, so he wasn't about to let some fish-stinking fisherman call the shots when the police had never been able to.

He had plans and dreams. One day, he was going to take over from Monty. And then there wasn't going to be any of this pussy-footing around with small—

A high-pitched squeal cut into his thoughts. McKenzie narrowed his eyes and turned to look at Zander to ask what the hell that fuckin' noise was, but when he saw Zander's nervous expression, he decided against it. He had never seen the skipper appear anything other than stony, and the realisation that something had rattled the man made him feel anxious too.

McKenzie glanced at the knife, wanted the comforting feel of its handle within his grasp, but it was out of reach at the moment. He chewed his top lip and looked out at the net.

The high-pitched noise caused Zander to flinch. He stared out, saw something hauling itself up the outside of the net, clawing its way along the mesh.

"Here they come," he said.

McKenzie stared at him. "What the fuck's going on?"

Zander pointed outside, saw McKenzie's expression turn to shock as the first of the creatures flopped onto the deck.

A large wave washed across the starboard bow. The boat listed precariously.

McKenzie jumped up and grabbed his knife. A small grin altered his expression as he opened the blade. "What are those things?"

"I told you, they're what took your drugs."

McKenzie narrowed his eyes. "If this is some fuckin' sort of joke … if you're fuckin' with me …Right, let's go see how they like the taste of cold steel." Then he turned, ran towards the door and disappeared outside.

Although not a religious man, Zander said a prayer then picked up his shotgun and followed McKenzie outside.

The wind roared around him, sea spray stinging his face. McKenzie ran on in front, slipping across the deck. He reached the nearest Fangtooth and started stabbing it with the knife. The blade pierced its body and the creature slashed out in retaliation, raking its wicked claws across McKenzie's arm, tearing cloth and parting flesh.

Zander raised his weapon and pulled the stock into his shoulder. He tensed his finger on the trigger and aimed, but couldn't get a clear shot as McKenzie kept bobbing in his way.

"Get down," Zander roared.

175

McKenzie dropped to the deck and Zander pulled the trigger, peppering the creature's chest with lead shot.

As McKenzie stood up, he grasped his arm, wincing. Blood rained from his injury, splashing the deck with lurid patterns

"Take that, you son of a bitch," Robinson shouted as he lashed out with a gaff hook.

Zander fired at a couple of creatures scrambling over the net, punching them back into the water. But behind those came more. Lots more and he couldn't reload fast enough to keep up.

One of the creatures lurched forwards. McKenzie slashed at it with the knife, but the creature ducked underneath the attack and sank its teeth into his stomach. McKenzie screamed, the sound reaching an ear-splitting crescendo as it tore its head back, ripping out a chunk of flesh. Loops of purple intestine and viscera slopped out onto the deck. McKenzie staggered for a moment, then collapsed in a heap.

Oblivious to Zander, the creature dropped down onto all fours and started chewing on the wound it had inflicted. Zander opened fire, lead shot tearing through the creature's body.

McKenzie scrabbled around on deck, trying desperately to push his intestines back into his stomach. "Help me," he whined.

Zander gritted his teeth. McKenzie was beyond saving. He levelled the barrel at McKenzie's head, finger tensed on the trigger. Despite his hatred of the man, he had never killed anyone before, and even though it would be a mercy killing, he couldn't do it. He exhaled and lowered the weapon. Shook his head.

McKenzie scrunched his face up in pain. "Please," he said.

Before Zander could reply, Jim ran past and rammed his knife into McKenzie's chest.

"Good riddance to bad rubbish," Jim said.

The boat listed, throwing Brad across the room. He picked himself up, heard the ear-piercing scream over the sound of the engines and he vaulted across the machinery, donned his oilskins and headed up towards the deck. What was going on up there?

The first thing he saw when he stepped out onto the deck was Zander firing from the hip. Then on the deck he saw McKenzie's eviscerated body, next to which lay a dead creature, its body slick with blood and seawater.

The rest of the crew was back peddling against the tide of creatures surging up the net.

Brad sprinted across the deck and grabbed the fire axe from the side of the wheelhouse.

Movement to his left caught his eye and he raised the axe, prepared to deliver a deathblow when a voice shouted, "Stop. It's me."

Brad focused his gaze and stared at Robinson. He shook his head. "I fucking nearly killed you, you idiot."

Jim appeared behind Robinson. "Might have knocked some sense into him at least."

Robinson whirled on Jim. "Now's not the time for your sarcastic comments."

"Might not get another chance," Jim cackled. His expression changed. "Behind you," he screeched.

Brad turned and glared at the creature making its way towards them across the deck. It walked on all fours until it was about seven feet away, then it raised itself up to stand on its rear legs in an almost humanlike way. It opened its mouth impossibly wide, revealing long, sharp fangs. Brad could see down its ribbed throat – it was like staring into the bowels of hell, the teeth the gates to Hades.

"Come on you mother," he said between clenched teeth. "If you wanna piece of me, come and get it."

The creature scurried forwards, head thrust out, mouth open ready to bite.

Brad heard a scream, thought it might have been Robinson but couldn't be sure. Well, nothing on this earth

177

was going to make him scream like a baby. Not when he could make it scream first.

With expert timing, he swung the axe up and around with all his strength. The sharp blade struck the creature on what purported to be its neck. Brad clenched his teeth against the bone jarring pain that shot along his arm, but he didn't stop following through. The creature didn't even have time to blink as the axe severed its head clean off. The headless creature still moved forwards at an alarming speed, and Brad stepped quickly aside. A geyser of blood gushed out of its neck, spraying the deck with gore as it sailed by. Brad felt a sense of power, and he was about to whoop with joy when he heard another scream. What was it with Robinson? Brad never thought of him as a big crybaby before. He turned, about to tell Robinson to can it, but the words died in his throat.

One of the creatures had Robinson's arm in its mouth. It shook its head from side to side, and Brad heard the bone-sickening crunch as it chewed straight through Robinson's arm.

Without the creature pulling against him, Robinson fell back. Blood gushed from the stump of his arm, spraying the air around him like a fire hose. At his side, Jim could only stand and stare. Blood spurted over his face to cover it like a gory mask.

Robinson's scream was the most disturbing thing Brad had ever heard. Spurred into action by the sound, he swung the axe around and buried it in the creature's head, splitting it in two like a ripe watermelon. The creature slumped to the deck, and globs of brain matter poured through the split in its skull.

The creature writhed on the ground, its talon tipped hands clenching in spasms, and Brad slammed the axe into its chest, opening up a large cavity out of which gushed a snake of innards.

He placed a foot on the creature and yanked the axe out, then he looked up and saw two of the creatures charging towards him, jaws open wide and fangs hinged ready to bite.

Chapter 33

Zander reloaded his gun then stared at the carnage and winced. This was all his fault. He saw Robinson flailing on the deck, blood spurting from his severed arm. He saw Jim, standing frozen in shock, blood dripping from his beard. He saw Brad, like a proud Viking warrior hefting his trusty axe. And he saw the two creatures bearing down on him like walking nightmares.

Brad flailed with the axe, swinging it in wide arcs, trying to keep the creatures at bay.

"Jim you old sod, give us a hand," Brad roared.

But Jim stood transfixed, his eyes glassy orbs in a bloodied face.

"Brad, hit the deck," Zander screamed.

Brad glanced over his shoulder, mouthed 'oh shit', and dropped to the ground.

Zander swept the gun around in an arc, spraying shot at the creatures, punching them back.

Once the coast was clear, Brad jumped to his feet. "Cheers, skipper."

Zander nodded, then saw movement as one of the downed creatures scrambled to its feet. "Look out," he shouted.

Brad spun around, slamming the blade of the axe into its mouth, splintering its teeth like icicles. With the next blow, he buried the axe in its shoulder and the creature dropped to the ground, writhing in pain.

"Come on, grab it," Zander said as he bent and took hold of the creature's legs. Brad dropped the axe and grabbed the creature by the shoulders, then together they lifted and threw it overboard. The sea appeared to boil as the other creatures started a feeding frenzy. In the beam of the spotlights, the sea turned red. Zander leaned over the side and watched. If they fed upon each other with such ease, what chance did humankind have?

The creatures clawed at the boat, scrambling up the net. He shivered.

They were relentless bastards.

Unable to look at them any longer, he turned and hurried to Robinson's side. As he approached, Muldoon shook his head.

"He's dead."

The guilt weighed heavy on Zander's shoulders and he slumped under the pressure. "I'm going to drop the nets to stop anymore climbing on board."

Jim ran his hand across his face, smearing Robinson's blood, then he fired his pistol at an approaching creature.

Zander licked his lips. The skin felt cracked and he could taste the saltwater. He knew the crew was going to blame him for this, and he knew they were right. Stupid pride had possessed him to come out here. He would never forgive himself.

He hurried back to the wheelhouse and stared down at the carnage on deck. He pressed a button, sending the nets into freefall.

But there were already too many creatures on board. Seeing that his men were losing ground, he picked up the microphone. "Fall back and barricade yourselves in. We're heading home."

He set a course back to Mulberry, pushing the engines as fast as he could.

Chapter 34

Bruce held his hands up. "Duncan, what are you doing?"

Duncan folded his arms across his chest. "Lillian's right. It's an age old tradition to offer a sacrifice to the sea or the land in return for a good harvest."

Bruce couldn't believe his ears. This was pagan claptrap. "Duncan, there are monsters out there. You can't be serious."

"Deadly."

"Gran," Jen said, "you saw those things. This is crazy."

"*She's* crazy," Jack said.

"Shut it kid," Duncan said. "You outsiders think you know it all. Well you don't. If it wasn't for us, this village would have shrivelled up and died years ago."

"My God," Bruce said. "The people who lived in the house before us. You killed them, didn't you?"

Duncan shrugged. Shazam growled.

"I'd shut that dog up before I do it for you," Duncan snarled.

Bruce patted Shazam on the head. "Shush," he said.

Duncan was a large man, but Bruce guessed he could tackle him. He chewed his lip, could feel his heart hammering away, palms sweating. How had they ended up in this mess? And to think he thought they were moving out of the city to escape trouble.

"Okay, that's enough of the pleasantries," Lillian said, tapping the wooden club on the top of the bar.

"This is bullshit." Rocky stood up and faced Duncan. "You ain't keeping me here." He started walking towards the door. When he reached Duncan, he stretched out a hand and touched Duncan's arm to move him aside.

For such a large man, Duncan reacted fast. He punched Rocky in the stomach, forcing him to double up in pain. Rocky retched, his hands clutched to his abdomen. "You piece of shit," he wheezed.

"Rocky!" Sara said as she ran to him.

181

Duncan widened his stance, hands on hips. "Look kid, this isn't personal. You've got to realise it's for the good of the village."

` Erin stubbed her cigarette out. "So what are you going to do, kill us all?"

Duncan ran a finger across his top lip and looked at Lillian. Lillian gazed around the room. "It's for the good of the village."

"*Gran*," Jen squealed.

Lillian sighed. "Jenny, stop whining. I sometimes wonder if you really are my granddaughter. You hear about people being given the wrong baby in the hospital."

"Gran, how could you? If mum and dad find out about this—"

"And what makes you think they don't already know?"

Jen shook her head. "No. They wouldn't. You're lying."

Lillian shrugged.

"Well you won't be able to take us all," Bruce said. "There's only two of you."

Lillian laughed–it sounded like a cackle; made Bruce shiver. "And where are you going to go?" Lillian asked.

It was a simple question, but the way she said it made Bruce hesitate. Was there something he didn't know? How many more villagers were in on this crazy idea? Were they waiting outside? It seemed ridiculous, but after what he had seen tonight, he would believe anything was possible.

Jen started crying. Jack put an arm around her shoulder. "Don't worry," he said.

"There's a police officer outside. He'll be back in a minute," Bruce said.

Lillian spat on the ground. "You think we're bothered about the law."

Bruce knew he was going to have to do something. But what? He fingered the lucky charms in his wallet. Make me lucky, he thought before he ran at Duncan.

Not usually an impulsive man, Bruce took both himself and Duncan by surprise. He rammed his shoulder into the shopkeeper, driving him back into the door and making it clatter in its frame. Before his opponent could recover, Bruce drove his fist into Duncan's chin, knocking the man's head back.

The blow seemed to have little effect. Duncan stood up straight and stroked his jaw. A slight grin curved the edges of his lips. Bruce saw the shopkeeper bunch his fist, and just as he was about to retaliate, Shazam bounded across the room and sank her teeth into his ankle. Duncan squealed and hobbled around, trying to kick the dog away with his other foot. Knowing it was now or never, Bruce grabbed Duncan around the neck, trying to choke him. Despite his predicament, Duncan was strong and Bruce struggled to maintain his hold. He linked his hands to strengthen his grip, but Duncan's neck felt like steel.

"Let me help," Jack said.

Bruce nodded and allowed his son to grab Duncan's arm.

Although it looked like David versus Goliath, with only a couple of deft Judo moves, Jack had Duncan on the floor with his arm pinned behind his back squealing like a pig.

Bruce stood up straight and sighed with relief. Then a wailing cry filled the air. He looked up just in time to see Lillian charging towards them, holding the wooden club aloft.

Although she was an old woman, he didn't doubt being hit with the club would hurt–a lot–and he put his hands up to fend off the attack when something flew across the room and he heard glasses breaking and a rain of glass poured down. He shielded his eyes with the back of his hand, and saw Erin and Jen bombarding Lillian with glasses from behind the bar.

One of the glasses struck Lillian on the head, knocking her aside. "You don't understand," she screamed. "We have to offer a sacrifice."

"You're crazy." Erin lobbed another glass, fragments exploding and striking Bruce in the face.

"That's why the creatures have come. That's why they're here," Lillian yelled. "You think this is the first time they've been? They've been here before, but we've kept them satisfied."

"They're here because they're hungry," Erin replied, "not because of you and your primitive beliefs."

Lillian backed into the corner.

Bruce didn't want to listen to anymore nonsense, so he stepped over Duncan and Jack, unlocked the door, and said, "Come on, let's get out of here."

Jen helped Rocky to his feet and they made their way outside followed by Sara and then Erin, who looked at Bruce as she passed and offered an encouraging smile.

When they were all out, Bruce tapped Jack on the shoulder. "Okay, let him go. Come on, we'll find Powell and let him sort this out."

Jack released Duncan and jumped to his feet to follow Bruce outside. As he shut the door, Bruce heard Lillian scream in anguish. The sound went through him. She was totally crazy. He wondered why no one had ever noticed that she needed to be locked up.

He thought Jen of all people should have noticed her relative's behaviour, but then he remembered his own nana was as fruity as a bowl of punch, and no one had bothered having her put away. But at least she didn't go around making pagan sacrifices.

He looked along the street, but Powell was nowhere in sight. Where were the police when you needed them? If he were speeding, no doubt an officer would appear out of the blue, but now when he needed one, the blasted idiot had wandered off.

Getting angry wasn't helping, but it felt good to let off a little steam. "Powell," he shouted.

"Dad, we've got to get out of here," Jack said.

Before Bruce could reply, Erin pointed. "Isn't that Zander's boat?"

Bruce looked out to sea where the running lights of the trawler reflected from the choppy waves. Bright spotlights illuminated the water around the boat, making it appear ethereal, like a ghost ship.

184

"She's coming in fast," Bruce said.

"Too fast," Erin replied.

Bruce heard the roar of the boat's engines as the craft sped towards the harbour. In the glow of her lights, he noticed ropes trailing in the water.

"Is that smoke?" Jack asked as he pointed at the boat.

Bruce ran across the road, vaulted the harbour wall and stared out to sea. Jack was right. A column of black smoke drifted from the boat, and although not an expert, he noticed the craft appeared to list sharply.

As the vessel drew closer, he was able to make out more details, the skeletal framework of cranes and the bristly sea urchin-like array of masts and aerials.

A shout issued from the boat, followed by movement on the deck. Now close enough to see more clearly, he saw someone or something had smashed the wheelhouse windows.

Erin stood behind the harbour wall. "Jesus," she said. "They're in trouble."

Rocky pointed. "They're going to ram the harbour."

"Shit," Jack said.

A white froth fanned out from the boat's bow as it sped towards the harbour. "You'd better stand clear," Erin said.

Bruce didn't move. He looked at the boat, his eyes narrowed. There was someone hanging from the crane. At least it used to be someone. Even from a distance, he could see the figure had been severed at the waist. A grisly mass of entrails hung down like obscene rigging. It looked as though something had eaten him while he tried to climb out of reach.

"Bruce, stand clear," Erin shouted.

Movement in the water caught his eye, and he stood transfixed at the sight of hundreds of dark objects swimming alongside the boat.

A shoal of Fangtooth. A pack of killer creatures shepherding the boat to its destination.

This was bad. This was very bad.

The sound of the boat grew louder. Bruce looked up, alarmed to see it looming upon him, a gigantic axe head of metal and wood. He jumped aside, rolled, banged his shoulder against the harbour wall. Pain shot through his body.

As the boat struck the harbour, it felt like an earthquake – a horrendous noise of tortured metal and pulverized concrete rang out. The ground underfoot shook violently. The light from the lampposts flickered, throwing wild shadows around the harbour. Someone screamed. Shards of concrete and metal started to rain down. Bruce shielded his face. A lump of concrete struck the back of his hand, sending a jolt of pain along his arm. He heard the boat creak and squeal as though in torment. He peeked between his fingers, saw the boat's bow sticking up in the air. A fallen mast lay feet away. Water poured from the side of the boat. The intermittent flash of sparks illuminated the boat's wheelhouse. Shadows danced among the sparks.

Concrete dust filled the air; hung like a fog obscuring his vision. Bruce coughed and stood up. His legs shook, made him feel unsteady. He took a tentative step towards the boat. The sound of squealing metal rang out and the boat slipped back a couple of feet, making him jump.

"Hello, can you hear me?" Bruce shouted.

Footsteps sounded behind him and he turned to see Erin approaching. "Jesus," she said as she surveyed the scene.

"Help me!"

Bruce heard the voice, but with the boat standing proud, he couldn't see anyone.

"Hello, where are you?" he shouted back.

"Help me!" the speaker croaked.

Bruce studied the boat; saw a tangle of ropes and chains hanging down.

"I'm going to have to climb aboard," he said.

Erin touched his hand gently. "Be careful."

"I'll come with you," Jack said.

Bruce shook his head. "No, you'd better stay here."

186

He stepped towards the edge of the harbour and looked down. For a moment, he felt dizzy and his heart thudded. The water looked cold, dark and foreboding. Sudden movement disturbed the surface, revealing the Fangtooth circling the wreckage. Some of them scratched at the boat, trying to find a handhold. Bruce gulped. He tried to swallow but found he couldn't.

The front of the boat was crumpled and dented, with jagged shards of metal jutting out at odd angles.

He grabbed hold of a hanging chain. It felt cold and wet within his grasp. Then with the help of the sharp metal protrusions created by the blow with the harbour, he started to climb.

Heights always made him a little apprehensive, but climbing up the side of a damaged boat, above Fangtooth infested waters, well, that was just plain crazy, and his sweaty palms, shaking legs, thrumming heart and spinning head told him so. But someone needed help, and he couldn't stand by and do nothing, so he climbed, hand over hand, foot over foot, one torturous, slow step at a time.

"Now do you see why we have to make the sacrifice?"

Bruce twisted his head at the sound of Lillian's voice. She stood at the edge of the harbour, a vitriolic glare plastered across her face. Blood dribbled from a cut on her forehead. In the light from the lampposts, it looked like an exclamation mark. Duncan stood behind her. He rubbed his wrist as though to relieve it from pain, his gaze fixed firmly on Jack. Since leaving the bar, he had armed himself with a wicked looking spiked hook.

"Do you want some more?" Jack asked, bobbing his head.

"*Jack*," Bruce shouted, hoping the inflection in his voice was enough to cool his son's bravado. They had enough trouble without creating more.

"Yeah," Rocky said, squaring up to Duncan, "you ain't gonna sucker punch me and get away with it."

Bruce bit his lip. This was turning into a testosterone showdown, and here he was, stuck up the side of a boat.

187

"Everyone calm down," Erin said. She waved her arms in the air and stepped between the warring factions. "We've got injured people to help here. We don't need this right now."

Bruce readjusted his grip. He felt relieved that Erin was taking control and trying to calm the situation. His feelings for her went up another notch. Growing tired hanging onto the boat, he continued climbing and clambered over the side and onto the sloping deck.

Holding onto the front of the boat to stop himself falling towards the wheelhouse, he looked back down at the harbour, his eyes opening wide when he saw Lillian raise the club. His heart stopped.

"Look out," he screamed, but he was too late. Lillian swung the club, hitting Erin on the head. Even from a distance, Bruce heard the sharp crack of wood on bone. Caught unawares, Erin's head snapped to the side and she staggered back. Bruce cringed.

Without hesitating, Lillian grabbed Erin by the shoulder and pulled her back.

"Accept this, our offering," Lillian screeched.

Bruce saw what was going to happen, but he was powerless to intervene. He screamed and then watched in vain as Lillian pushed the still stunned Erin off the harbour. She fell heavily, and landed with a splash, surfacing seconds later, spluttering and treading water.

"*You're crazy,*" Jen screamed.

Before Lillian could react, Jen pushed her grandmother off the harbour. Lillian flailed in the air, and then disappeared over the edge. She landed with a loud splash and Bruce looked down in time to see her sink below the water, only to bob back up moments later with seaweed stuck comically on her head. She stared up at the people on the quay, and instead of the anger Bruce expected to see, she was grinning.

Attracted to the commotion, Bruce saw a swirl of displaced water as the first of the Fangtooth swam to investigate.

With Lillian being the closer of the two, the creatures made a beeline for her. Bruce watched wide-eyed with shock as the first Fangtooth sank its teeth into her shoulder, severing flesh with one bite. Although she must have been in agony, Lillian didn't scream. A corona of blood spread out around her body, and the water became a whirl of motion as other Fangtooth joined in the feeding frenzy. Moments later, the creatures dragged Lillian under the water, her last breath a few bloody bubbles that popped on the surface of the sea.

With no time to lose, Bruce looked around, grabbed a length of rope that had unravelled along the tilted deck and wound it up into a loose bundle.

"Catch," he shouted, throwing the rope as far as he could. It hit the water with a splash and Erin grabbed the end. Bruce started to pull, dragging her towards the boat, when he heard something bang behind him.

He turned his head and in the meagre light, less than eight feet away, he saw twin rows of vicious fangs and a pair of luminous eyes.

Chapter 35

Upon hearing the commotion, Powell ran towards the harbour. Along the way, residents started emerging from their houses.

"Stay inside," Powell shouted. He ran out of a backstreet, his eyes growing wide when he saw the boat that had rammed into the harbour. Smoke billowed into the sky and firelight flickered in the wheelhouse. "Jesus," he whispered. The people he had been talking to in the bar stood by the harbour wall, waving frantically.

"*Help me!*"

Powell looked up at the wreckage to see Bruce hauling Erin up the side, and just behind him, scampering up the deck, something monstrous ...

With no time to lose, Powell pulled the taser gun out of his belt. He aimed, but his hand was shaking.

Powell held his breath, steadied his aim and squeezed the trigger. The two barbed darts struck the creature in the chest, delivering an initial 50,000 volts, and it flopped back. For the first time in his life he wished that British police were armed with guns.

He quickly radioed base and relayed what he knew of the situation, which wasn't much, then he started to clamber up the boat using a chain that hung down the side.

Powell glanced down at the water to his left, saw things swimming just below the surface. His police training had never prepared him for anything quite like this.

His wife, Juliet, would go ballistic if she could see him now. She had never liked him being on the police force, thought it was too dangerous, and her pregnancy didn't help. For the last couple of months she had been overly emotional, bursting into tears at the slightest thing. Seeing her husband now would likely be the last straw.

The bow of the boat projected into the air—*it must have hit at some speed to end up like this*, he thought. The chain he used to clamber up the side rattled and clanked against the hull. He thought he heard a groan, but the sound of the chain drowned it out.

He wondered what had happened to cause the boat to crash. Wondered what morbid sights awaited him.

At the top of the boat, he scrambled over and sat on the bow to catch his breath. Across from him, Bruce hauled Erin on board and then gave him a wave of thanks.

Powell nodded, then glanced down at the mayhem on deck. Nets, ropes, buoys and baskets lay scattered all around. Intermittent sparks illuminated the interior of the smashed wheelhouse. A column of black smoke rose from somewhere further back on the boat, and the caustic smell of burning rubber and plastic filled the air.

"Hello, is anyone on board?" he shouted. He surveyed the wreckage below for any sign of movement, but apart from a swaying boom and the clank of chains, there was nothing.

Keeping hold of the side of the boat, he slowly started to descend. The acute angle of the deck made it hard to keep his footing, and if it hadn't been for part of a broken boom, which doubled as a ladder, he would have been left dangling.

The lower he went, the more pungent the smell of burning became. It seemed to cling to the back of his throat, making him choke. When he reached the wheelhouse, he swung himself across and entered through the already open door. The inside of the room was a mess of broken equipment. Sparks shot out from the front panel and skittered towards the back of the room. Bracing himself in the doorway, Powell removed his torch from his belt and shone it around the room. The severity of the damage amazed him. It looked as though someone had literally torn the place apart.

Something clattered against the wall, made him flinch. He shone the torch towards the back of the room, but couldn't see anything.

Although not one to be overly sentimental, Powell looked forward to the birth of his son; had decorated the spare room in blue, stuck Disney transfers to the walls, hung a Winnie the Pooh mobile, even purchased a remote control Porsche.

191

He remembered Juliet laughing when he purchased it, saying he didn't need to use the baby as an excuse to buy a toy. Of course he played with it–just to check that it worked–it's not as if his son would be using it for a while.

The noise came again, bringing him out of his reverie. He shone the torch around, then started to descend through the wheelhouse towards the bank of fallen equipment that lay jumbled against the rear wall. "Is anyone there?" he asked. No one replied.

The angle of the boat made the descent difficult. Anchored to the floor, the skipper's chair presented a good starting point. From there, he reached across and grabbed the edge of a desk, then scuttled down.

The equipment lying against the rear wall consisted of monitor screens, a broken tabletop, radio equipment and other electronic tackle whose purpose Powell couldn't even guess at.

When close enough, he slid the last few feet and arrested his fall by placing his hands against the wall.

About to squat down and investigate the clutter, a bloody hand shot out of the jumbled equipment and grabbed his ankle, taking him by surprise

"Help me," a voice said.

Powell took a couple of breaths to steady his beating heart, then squatted down. He lifted a monitor screen aside, then shone his torch into the debris. A face stared back at him, the haunted features scratched and bloodied. Powell recognised the stubbly chin and short brown hair as that of Zander, the man who had run out of the bar when he tried to question him earlier.

"Are you okay?" Powell asked.

Zander grimaced. "My leg's trapped."

Powell peered over the rubble, saw a piece of heavy equipment lying across Zander's legs.

"Are they broken? Can you move your toes? Are they cut?"

Zander shook his head. "For Christ's sake, just get it off me before the creatures come back."

Powell crouched down, took a hold of the equipment and used all his strength to lift.

Something squealed; he realised it was Zander. "Shit, I'm sorry."

"Just get it off."

Powell nodded, rubbed his palms against his trousers to remove any sweat, then grabbed the equipment and lifted. His arms strained, and he felt the muscles in his back pull taut. After a moment, the apparatus shifted, then came clear, and Powell gently laid it aside. He took a breath, needed to get down to the gym.

Zander sat up and rubbed at his legs. He rolled the bottoms of his pants up to caress the spot where the apparatus had lain, then he gingerly got to his feet.

"I've got to help my men," Zander said.

"How many were on board?"

Zander started clambering towards the door.

"Zander. How many?"

Zander turned. His face looked pale. "Six. McKenzie's dead. So is Robinson, perhaps Brad too. I don't know."

"So there might be two or three more people on board. Is that right?"

Zander nodded, then he pulled a knife out of a sheath in his waistband and clambered towards the door.

Powell hesitated a minute, and then followed.

Chapter 36

Zander surveyed the damage to the boat and his heart sank. The insurance would cover the cost of the vessel, but what about those who died? Nothing could repay their loved ones for the loss.

He stared towards the stern where Robinson's half-eaten body lay. A pain burned in his stomach, remorse. He felt sick; fought to restrain the feeling.

Powell joined him at the wheelhouse door.

Zander gripped the handle of his knife tight enough to make his knuckles go as white as his face. Years at sea had hardened him, but nothing prepared him for this. He had lost his gun during the crash, and the knife felt like a poor substitute.

He slid down the deck, using the fallen masts and derrick to stop himself from falling too far. Smoke poured out of a hatch leading to the engine room and he coughed as he breathed in the acrid vapour.

Waves slapped over the submerged stern. Zander narrowed his eyes, spied creatures lurking in the surf. A couple scuttled onto the deck. They looked up at him, opened their mouths and hissed, their long, curved fangs dripping saliva.

Zander clenched his teeth. "Come on, we've got to be quick."

He clambered down and swung around the side of the wheelhouse. The door to the lower decks hung open, and he gripped the door frame and hauled himself through. Smoke crept across the ceiling, shrouding the flickering light to create a stroboscopic miasma.

Powell scrambled in behind him. "I don't believe it. Those things, whatever they are, they're coming."

Zander nodded. "And they're hungry."

In the flickering light, the passageway looked foreboding. Zander swallowed to wet his throat, but he couldn't produce saliva. His tongue felt like a bloated slug in his throat.

Utilizing the walls, he dragged himself up the passage. At the end, a ladder led down to the engine room. A door to the side led to the crew's quarters, fitted with coffin bunks. Another door led to the galley and the head. Smoke poured up from where the ladder descended.

Moving cautiously, Zander made his way towards the ladder. He heard Powell bringing up the rear. Once at the ladder, Zander descended into what he could only describe as a cloudy hellhole.

Smoke poured from the engine and sparks flickered from the tangle of electrics on the back wall. Almost indiscernible from the smoke, steam gushed from a broken pipe and scalded Zander's hand, making him wince.

"Brad, are you down here?" Zander shouted.

A sudden bang made him jump, and he peered over the top of the engine as Brad emerged from a space beside the equipment.

"Skipper, am I glad to see you. I thought everyone was dead."

"Is Jim here with you?"

Brad shook his head and stood up. He looked at the engine and sighed. "She were a lovely old girl."

"We haven't got time to stand around and mourn the fucking engine. Those things are still aboard. Let's go."

Brad rolled his shoulders, clucked his tongue, nodded, and then picked up the axe and followed Zander up the ladder.

At the top, Zander nodded at Powell. "We've got a live one. Come on, those engines could catch fire at any time and I don't want to be caught standing on top of them when they do."

Zander brushed past Powell and took the lead. He reached forward to grab the edge of the doorway to his right; the boat shifted, Zander slipped, missed the doorway, his hand entered the room–and touched something scaly. His heart missed a beat.

Recoiling, he snatched his hand back and withdrew the knife. A loud hissing noise emanated from the doorway, and one of the creatures stepped through. Its body glistened, quicksilver eyes reflecting Zander's terrified features. It opened its mouth, revealing the long fangs.

Powell gasped. Brad swore.

Zander knew he had to act quickly. Without hesitating, he released his hold on the opposite wall, grabbed the knife handle with both hands, and flew at the creature.

Although he tried to aim for its eyes, he missed. The blade skidded across the creature's head, throwing him off balance. The creature snapped its jaw as it tried to take a chunk out of Zander's arm. Still moving forwards, Zander rolled around the creature until he ended up at its rear. Wicked spines rose from its back, and Zander narrowly missed impaling himself.

He heard a roar, watched Brad charge at the creature, axe raised. The grease and muck on his face looked like camouflage paint, made him appear fearsome.

The axe head split the creature's head, and a viscous fluid spurted out and coated Brad's arm.

"Not quite the trip you had in mind, hey, Skipper."

Zander shook his head.

He noticed the hatches to the gutting room were open, and he scrambled towards the entrance. He peered down the chute used to drop the fish below, but couldn't see anything.

"Brad, Powell, keep a watch," he said, then he slid down.

Jim stood by the conveyor. As Zander crashed down, he raised his gutting knife, prepared to strike.

"Whoa, Jim, it's me."

"Skipper. Have you seen those things? What a size. Should be worth a fortune." Jim raised a creature's gutted carcass. The beast's innards lay in a sloppy pink congealed mess in a basket.

Zander grimaced. "For God's sake, man. Get a grip. We've got to get out of here. Those things, they're …" His words trailed off when he saw Muldoon's eviscerated body lying on the ground.

Jim shook his head. "First decent catch we've had in ages, and you want to leave it. Me and the boys, we've got bills to pay too, you know."

"Jim. Listen to me. Look what's happened. Look at Muldoon." He pointed at the body. "Do you know where we are? We've run aground in the harbour."

Jim laughed. "Then we'd better get the haul ashore."

"Skipper," Brad hollered. "You'd better shake yourself. We've got company."

Zander gulped. "Come on Jim. We'll gut the catch later."

Jim's eyes twinkled maniacally. "You bet we will."

Zander grimaced.

He followed the conveyor towards the exit, peered out at the ladder leading up, then slowly ascended. He kept glancing back and to the side, wary of something jumping out on him. When he reached the deck, he saw the creatures scrambling towards them. He counted four, the sight turning his blood cold. He turned back, grabbed Jim by the arm and hauled him out.

"Come on, man, hurry."

Jim came topside and stared at the creatures. "More money for the pot," he said, rubbing his hands. "Come on ya fuckin' monsters, let's be havin' ya."

Zander gritted his teeth. "Jim, get ashore."

Powell withdrew an extendable baton and started hitting the nearest creature, but it had no effect, so he scuttled away.

"Duck," Brad shouted.

Zander looked back up the deck to see Brad levelling the high-pressure hose his way. Operated by the auxiliary donkey engine, it didn't need the main engine to operate, and as he opened it up, a jet of water shot out and lifted the lead creature off its feet and slammed it back into the sea.

"*Don't lose the bastards,*" Jim shouted.

Zander grabbed Jim by the arm and manhandled him back up the deck towards the bow. Powell followed. Brad kept them covered.

Once they reached the bow, Zander sat astride the edge and forced Jim to clamber over the side.

197

"Brad, you go next. Make sure Jim gets down," he said.

Brad nodded and squeezed past. Then Zander reached back for Powell, but a creature scuttled out of the wreckage and grabbed Powell's foot.

"No," Zander shouted. He stretched to grab Powell's hand, the officer's fingers only millimetres away, but the creature pulled him down.

Powell screamed as the creature sank its teeth into his stomach, twisting its head. It pulled its head out, trailing a length of intestine from its jaw, formed the semblance of a grin, then chugged down the morsel of flesh.

Zander tore his gaze away, hopped over the side of the boat and scrambled down to shore.

Chapter 37

Bruce helped the men clamber off the boat. When Zander climbed down, he said, "Where's Powell?"

Zander shook his head. "Those monsters, they got him."

Local residents ran across the road to help. Bruce waved his arms at them. "Get back inside," he shouted. The people stared at him as though he were mad.

"What's going on?" an old man asked.

"There's been an accident," Bruce replied. "Chemical leak. Everyone get inside." He didn't think they would believe him if he told them the truth.

"I can't see any chemicals," the man said, screwing his face up like a wizened old owl.

"They were on board the boat. Highly toxic. Now fucking get inside." The old man sucked his lips in, then turned and ran back across the road.

"We'd better get out of here, too," Zander said.

"Yes, what's the quickest way out of the village?" Bruce asked.

"I think it's too late for that." Zander pointed along the street.

Bruce turned and stared, horrified to see the creatures scrambling towards them.

"Shit!" He didn't like the idea of staying in the village, but there seemed to be little option. "Let's go back to the bar," he said. "It's closest."

Without any argument, everyone started to run across the road. The teenagers piled through the doorway, followed by Erin and then Zander, and a couple of men Bruce assumed to be members of Zander's crew, one with ginger hair, the other with a beard and a blood covered face. Bruce entered next. He turned at the door, saw Duncan waiting outside. The shopkeeper looked sheepish, anxious.

"You can't leave me out here," he said

"And why not? You wanted to sacrifice us, you bastard."

Across the road, a drain cover clattered aside and Bruce looked over to see a Fangtooth emerging from the ground.

Duncan's expression hardened. "But I didn't. It was all Lillian's idea. I got caught up in her madness. I'm sorry. Jesus, they're coming. You can't do this."

Bruce didn't doubt Duncan was sorry now that his ass was on the line, but the bastard had tried to kill them. He didn't deserve to live, but if he left him outside to die, that would make him just as bad, so he grudgingly stepped aside. "You make one wrong move, and you'll be back out that door before you can blink," he snarled.

Duncan nodded and scurried inside. Bruce slammed the door shut and threw the bolts across top and bottom. Seconds later, he heard wicked claws tearing at the timber. The door was old and made of sturdy, thick wood, but he didn't think it would prove an obstacle for too long.

"Zander, help me shove that table in front of the door." He indicated a sturdy, wooden table. Zander took one side, Bruce the other, then they turned it on its end and rammed it against the door.

"Can someone tell me what the fuck's going on?"

Bruce turned and looked at the landlord, Graham. He stood behind the bar nursing his head.

"And if I find out who hit me over the head, I'll fuckin' kill him," he groaned.

Bruce looked at Jen, and she turned away and stared down at the ground. He was tempted to say someone had beaten him to it, but he kept his mouth closed. Whatever the repercussions, he would always be grateful to her for pushing her grandmother into the water, giving Erin a chance to escape.

"Call the police," Bruce said. "Tell them anything, but get them to come out and investigate. Anyone else with a phone, do the same thing. They might not believe one person, but they can't ignore two or three or more."

Jack nodded, took his phone out and dialled. Sara did too.

The sound of the Fangtooth scraping at the door grated on Bruce's nerves. He looked around the room. The occupants

200

were dishevelled, postures slumped as though in defeat. The two men who accompanied Zander sat at the bar.

"Of course it's an emergency," Jack said. He paced the floor, talking animatedly. "Yes, there's been a murder." He glanced quickly at Jen, bit his tongue then turned and walked the other way. "Send as many police as you can." He gave them the name of the village, then disconnected the call.

"Graham, whisky," said the bearded man at the bar. "Make it large."

"Make that two," said the grease covered man who sat next to him.

The landlord rubbed his head. "Whisky! Someone clocked me on the head, and you want whisky. Can someone tell me what the fuck is going on?"

"It's like we told you," Erin said. "There are mutated creatures outside."

Graham looked unconvinced. "Why have you barricaded the door? If you've scratched that table, you'll have to pay for it."

"Graham, pour me a fuckin' drink before I come round there and pour my own," the bearded man said.

Graham continued as though he hadn't heard or wasn't listening: "And who the hell's scratching on my door? Where's that police officer gone when I need him?"

"He's dead," Bruce snapped. "They're all dead. Now shut the fuck up and pour the men their drinks."

The landlord opened his mouth to respond, but Bruce glared at him, and Graham seemed to decide against it.

Bruce felt everyone staring at him, but he didn't care. The wolves were literally at the door, so what people thought of him was the least of his worries.

Erin stood in the middle of the room. He looked at her and offered a weak smile.

Erin's eyes went wide; her mouth opened, but no words came out. Bruce followed her line of sight. The window cast a reflection of the room's occupants, but outside, its features bathed in light, a Fangtooth peered through the glass.

Bruce felt sick; felt like an animal in a cage. The glass misted over as it breathed, making its features appear ethereal.

"Graham, switch the lights off," he ordered.

"I've only just got them back on again," he grumbled. "Someone had put a piece of paper between the fuse and the connector so it wouldn't work."

"Graham, look at the fuckin' window."

The landlord begrudgingly turned and stared at the window. Although Graham only had one eye, Bruce watched it enlarge to cyclopean dimensions. His jaw went slack, his features growing pale as the blood drained away.

"Fuck," Graham said. "There's a goddamn monster out there." He lurched across the room and smacked the light switch, plunging the room into darkness.

Bruce waited for his eyes to adjust, then he said, "Everyone, help me stack tables against the windows." He turned to Graham. "We need something heavy. Something to brace the tables with."

Graham stroked his jaw. "The cellar's full of barrels. Will that do?"

Bruce nodded.

"I'll need a hand," Graham said.

Bruce ran forwards. "I'll come with you."

Zander waved an arm. "Brad, Jim, help me with these tables." The grease covered man seated at the bar jumped to his feet and ran across the room.

"Brad," Zander said as the man reached his side, "grab that end."

The man with the beard stood up. "The sooner we get back to fishing and make some money instead of messing about, the better," he mumbled.

Bruce motioned towards Jack. "You and the others see if there's anything we can use as weapons. We've got to hold out until someone comes to help us."

"Try in the kitchen back there," Graham said. "You'll find some carving knives and the like." He pointed towards a door to the left of the bar.

202

As Erin walked by, Bruce took hold of her gently by the arm. "Look after him for me. He's all I've got left."

She nodded. "He's not the only one you've got, though." She smiled, then she followed Jack and the other teenagers through the door.

Chapter 38

Bruce peered down the steps into the cellar. Something niggled at the back of his mind, but he couldn't recall what.

He watched Graham descend, his body almost filling the narrow staircase. A single lamp glowed at the top of the stairs, and further light filtered up from below, throwing a corona around the proprietor. Bruce inhaled. The air smelled of a combination of mould and stale beer.

"You've barricaded my bar, lost me customers, the least you can do is help," Graham called up the stairs when he realised Bruce hadn't accompanied him.

"Don't blow a gasket, I'm coming," Bruce said.

Cracks ran through the walls of the white painted stairway, gashes large enough for Bruce to insert his hand inside.

The concrete steps seemed well maintained, and he jogged down to find himself in a large room full of alcoves stacked with crates, barrels and boxes. Pipes connected to the beer pumps upstairs snaked through the ceiling. The smell of stale beer seemed a lot stronger in the basement. He judged the room to be as wide as the bar upstairs, at least twenty feet, but it seemed a lot longer, although he couldn't tell how long because the further reaches of the room basked in darkness.

The cold permeated Bruce's bones. He shivered.

"Didn't you think to put bulbs all the way through?" he asked.

Graham glanced at him. "No point. Everything we need is here at this end. Back there only gets used on the days when I have the barrels delivered, and then it's daylight. Do you know how much it costs to run a bar? Every little bit helps."

That's when Bruce remembered seeing the barrels delivered a few days ago; remembered the hole in the pavement, an access to the bar.

He peered into the dark reaches, trying to decipher the strange shadows that lurked just out of the light.

"Graham," he whispered.

Having squatted down to lift a barrel, the landlord looked up. "What?"

Bruce wished he wouldn't speak so loud. "How many other entrances are there to the bar?"

"There's the front door, the back door, a side door in the kitchen and the trapdoor over there in the corner."

Bruce could see the cogs turning in Graham's mind, his eye narrowed, mouth pursed as another revelation threatened to blow his mind.

"You think maybe—"

Something clattered in the shadows, cutting Graham off mid-sentence. He stood up with a start. "Shit," he said, "You don't think …"

Bruce didn't know what to think. His chest constricted, felt as though someone had dropped a lump of lead between his ribs. He felt a knot tighten in his stomach, his intestines tied in a tight loop. Goose bumps raced down his arms and his fingers tingled.

He took a step back, eyes trained on the darkness.

Another clatter. This time closer. His cheeks prickled in response. He caught sight of movement. A cry caught in his throat. Something ran out of the shadows. Ran towards him. Something black, travelling close to the ground.

"Oscar," Graham said. The black cat ran to Graham's side and rubbed itself against his leg. Graham crouched down and stroked the cat behind the ear. "You nearly gave me a heart attack." He looked up at Bruce. "Best damn mouser I ever had. Found him as a stray."

Bruce exhaled slowly. His pulse still raced.

A sudden scream echoed down the stairs. Bruce jumped. The cat arched its back, hackles raised. It hissed loudly, sharp teeth bared, reminding Bruce of a miniature Fangtooth. He turned towards the door, couldn't work out whether the scream was male or female.

Temples throbbing, he ran through the door and bounded up the steps, taking them two at a time in his haste.

The bar's kitchen wasn't large, but it looked clean and tidy. Erin gazed around the room, looking for anything to use as a weapon, something long and very sharp if they wanted to stand any chance of defending themselves.

A range ran along the back wall, above which a stainless steel extractor threw a warped reflection of the room. A worktable ran down the middle of the kitchen, laden with pots, pans, spices and utensils, none of which were suitable as a weapon. A rack to the left of the range held a row of knurled metal handled knives. She walked across and withdrew them, putting aside the paring knife, vegetable knife and bread knife to take a meat cleaver, a 20cm long bladed cook's knife, a carving fork, a filleting knife and a large knife with a fluted blade.

"Jack, take this," she said, handing him the meat cleaver. "Rocky, you have this." She handed him the filleting knife, then passed Sara the carving fork and Jen the 20cm long bladed cook's knife. She kept the blade with the fluted edge for herself. "Right, let's see what else we can find."

Duncan stood in the doorway. He still had the hook with the wooden handle; he stared at Erin, his face pinched, lips sucked in to create a thin gash where his mouth should be.

"You know this is pointless," he said.

"If you've got nothing constructive to say, button it," she replied, jabbing the air with the knife to punctuate her words.

"Yeah," Rocky barked. "Or I'll button it for ya." He clenched his jaw, his eyes narrowed into slits.

Erin heard something moving outside, something that clicked across the ground at a fast pace. Next minute, the side door burst open and a Fangtooth scurried inside. It twisted its head left and right as though selecting its prey. Then it opened its mouth.

Sara screamed, almost deafening Erin at her side.

Erin held the knife out, the fluted blade wavering within her grasp. She thought of Kevin, remembered his body bitten in half. The memory made her nauseous. It also made her angry.

206

Another Fangtooth appeared in the doorway. She saw that to enable them to move quickly, the creatures ran on all fours, but when they moved in to attack, they raised themselves on two legs, which is what the lead Fangtooth did now.

From the corner of her eye, she noticed Jack usher the other teenagers towards the corner of the room where they had more protection. Erin meanwhile stood before the range, while the Fangtooth approached along either side of the worktable. She saw Duncan standing behind the door, a look of awe on his face.

Her mouth felt dry, tongue glued to her palate. Compared to the many teeth and claws at the Fangtooth's disposal, her knife seemed ineffectual. She needed something better, and although she wouldn't know how to use them, she wished for a shotgun, a machine gun, or a bazooka. Soldiers charging headlong through the door would also be a heartening sight. But she didn't have any of those, only a knife and her wits.

Her gaze fell upon a can of spray polish on the worktable. She grabbed it, placed the knife on the edge of the table, then realised she didn't have a light.

"Here."

Erin looked across at the sound of Jack's voice. As if he had read her mind, he threw her his lighter, which she caught in midair. Using her thumb, she flipped the lid off the can, sparked the lighter and pressed down on the plunger. The spray ignited with a satisfying whump. A wave of heat wafted over her and she aimed the yellow flame at the nearest Fangtooth. As she'd hoped, the universal fear of fire stilled the beast's approach. It reared back, raking the air with its claws, teeth bared. A grumbling sound emanated from its throat, which sounded like anger and hunger combined. She tried not to think what might happen if the flame entered the pressurized can in her hand.

She let go of the plunger and the flame went out. She moved aside, placing herself between the teenagers and the creatures. She didn't know how much gas remained in the can, but she hoped and prayed there was enough to allow them to escape.

"Follow me–slowly," she said.

Although she felt like running, she knew she couldn't. She let loose another blast of flame, warding the creatures away. She only hoped more monsters didn't rush into the room.

The flame flickered and stuttered. Erin's heart rose into her throat. She took her finger off the plunger and shook the can. It sounded nearly empty.

Zander appeared in the doorway leading to the bar. He surveyed the scene, jaw clenched. He had a large tumbler of whisky in his hand, which he threw over the nearest Fangtooth.

The Fangtooth turned and bared its teeth at him. "Torch that fucker," Zander said.

Erin moved towards the creature, pressed the plunger and struck the lighter. A jet of flame shot out, igniting the whisky. A throaty roar echoed from the Fangtooth's throat. Cloaked in a blanket of flame, it raked its claws in the air and crashed against the worktable, sending pots and pans flying. The second Fangtooth dropped to all fours and backed away. The pungent aroma of roasting fish filled the air. Burning scales flaked off the Fangtooth's body and fell to the ground.

"Quick," Erin said, "around the other side and through the door."

Jack and the others moved where she indicated. She noticed Bruce appear in the doorway, his hand out to help pull them through.

"Come on," he shouted.

Jack shook his head and ushered the others back. "We can't get past." He pointed at the Fangtooth barring the way.

The flames from the burning Fangtooth licked the ceiling, setting off the ear-piercing wail of the fire alarm. Erin could hardly hear herself think. She winced.

Seeing the predicament the teenagers were in, she slid around the table, wary of the burning Fangtooth. The second

208

Fangtooth regarded her from its lower position. Its jaw hung open, the spines on its back bristling in anticipation. Erin raised the can, struck the lighter and pressed the plunger, only to find the can empty.

"Shit," she said. She threw the can at the creature and stepped back. Her fingers brushed the tabletop, felt the cold handle of the fluted knife. She grabbed hold of it with both hands and, without thinking, she leaped at the Fangtooth and plunged the blade through its eye.

The blade met resistance as it sank through the eye socket. A clear liquid spurted out, struck her cheek, making her cringe. The creature bucked like a bronco, slashing with its claws. Erin kept it at arm's length, the vicious spines along its back dangerously close to her eyes. She pushed with all her strength, her triceps aching with the strain. Blood seeped around her fingers, weakening her grip on the handle. She bit her lip, held on for dear life. The Fangtooth felt cold and dry; its sharp, rough scales sliced through her wrists with the same pain as a paper cut. Erin winced, tears blurred her vision.

The blade met further resistance. She pushed. Hard. Seconds later the tip of the blade punctured the Fangtooth's palate, resembling another wicked tooth as it protruded through its mouth. She twisted the blade, gouging a hole, causing maximum damage. She felt the fluted edge grind against the creature's eye socket, splintering tough bone. Next minute the Fangtooth shuddered and collapsed to the ground. Its jaw struck the tiles, forcing the knife back out.

Erin jumped to her feet. She turned towards the side door to confront Duncan, only he was no longer there.

Enraged, she ran across, slammed the door shut and leaned against it, breathing heavy. If he wanted to be fish food, so be it.

Chapter 39

Duncan peered through the narrow gap in the pantry door, his heart pounding. He saw Erin slam the side door shut, then lost sight of her. The alarm drowned out any noise he might make. Coupled with the distraction of the creatures, it had also helped him enter the pantry without anyone noticing.

Tins of food filled the shelves. The tins clinked at his back as he adjusted his position, his hands and legs shaking. Fear had driven him to hide, and now embarrassment made him stay. His only choice now was to escape and flee the village.

He tightened his grip on the gaff hook and pressed his ear to the door to see if he could hear any conversation, but apart from the alarm, all seemed quiet.

He assumed those monstrous creatures–what did that bitch call them, Fangtooth–had arisen because of the failed sacrifice. The ocean's way of making amends, to teach them a lesson.

The sound of hammering broke his chain of thought and he peered through the gap to see Zander and Bruce nailing a small wooden table across the door. A moment later, the fire alarm fell quiet, although Duncan's ears continued to ring for a few minutes after.

His legs ached from standing in one place, but now that the alarm had fallen silent, he didn't dare move in case he made a noise and he did his best to control the shakes that still coursed through him.

The hammering continued for a while. They were battening down the hatches, for what good it would do them.

Finally satisfied there was no one left in the kitchen, he eased the door open and peeked out, the gaff hook held ready to strike at anyone that might be loitering around. Relieved, he stepped out and studied the table they had nailed to the door. He had planned to pull it off, but there was no way he could remove it without being heard.

210

The two dead Fangtooth lay on the ground. One toasted, the other stabbed. Duncan looked at them, repulsed but also slightly impressed by their appearance. Blood pooled around the stabbed creature, and he knelt down, ran his fingers through the red liquid, and smeared the gore across his cheeks. He hoped it would be enough to convince the Gods of his devotion–that in the coming slaughter, they would deem him worthy and spare his life.

The door to the bar was ajar, and Duncan crept towards it and peered through the gap. Erin sat at a table drinking what looked like brandy. Bruce sat next to her, his arm around her shoulder. The teenagers sat in the corner; Rocky twiddled with his knife, spinning it on the tabletop. He couldn't see anyone else, and he daren't open the door too far as the dog would be somewhere, and the slightest thing might alert it to his presence.

The position of the counter meant he could duck down and no one in the bar would be able to see him, so as long as there was no one behind the actual counter itself, he could crawl through to the back of the building.

He knew it was no good holing up in the kitchen, as someone would be bound to return soon.

Dropping to his knees, he leaned as far around the door as he dared. Satisfied no one could see him, and that no one stood behind the counter, he crawled cautiously out of the kitchen. The pungent smell from the slop trays below the pumps made his nose itch, and he fought not to sneeze.

A draft emanating from a door a few feet further on blew around his body, making him shiver. Duncan crawled towards the door and found himself staring down a set of steps towards the cellar.

As Bruce and Graham had been down in the cellar to fetch barrels, he surmised they wouldn't have any need to venture down again.

The steps weren't too steep, and he slid cautiously down the steps. Halfway down, he heard a voice muttering from below and he froze on the spot.

Still too high up to see into the cellar, he took a couple of deep breaths, and continued down.

The person in the cellar continued to mutter away, so he guessed they hadn't heard or hadn't registered his presence. Now closer, he recognised the voice as that of Graham, the proprietor. As no one else spoke, he guessed–hoped–the barman was alone.

Duncan crept down one step at a time. Once low enough, he ducked to see below the door frame, saw Graham bending over a barrel in the corner and tiptoed across the room as fast as he dared.

Beer shot out of the barrel Graham was messing with, soaking his front. "As if I haven't got enough problems," he mumbled.

"And here's another to add to the list," Duncan said.

Graham turned at the sound of Duncan's voice, his one eye going wide as he spied the raised gaff hook.

"What the blazes …" he shouted.

Duncan slammed the hook into Graham's throat and yanked hard, as though landing a fish. The point ripped through his skin and out the other side of Graham's neck. The flesh pulled taut, stretched. Blood spurted out. Graham raked Duncan's face with his hands, opening up a vicious cut down his cheek.

Duncan grimaced and wheezed. Graham was a big man, and Duncan thought he had underestimated his opponent.

Using all his strength, Duncan snatched the gaff hook back and the skin ripped open like a wet paper bag. The lower section lay as a flap of purple and red bunting. As Graham exhaled, the top flap lifted, spraying blood across the ground. Graham gagged. He staggered back, hands at his throat. Blood poured between his fingers. His eye rolled in its socket and he dropped to his knees. Blood bubbled from between his lips as he tried to speak. Duncan couldn't understand what Graham was trying to say, but it wasn't anything he wanted to hear.

He raised the hook again, swept it down and across, spearing the landlord's cheek. The tip of the point slid from between his lips where it had impaled his tongue. Without hesitating further, Duncan pulled hard. For a brief moment, Graham's tongue appeared in the gash in his cheek, then the skin tore open and the tongue split in two like a snake's.

Graham fell forward, his head striking the ground with a loud crack and Duncan slammed his foot down on Graham's head until the barman stopped moving.

Duncan felt strangely buoyant, empowered. His cheeks flushed. His hands tingled. To anyone who didn't know, Graham had been attacked by a Fangtooth.

Blood pooled on the ground in a widening circle. Duncan stepped over the puddle and entered the shadows where the light didn't reach. When his eyes adjusted, he spied a pale rectangle of illumination overhead that outlined the trapdoor leading to the street. He grinned, traced around the edge to locate the retaining bolts, then slid them across.

Chapter 40

Bruce stared through a slim gap in the barricade of tables and barrels they had fashioned over the window. He thought he heard someone scream outside, but couldn't be sure. He couldn't see much, but he perceived things moving, the click of sharp claws scurrying across concrete.

Erin came up beside him. Her hand trembled, making the cigarette clenched between her fingers shake.

"I really can't believe this is happening," she said.

"Me neither. All I wanted was a home by the coast, you know, a quiet place. But this …" He raised his hands, didn't know what else to say.

Erin sucked on her cigarette, exhaled a pale cloud of smoke.

Bruce rubbed his hands across his face. His muscles ached. "I can't believe what Duncan and Lillian were prepared to do. It's like something from pagan times. I shouldn't have let him in. Should have left him outside in the first place."

"Well he's gone now. And good riddance."

"Yes, but I should have—"

Erin placed her finger over Bruce's mouth. She removed it moments later only to replace it with her lips. Bruce didn't resist. He closed his eyes, the kiss creating a warm feeling in the pit of his stomach. She tasted of cigarettes, but he didn't mind. He slipped his arms around her waist, pulled her towards him, her body warm against his. He felt the crush of her breasts against his chest–it felt good.

When they parted, Bruce opened his eyes, saw Jack looking at him. Although he expected Jack to be furious, he was surprised when his son nodded to offer his approval before turning away to give them a little privacy.

Bruce returned his gaze to the gap in the window, but he didn't let go of Erin's hand.

Brad knocked back another whisky. Not wanting to pass up a free bar, he topped off his glass from the bottle on the counter. The golden liquid felt as warm as it looked as it rolled down his throat. He licked his lips and noticed Zander look up from his perusal of the ground long enough to glance at him then turn away.

Graham seemed to be taking his time. He said he was only going to change a barrel, although Brad couldn't see the point. It was not as if they were suddenly going to be snowed under with customers, but he guessed the man wanted to keep busy as a distraction from what was happening.

The wrecked boat meant he was out of a job, at least for a while–his brother always said there was a place for him at the garage, but Brad had always refused. He didn't think it was a good idea to mix family and business. Now it looked as though he had no choice, reason enough for another drink. He swallowed most of the contents of the glass and was about to pour himself another, when he thought he heard something from down in the cellar, a sort of muffled groan.

"Did you hear that?" he said to Zander.

Zander shrugged. "Didn't hear anything."

Brad set his glass on the counter and stood up. "Jim, did you hear it?" Jim mumbled something through his beard. It sounded like, "Mine's a double."

"Graham's down there," Zander said, "so you're bound to hear something."

"No, this was like a groan, you know." He turned towards the cellar door, leaned across the counter and peered down the steps. "Graham," he called, "you okay down there?"

No one replied.

"Graham," he shouted again.

"This happened before," Bruce said, "when the lights went out. He said he couldn't hear through the thick walls. It's nothing to worry about." The dog growled, her hackles raised as she stared towards the cellar door.

Brad narrowed his eyes and turned to look back down the steps when he saw a quick blur of movement. Then a sound, the sharp click of claws on stone as a Fangtooth scurried up

215

the steps on all fours, head held high as though sniffing the air.

"They're here," Brad shouted. He vaulted the bar, grabbed the axe from the counter, and plunged it into the Fangtooth's head as it reached the top of the steps. The blade crunched through thick skull, killing it instantly. "Take that, you piece of shit."

"Graham's down there," Zander said.

Another Fangtooth started up the steps, more followed behind. Too many to count. Brad pushed the carcass down the steps and slammed the door shut. "If he is, he's dead now." He leaned against the wood. The door had not been designed to keep people out, and it didn't have a lock. Something clattered on the other side, and the door banged. The bottom of the door moved inward, the flimsy wood bending.

"This ain't gonna hold 'em," he roared.

The dog started barking, tail between its legs.

Panic seemed to flow around the room. Sara sobbed.

Jim stood up and shook his head. "You're throwing away good meat," he said. "Let them in, I'll show you how it's done." He brandished the knife in his hand.

Brad shook his head. This was no time for Jim to lose it.

Jim grinned. "Come on, let the fuckers in. It's gutting time."

Zander grabbed Jim by the shoulder and spun him around. "Be serious, man. Those things, they'll kill ya."

Jim shook Zander off and rolled his sleeve up to reveal a six-inch scar. "If that shark we had tangled in the net couldn't do it, then no fucking bottom feeding piece of mutated scum sucking fish bladder is going to either."

Brad braced his legs against the counter, and ground his teeth together. How many of the bastards were there on the other side of that blasted door?

"I won't be able to hold them for long," he wheezed.

"Then let the bastards in," Jim said.

Brad didn't like the maniacal glint in Jim's eyes. Didn't like the way he held the knife with a caressing touch. He

216

knew some men formed a sort of bond with their knives on board a trawler, and woe betide the man that touched another man's knife.

"Don't talk daft, man," Zander said.

Jim waved his knife around. "Me and this 'ere knife, we'll slice and dice the fuckers, mark my words."

The creatures scratched at the door at Brad's back. He could literally feel each claw scraping across the wood; half expected one of the brutes to break through at any minute.

Bruce ran around the bar, placed his hands on the door, and pushed to help keep it shut. Splinters of wood skittered through the gap at the bottom.

"We won't be able to hold them much longer," Brad said. "The door's not strong enough."

"Here, wedge this between it and the bar," Zander said as he passed over a chair. "It'll give us long enough to get upstairs."

"Then what?" Erin asked. "Upstairs or down, they're going to come for us. We can't hole up there forever."

"So what do you suggest?" Zander asked.

"We need to get away. Out of the village."

"How? Those creatures are out there."

"Fire keeps them at bay. We can use it to help make an escape."

"And where are we going to get something to burn?" Zander asked.

"Will these do?" Jack held a chair leg aloft.

"Perfect," Erin said. "Now we need to wrap them in something that will keep burning."

"Graham won't need them anymore, look for some clothes upstairs," Brad said.

Jack started towards the door leading through to the stairs. "I'll go."

"Me too," Jen said as she hurried after him.

The bottom of the cellar door clattered and banged. "And be quick," Brad shouted.

The bare bulb at the top of the stairs illuminated the stairway. Jack felt nervous as he climbed; couldn't help wondering what had happened to Graham, and although he had reservations, he was glad that Jen had accompanied him.

"This is turning into one crazy night," Jen said.

"Yeah, I've had better," Jack replied.

"I'm trying not to think about it. I still can't believe what my grandmother's done though. I keep thinking this is just a nightmare; that I'll wake up soon."

"You and me both."

"Do you think the police are going to come?"

"I think we'll need more than the police to put a stop to this." Jack turned and hurried up the stairs to a short corridor. At the top, four doors led off, two of which he would have to double back to check. The first door opened onto a sparsely furnished sitting room. Light from the landing illuminated a settee, a small bookcase, a coffee table on which lay a men's magazine opened at the centre spread and a footstool. The next door led to a small kitchen, where he found the cat drinking milk from its bowl. It looked up and regarded Jack, then resumed lapping its milk as though he wasn't worth bothering about. Dirty bowls, plates and cutlery were stacked up in the sink and over the draining board. The tap dripped. Jack wondered who would come and clean up when this was all over. Wondered who would look after the cat.

Exiting the room, he walked back along the corridor to investigate the other two doors, both of which were shut. He pushed open the first one he came to, but couldn't see anything inside as the curtains were drawn and the light on the landing didn't reach this far. He swept his hand across the wall until he found the light switch and flicked it on.

The first thing he saw was a face staring at him, and his heart did a somersault. He opened his mouth and let out a gasp, only to realise he was looking at his own reflection in a mirror on the wall.

"You okay?" Jen asked.

218

Jack nodded. "I may not be the best looking lad in the world, but it comes to something when my own reflection makes me jump."

"You look pretty good to me."

Jack entered the room to hide his embarrassment. A single bed occupied one wall, across from which a wardrobe held the promise of clothes. Jack strode across and opened it. He thought it felt macabre rifling through the jackets and shirts of someone probably now food for the monsters but he put his feelings aside as he selected things which would burn well, and which would continue to burn, such as a stack of polyester shirts.

"Here, take these," he said, passing an armful to Jen.

He grabbed a couple of pairs of polyester pants. "That should be enough. Come on, they're waiting for us."

Jack ran down the stairs and back into the bar. Brad and his dad were holding the door shut.

"Hurry up, kid," Brad said.

Rocky, Sara and Erin were stamping on chairs to snap the legs off. Jack and Jen dropped the pile of clothes next to them, then helped wrap each item tightly around the jagged end of each leg.

"We'll need some alcohol from behind the bar to soak them in," Erin said. "Rocky, help Jack pick bottles with the most alcohol as that will burn better. Look for liqueurs and rum with high alcohol content."

Jack looked at Rocky, wondering whether there was still going to be any animosity between them. Rocky stared back, nodded, then proceeded to the bar where he started removing bottles of alcohol from the racks on the wall.

Jack joined him, and said, "I know you don't like me, but thanks. You know, for helping us when we were stuck on the rocks."

Rocky looked at him. "Least I could do in the circumstances."

"Me and Jen, we're ... well ..."

"I know." He leaned closer. "Tell you the truth, I never liked her that much. Don't tell her, though. Don't want her to get all upset and the like. Now you see Sara though, she's a fox."

Jack looked at Sara and smiled.

When they had enough bottles, Jack and Rocky carried them back to Erin and she started dousing the makeshift torches in alcohol. The pungent aroma of the spirits soon filled the air, and Jack wondered if you could get drunk from the fumes.

"Okay, we're all set," Erin said. She passed the torches around. "I don't know how long they'll last, so use one at a time. Now who's got a light?"

"I've got one," Jack said.

Zander nodded. "And me."

"Those who haven't got one, grab some of the boxes of matches from behind the bar," she said.

She placed Brad's and Bruce's torches on the bar. Bruce turned to Brad. "You ready?"

The engineer nodded. "As I ever will be."

Erin lit a match and ignited one of her torches. Acrid black smoke spiralled towards the ceiling as people stepped forwards to light their own torch from Erin's. Finally, Jack lit his dad's and Brad's. Then he held them out, and they jumped away from the door, grabbed the torches and moved clear.

A series of bangs rattled the cellar door in its frame. It wasn't going to hold much longer. The heat from the torch warmed Jack's cheeks. He looked at his dad; felt more for him at that moment than he ever had.

"Let's get out of here," Bruce said. He hurried towards the front door, slid back the bolts, opened the door, brandished his torch before him, and then stepped outside.

Chapter 41

Bruce gingerly surveyed the street. The harbour lights threw a sheen of illumination across the surface of the water, making it appear almost picturesque. Shazam's ears went up and her hackles rose. She bared her teeth, growled.

"Come here. Heel," Bruce said.

The sound of skittering claws scraping across the ground reached his ears. He turned, looked down the street and saw a number of Fangtooth heading their way. Some ran on all fours, others moved upright. However they moved, they all looked menacing. Lamplight reflected from their teeth, made them appear even longer and sharper.

He counted at least six creatures, but God knew how many others lurked in the shadows.

The torch in his hand flickered, creating misshapen shadows that danced across the walls and the ground.

"Form a circle," Bruce said.

He felt people gather at his side and back. "Right, we need to move as a unit."

"Move where?" Zander asked.

"We need to get out of the village. My car's parked over there and I can get five in with a squeeze. Who else has got a car?"

"And what about everyone else in the village?" Zander asked. "We can't just leave them."

"The police will be here soon."

He noticed the entrance to the cellar door lying open. "What's with the torches?"

Bruce looked across to see the old man that had spoken to him before. Still dressed in his pyjamas, he leaned against his front door and looked out. An old woman peered over his shoulder.

"Albert, what's going on?" she asked.

"That's what I'm trying to find out, Doris. You get inside; let me deal with it."

"You get the fuck inside too," Zander roared. Albert's expression changed, became indignant. "There's something dangerous out here," Zander said.

"Is that you, Zander?" Albert asked. "What's going on?"

"For God's sake, man, get the fuck inside and lock your door."

Albert stepped out into the street. "I don't know what the meani—"

The word caught in his throat as a Fangtooth scurried from around the side of the house. It looked at Bruce and the torches, hissed, turned and saw Albert.

The old man stood frozen to the spot, his jaw hanging open. He babbled something unintelligible, raised his hands in a feeble attempt to ward the creature off, then screamed as the Fangtooth sank its teeth into his hand, severing it at the wrist. A plume of blood jettisoned from the severed limb, spraying the ground with abstract gore.

"Shit," Zander said. He broke free from the others and ran towards the creature, furiously waving his torch.

Bruce sensed the unease in the rest of the group. Next minute, Jim broke free. He dropped his torch and pulled out his knife.

"You don't think I'm gonna let you take all the spoils, Skipper," he said as he danced across the road.

Brad shook his head. "The damn fool." He ran after Jim.

Bruce grimaced. They needed to stick together. Safety in numbers.

He watched as Zander parried and thrust with the torch. Bits of burning cloth and sparks fell to the ground. The Fangtooth scuttled back, chomping Albert's hand as it moved. The firelight appeared to dance in its eyes.

"*Albert*," Doris screamed as she ran out of the house. Blood sprayed over her nightgown as she reached her husband's side. Without hesitating, she started to drag him back towards the house.

By now, the other Fangtooth had reached the group. Bruce and his companions warded them off with the torches.

222

The Fangtooth circled around, snapping at the air with their teeth.

Alerted by the commotion, other people ventured outside. Then the screaming really started.

Bruce saw a small, middle-aged woman open her door to find a Fangtooth on her porch. The creature moved with almost fluid grace, taking a chunk out of her waist with one bite. In a strangely silent manner, the woman grabbed her wound and a length of intestine slopped over the top of her hands to hang down her side. She staggered back, stumbled, and another creature leaped upon her prone body and buried its head in her stomach. Bruce heard its jaw chomping, and he turned away, sickened by the sight.

A young blond-haired boy ran into the street. His mother called him back, but it was too late. A Fangtooth pounced, raking the boy's back with its claws and tearing out ribbons of flesh. The boy screamed and fell to his knees, the creature on his back. The boy's mother, heedless of her own safety, ran out and started hitting the creature with her bare hands. Loud sobs burst from her mouth. Another creature loped across, sank its teeth into the woman's leg, severing her ankle. She collapsed to the ground, still trying to wrestle the creature from her son.

Bruce didn't know how much more he could take. He wanted to shut his eyes to blank out the horror, but he couldn't. He had to stay alert.

Terrified faces peered out of windows. Gunshots rang out as some of the villagers took the initiative.

The creatures were in a feeding frenzy. Blood shone from their heads, dripped from their teeth, between which lay strands of human flesh. They attacked indiscriminately, old or young, male or female, it didn't matter.

Jim jumped onto one of the Fangtooth, riding it like a cowboy. Brad joined in, jabbing at it with his torch. A spine along the Fangtooth's back pierced Jim's leg, but he seemed unconcerned. He stabbed it with his knife, raking the blade across the creature's eyes. The creature roared in pain, which brought a grim smile to Jim's lips.

Bruce's torch burned low and he lit his other one from the embers. It wouldn't last long, and he wondered what he would do when it burnt out. "We need to move faster," Bruce said.

"We can't leave them," Erin cried.

"We'll come back for them in the car, but we've got to move, now." Four Fangtooth blocked their path. One of them chewed on a man's carcass, tearing chunks of meat out. Bruce never would have thought human skin could stretch so far. With each bite, the creature shook its head to snap the tenuous strands connecting the flesh to the body.

The Fangtooth reminded him of a cross between sharks and crocodiles, both true carnivores with a penchant for raw meat.

Two of the creatures moved to intercept the group. The nearest Fangtooth lunged for them. Bruce dodged aside, lost his momentum and almost tripped. Shazam growled and snapped her teeth at the creature's legs, distracting the Fangtooth from her master and allowing him to regain his balance. The Fangtooth dropped down to Shazam's level, cocked its head and lunged for Shazam's throat. Bruce felt his heart stop and his stomach sink. A lump blocked his throat, making breathing difficult.

Shazam jumped out of the way, and the Fangtooth's teeth snapped on empty air. Bruce squeezed out a thankful breath.

Another Fangtooth scuttled across. Shazam ran to intercept it; her agile body and faster legs helping her avoid the creature's attack. Bruce shoved the torch towards the creature's face, causing it to rear back, and allowing him to skip past. Although only twenty feet away, the car may as well have been on another continent.

The Fangtooth feasting on the carcass looked up. Blood dripped from its face, giving it a menacing sheen. It opened its mouth, revealing half-chewed organs. Bruce cringed, his stomach curdling at the sight.

He waved the torch, and remnants of burning cloth fell off to lie smouldering on the ground.

The Fangtooth advanced on all fours, one step at a time. The other Fangtooth stood before the car, as though it knew his destination.

As the bloodied Fangtooth moved in for the kill, it rose up on two legs and opened its mouth to roar. Bruce didn't hesitate as he thrust the burning chair leg down its throat, searing flesh. The creature moved back. Bruce let go of the torch, leaving it jutting from the creature's mouth. Smoke from scorched flesh drifted out of its mouth, making it look even more hellish.

Bruce's companions waved their torches and shouted menacingly to try to drive the creatures away.

The Fangtooth guarding the car twisted its head to look at its wounded companion. With no distinction of where its next meal came from, and seeing an easy target, it moved in and started to bite the wounded creature. With the stick jutting from its throat, the stricken creature couldn't defend itself and it fell to the ground, the other creature moving to stand above it before driving its teeth into the other Fangtooth's body.

"I'm going to make a run for the car," Bruce shouted. He extracted the keys from his pocket; pressed the key fob button to unlock the car, ran across, yanked the door open and tumbled inside. Shazam bounded across and jumped over him to sit in the passenger seat. Bruce shoved the key in the ignition and turned it. The engine started up; it was the most beautiful sound he had ever heard. Grinning to himself, he looked across to his companions, only to see another group of Fangtooth had arrived and cut them off.

Chapter 42

Bruce saw Erin and the group sweeping their flaming torches around to ward off the creatures surrounding them. Zander and his crew had disappeared. Bruce put the car in gear, pressed his foot down on the accelerator and sped along the road. When he drew close to the nearest creature, he switched the headlights on and pressed the pedal to the floor.

The Fangtooth swivelled and stared at the approaching vehicle, but it reacted too slowly. The car struck it with a sickening crunch; sent it bouncing along the road, rolling end over end. Without easing off the accelerator, Bruce headed towards the next Fangtooth. The car stuck it, the front wheel rolling over its body and momentarily leaving the road as it careered over the carcass. Bruce thought he heard something snap.

Shazam barked in his ear.

The group cheered, waving their almost burnt out torches in the air. The remaining Fangtooth scattered, looking for easier prey.

Bruce stopped the car. He glanced in the rear-view mirror, saw movement against the harbour wall and twisted his head to see Duncan. He glared at Bruce, his lips mashed together in a tight grimace. A knife glinted in his hand. Bruce revved the engine, slipped it into reverse, eased off the clutch, spun the car around and steered a course towards Duncan.

Seeing the car heading towards him, Duncan stood up and started to run. The group was busy focusing on the remaining Fangtooth and they failed to spot him until it was too late. He flew into the group, knocking Jack and Sara aside before grabbing Erin. He sliced the knife across the back of her hand, forcing her to drop her weapon, then placed the knife to her throat.

Bruce slammed on the brakes. Erin stared back at him, her face contorted by fear that made him feel physically sick.

226

Bruce jumped out of the car. He heard sirens in the distance; saw flashes of red and blue lights on the track leading down to the village.

"Duncan, it's over. Let her go."

Duncan laughed. "It's never going to be over."

"The police are here. Don't make things worse for yourself than they already are."

"I don't think you're in any position to tell me what to do."

Over ten feet separated them, ten feet that Bruce couldn't cross in time. He caught sight of movement out of the corner of his eye, a flash of white creeping through the shadows beside the harbour wall: Shazam.

"Look, what good is holding Erin hostage going to do?"

"Who said anything about holding a hostage?" Duncan turned, keeping a tight grip on Erin.

Bruce saw a thin line of blood at Erin's throat. Saw the fear in her expression.

Shazam was less than eight feet from Duncan. She crawled along the ground, a canine predator.

"Now it's up to you girl," Bruce whispered. As though sensing what to do, Shazam slinked closer, closing the gap. Once close enough, she jumped up and started barking.

Taken by surprise, Duncan spun around, the knife coming away from Erin's throat enough for her to lever her arm underneath his to hold the knife away. Bruce didn't hesitate. He charged, slamming into Duncan's side, knocking him and Erin over.

Momentum carried Bruce further and he rolled painfully across the ground. Behind him, Shazam grabbed the bottom of Duncan's trousers between her teeth and tugged at the shopkeeper's leg. A low growl emanated from the back of her throat.

Duncan slashed out with the knife. Bruce clambered to his feet, but he was too slow. The blade cut Shazam across the back, opening up a pink stripe in her black and white fur. The dog let go of Duncan's leg and yelped.

Erin scuttled backwards. Duncan jumped up and bent to grab hold of her again.

Incensed, Bruce let out a roar of anguish and charged towards the shopkeeper. Without any heed towards his own safety, he crashed into Duncan, sending him sprawling across the ground.

Duncan landed on his back, arms above his head. The knife skittered away. Bruce jumped astride the prone figure and started hitting him in the face, blow after blow connecting with a sharp smack.

A moment later, Erin grabbed his arms to stop the onslaught.

"That's enough," she said.

Bruce looked down, saw Duncan's bloodied face–his cut lips, broken nose, left eye already swelling–and the anger drained from his body, leaving him feeling strangely empty. He hadn't thought he possessed the capacity for such aggression, but driven to the edge, he had responded with raw anger. He rolled away from Duncan and crawled towards Shazam.

The dog lay on the ground, panting. Her tongue lolled from the corner of her mouth. Bruce stroked her fur and Shazam arched her head to lick his hand.

"Good girl," Bruce said.

He gingerly inspected the vicious wound on her back, and tears stung his eyes.

Shazam rested her head on his leg.

"She'll be okay," Erin said as she crouched beside them. "We'll find some antiseptic cream and bandages. The wound doesn't look too deep."

Bruce looked at her, unable to see clearly through the tears. He nodded.

"You're going to pay for this," Duncan said.

Bruce looked up, saw the shopkeeper on his feet. Blood dripped from his nose, and he spat a thick wad of blood onto the ground. The reclaimed knife winked in his hand.

Bruce felt his heart sink. Screams and shouts echoed throughout the village. Horrible, terrifying sounds originating from the mouths of people being eaten alive; people battling against a horror more terrifying than anything their minds could conjure.

"No, it's you who's going to pay," Jack said.

Duncan turned, raising the knife in his left hand. He blinked his swollen eye, his mouth hanging open in surprise as the smouldering chair leg struck him across the side of his head, sending him sprawling back towards the edge of the harbour.

He teetered on the edge, arms flailing in the air before regaining his balance. He grinned, revealing bloodied teeth. But Jack was too quick for him. He drove the glowing tip of the chair leg into Duncan's stomach, sending him plummeting over the edge.

Bruce heard him land with a loud splash. Next minute he heard the sound of churning water, a scream, and then silence.

Bruce ran across and hugged his son close, ignoring the protests when he squeezed him too tight.

Chapter 43

Zander looked across at the settee where Doris tended to Albert's wound. Blood soaked through the bandages, turning them into a sodden mess. The old man gritted his teeth.

"It hurts," he said.

"Shush," Doris said. "I've phoned an ambulance."

Zander turned and peered through the window. He wondered how an ambulance would ever manage to get through, but decided not to comment.

The old-fashioned living room smelled faintly of mildew. Probably white once, the flowery wallpaper had yellowed with age. Apart from the settee, the room held an armchair, a small brown cabinet and a glass fronted display case filled with a selection of mismatched ornaments, probably gifts from when their children were young. A newspaper sat on the arm of the chair, along with a pipe and an ashtray. Above the coal fireplace, an oval mirror cast a reflection of the room. Orange curtains had been drawn against the night and all it harboured.

"We can't sit here doing nothing," Brad said.

"There's nothing we can do," Zander replied.

Brad waved the knife he had acquisitioned from the kitchen. "I've never run from a fight before."

Zander rolled his eyes. "This isn't a fight. It's a massacre. We're staying here."

Jim scratched his beard. "You may be the skipper at sea, but on land it's every man for himself. There's money out there and I intend to take my share so you won't stop me from going out."

"Jim, listen to yourself. The only things out there are monsters."

Jim harrumphed loudly. "I've seen worse."

Zander rubbed his brow. "No, you haven't. Those things, they're eating people. Look at Albert, he's lost his fucking hand." *And you've lost your fucking mind!*

Jim cast a quick glance in the old man's direction. "He was careless."

"He was attacked."

Doris tutted loudly. "Can you not talk about my Albert as though he's not here."

Jim snorted. "I can look after myself."

"No offense, Jim, but you couldn't look after jack shit."

"I ain't gonna stand here and listen to this. Brad, out of my way." Brad looked at Zander and the skipper nodded. As much as he wanted to, he couldn't hold Jim against his will. They had enough problems without trying to restrain a cantankerous old man hell-bent on getting himself killed.

"If you want to go, the door's there," Zander said.

Without another word, Jim walked towards the door, opened it and stepped outside.

"Jim's right," Brad said as Zander closed the door. "We can't just hole up here waiting for the cavalry to arrive. Those things are going to get inside."

"So what would you suggest we do?"

Brad sucked his gums. "Well, we know they're afraid of fire, so what about making a huge bonfire? Get everyone to gather as much burnable material as they can, and then use it to keep us safe until we can get out of here."

Zander tapped his fingers against the windowsill. He saw the logic in Brad's idea, but there were problems. "We would need one hell of a lot of fuel."

"Then let's find it. Houses are full of furniture. I don't think anyone's going to cry over an old settee if it could help save their life, do you?"

"Then what are we waiting for? Doris, I know this isn't the best time to ask, but have you got something we can use to start the fire? You know, furniture you don't mind losing."

Doris looked up at him, her wrinkled face a mask of sorrow. "You're asking for my furniture … Albert's lying here with his hand bitten off, and you want to take my furniture."

Albert grabbed Doris' hand. "Let them take whatever they want," he said through gritted teeth. "If it's the only chance we've got to live through this nightmare, they can take it all."

Doris looked at her husband and said, "Hush, dear. Don't get upset. The ambulance is on its way." She turned towards Zander. "Take whatever you want, just please, don't let Albert die."

Although he knew it was ridiculous, Zander felt somehow responsible for what had happened, and his head bowed under the immense weight of guilt he carried.

"Brad, help me with this chair."

With Brad on the other side, Zander lifted the brown faded armchair and carried it towards the front door. He quickly checked that the coast was clear, then opened the door and hurried across the road with it. They then ran back to the house and picked up a small cabinet. Doris emptied it before they carried it out, pawing over the assembled contents of letters, cards and accumulated knickknacks collected over a lifetime, which she was probably loathe to throw out.

As they deposited the cabinet next to the armchair, Zander noticed they had attracted the attention of a Fangtooth. The creature raised its head as though sniffing the air, then it started to advance, its claws scraping the ground.

"Quick, light the fucking furniture," Brad said.

Zander crouched down and hacked at the chair with his knife, pulling out stuffing and shredding the fabric. Then he struck a match and held the flame to one of the strands, but the sea breeze extinguished the flame before it had a chance to ignite the furniture.

"Shit," he mumbled, striking another match.

"You'd better be quick," Brad said.

The second match blew out too. Now desperate, Zander stuffed the box of matches into one of the rips in the fabric, half opened the box, withdrew a match, struck it and ignited the box's contents. A yellow flare erupted, the caustic smell from which stung his nostrils.

"Come on, let's get out of here," he said as he stood up and headed back towards the house. He only hoped the fabric would catch light.

When they reached the house, they ran inside and slammed the door shut. Seconds later, the Fangtooth arrived at the step and started clawing at the door.

"Now you've brought one here," Doris screamed.

Brad leaned against the door. "Don't you worry Doris, it'll not get in here."

Zander peeked through the curtains. Across the street, a flicker of flame started to dance on the armchair. Come on, he urged, burn, you son of a bitch.

Despite what fire precaution advertisements showed, the armchair seemed in no rush to burst into flames.

"Doris, have you got any white spirits, anything like that?" Zander asked.

"There might be something under the sink in the kitchen."

"Brad, you just make sure that creature doesn't get inside. I'm going out the back. I'll distract the creature and get the fire going. Then shout the devil down and get everyone to pile the fire high."

Brad nodded. "You be careful, Skipper."

"Always am, my friend. I always am."

Zander dashed through the house, noticing how neat and tidy the place was. Like the living room, the decoration in the kitchen was old-fashioned. Fine china crockery and plates hung on the walls.

He crouched down, opened the sink and sorted through the bottles of cleaning fluid, candles, batteries, and pots and pans until he found some white spirits. Spotting a lighter, he shoved it in his pocket. He also grabbed a bottle of cleaning bleach, which he dropped into a plastic carrier bag with the spirits.

Bag in hand, he opened the back door, stepped outside and closed it behind him.

He found himself in a small backyard bordered by a high wall, in the cracks of which weeds had seeded themselves.

233

The only additions to the yard were a couple of wooden chairs.

Thinking the chairs would make excellent firewood, he picked one up and carried it with him to the rear gate. Although noise rang out around the village, the back alley sounded relatively quiet and he undid the latch on the gate and eased it open. He looked left, then right, and judging the coast clear, he hurried out and headed towards the road.

A sudden noise at his rear caused him to spin around, holding the chair out like a lion tamer. Running all the way behind the houses, the dark alley provided numerous hiding places and he narrowed his eyes to see more clearly. His heart thundered in his chest.

Unable to see anything, he was about to continue when a Fangtooth shuffled out from a side alley. Remnants of flesh and gore hung from its mouth. Its eyes, more accustomed to the dark from its time in the black abyss, fixed upon Zander, and it opened its mouth to display the sharp teeth, a walking mantrap.

"Son-of-a-bitch," Zander said. Keeping one hand on the chair to act as a shield, he hung the bag from one of the arms, removed the bottle of bleach, unscrewed the cap and pointed it towards the Fangtooth.

When it came close enough, he sprayed the solution at the creature's eyes, causing it to cry out in anguish. Unable to quell the pain, the Fangtooth slashed out blindly, its claws scraping across the wall at Zander's side.

Zander felt a small sense of satisfaction seeing the creature in torment, and he cracked the chair across its head, shattering the wood and leaving him holding two wooden legs. The creature slumped to the ground, unmoving.

The white spirits had fallen out of the bag in the melee, and he dropped one of the chair legs and bent to pick the bottle up when the creature slashed out, catching him unaware. Its claw raked through his ankle and Zander jumped in surprise and fell onto his bottom. The Fangtooth raked out again, slicing through the plastic bottle in Zander's hand and spraying the white spirits across his chest. The pungent, sweet smell of the liquid filled his nose.

Angry, Zander dropped the bottle, lifted the wooden leg and slammed the jagged end through the Fangtooth's eye. Liquid spurted around the sides of the wood and the creature writhed in torment. Zander twisted the stake in further, relishing in the creature's death.

Eventually the creature stopped moving and Zander sat back, panting with exhaustion. Bursts of white-hot pain radiated from his ankle and he winced. He wiped his gore and blood-covered hands on his jeans. The spilt bottle of spirits lay on the ground. Zander picked it up and staggered to his feet. He looked at the spoonful of liquid left in the bottom of the container and his spirits flagged. There was more on his clothes than in the bottle, and realizing the best idea would be to take his sweater off and use it to ignite the furniture, he tugged it over his head and stuffed it under his arm.

When he reached the end of the alley, he peeked around the corner, looked left, then right. The Fangtooth still clawed at the entrance to Doris and Albert's house, and large splinters of wood hung off the door. A couple of other Fangtooth scuttled around by the harbour where Bruce and the others battled to keep them away. More creatures were visible in the distance, along with small groups of people who had decided to fight. A few of them had guns, the reports from which echoed through the night. Ravaged bodies lay in the street, blood running along the gutter as though a gory shower had fallen upon the village.

The smoking remains of his boat jutted up from the harbour. The sight of it filled his heart with sadness. How could he ever make recompense for what he had done? Innocent men had lost their lives through his stupidity.

"So you decided to join me."

Zander turned at the sound of Jim's voice to see him crouched over a creature's carcass. He had gutted it and pulled its innards out, leaving them in a steaming pile beside the corpse.

The sight made Zander wince. "Jim, we've got a plan. We're going to build a bonfire big enough to shelter around, but we need to gather anything that will burn."

Jim barked a short, sharp laugh. "You call that a plan?" He buried his hands in the creature's innards and held them up. "What do you think, fry them with a little oil, add a few herbs. People would love it."

Zander couldn't believe what he was hearing. "Get a grip, you stupid old fool."

Jim pursed his lips, wrinkled his brow and glared at Zander. "You just want it all for yourself. You've always been a greedy bastard."

"Think whatever you like, but I don't want anything. You can't sell these things. They've goddamn eaten people; you really think someone would pay to buy one."

"'Course they would. Eat or be eaten, that could be the slogan. Catchy, ain't it?" He mouthed the words silently, as though trying them on for size.

Zander had heard enough. He checked that the coast was clear, then hobbled across the road towards the armchair. Once he reached it, he crouched down. Despite having lit the whole box of matches, the material had failed to burn and only residual smoke drifted out from a blackened patch. He wondered whether the material was flameproof.

He grabbed the sweater from under his arm and threw it onto the chair. Then he pulled the lighter out of his pocket and ignited it when Jim shouted, "Look out, Skipper."

Zander whirled around just in time to see a Fangtooth scampering towards him. Too late to move out of the way, he stumbled onto the armchair. He landed precariously, knocking the hand with the lighter underneath his other arm. The flame touched his spirit soaked bare arm and the hairs caught light like lamp bulb coils. The sudden heat was incredible. Flames roared along Zander's arm until reaching the T-shirt. He slapped at the flames, struggled to pull the burning item of clothing off, but it was no good. The flesh on his fingers blistered as he struggled to get a grip. He opened his mouth and screamed. The flames ignited the hair

236

on his head, turning him into a human torch. The heat seared his eyes, and one of his eyeballs actually felt as though it popped. For a moment, he thought that he could smell his own flesh cooking in the heat.

After a moment, Zander stopped struggling and settled back in the armchair.

He looked through his one good eye; saw Jim stabbing the beast that had charged towards him. Beyond Jim he saw the villagers, people he had known all his life. People he had grown up with. People he knew would blame him for the deaths of their loved ones on board *Storm Bringer*. He glanced at the furniture around him. Knew that for it to catch light it needed a source of flame.

Despite the torturous heat, he felt oddly at peace. He closed his eye as best he could and gritted his teeth against the searing pain.

It would never bring his crew back, but he hoped that his sacrifice would be his salvation. That through his death, others may live.

Chapter 44

Bruce stared across the road, shocked to see Zander engulfed by flames. He considered running across to help him, but he could tell that he was too far gone, his skin already charring. Strangely Zander didn't struggle; actually seemed to accept his fate.

He didn't understand what an armchair and a small cabinet were doing in the road in the first place, never mind what Zander was doing with them. The flames from Zander's body ignited the armchair, and a yellow and orange conflagration danced above the furniture. Behind the fire, Bruce could see Jim battling with a Fangtooth.

"Jesus Christ. Did you see that?" Bruce said.

Erin nodded, her face pale. "Here comes another Fangtooth," she said, pointing her knife in the creature's direction.

"There are too many of them," Jack said.

Bruce gulped. He didn't know how much longer they could hold out. He glanced at the car, contemplated running towards it, then looked back at Zander and the burning furniture.

He put a hand to his forehead as the realisation struck. "Jesus. He's using the furniture as a shield to keep the creatures away. Come on, we've got to head towards the fire."

Bruce bent down and carefully lifted Shazam. The dog's head lolled over his arm and he carried her across the road. The heat from the flames washed over Bruce as he drew near and he went as close as he could. The heat prickled his face; made the hairs on his arms tingle as he laid Shazam as close as he dared. The rest of the group joined him, standing around the fire. It was hard to look at Zander. The flesh on his body had blistered and popped, and his eyeballs had literally exploded in their sockets. The smell of burning flesh permeated the air. The aroma made Bruce gag.

The sound of breaking glass rang out. "Here, put this on the fire."

Bruce looked up to see Brad hanging out of the bedroom window of the house across the road. Next minute he disappeared and when he returned, he squeezed a mattress through the gap, letting it fall to the road. Next he threw out clothes and books.

"Come on, help me carry them," Bruce said.

He ran across the road, and Jack helped him carry the mattress back to the fire. They tossed it into the flames, dislodging Zander's now blackened corpse and causing the burnt skin to flake from his body. Sparks flew into the air, twinkling like stars as they sailed into the night sky.

The other teenagers gathered the clothes and books and threw them into the fire. Bruce couldn't help but be reminded of Fahrenheit 451 as he watched the books burn.

Windows and doors started to open along the seafront and terrified people peeked out.

"The fire keeps them away," Bruce shouted as he threw a pair of trousers into the inferno. "You'll be safe here. Gather anything you can that will burn, and bring it with you."

Moments later, items started dropping from windows. More books. Newspapers. Bookcases. Cushions. Plastic bowls. Anything that would burn poured down in a rain of bric-a-brac.

People started running from their houses, trailing clothes and blankets in their mad dash to reach the safety of the fire.

A number of Fangtooth hovered on the periphery, kept back by the flames. They scurried around, snapping at each other in their fury and hunger.

As the fire grew bigger, Bruce moved Shazam further from the heat. The dog's chest rose and fell at a steady pace.

Flashing lights appeared at the end of the road, and Bruce looked up to see a police car arrive. The man and woman in the car stared at the scene with their mouths open, as though unable to believe their eyes.

During the night, they raided every house, threw every available piece of furniture onto the bonfire, and then sat out the night in a huddle, sitting close to the flames. The searing heat turned people's skin a rosy red colour. Those who were armed took pot-shots at any creatures that braved the flames and came too close.

Soon after sun up, the first army convoy arrived, followed by a fleet of ambulances. Bruce watched the soldiers disperse throughout the village, and the sound of automatic gunfire rang out.

Erin had her head on Bruce's lap, where she had lain for most of the night. He stroked her hair and stared at the faces of those huddled around the fire. Despite the rosy skin, their faces reflected the horror they had endured. Their haunted eyes gave them a vacant, lost expression. Even though they hadn't seen a Fangtooth for a while, none of them seemed in any hurry to leave the protective circle of the fire.

Helicopters buzzed overhead, and the odd jet plane screamed across the sky.

"I don't suppose the army ever imagined their enemy would originate from the sea," Erin said as she turned to face Bruce.

"I don't think I did either."

"Dad, me and Jen are going to check if her parents are okay," Jack said. "She's looked around the fire for them, but they aren't here."

"Well, you're not going on your own. I'll come with you."

"And me," Erin said.

Jen nodded. "I'm sorry about my gran. If I had known …" She wiped tears from her eyes.

Bruce put his hand on her shoulder. "You're not responsible for what she did."

"Yeah, but—"

"There are no buts. Right, come on, we'll take the car." Bruce crouched down and picked up Shazam. He carried the dog to the car and placed her on the backseat between Jack and Jen. Then he jumped in the driving seat, Erin beside

240

him. He glanced at the lucky horseshoe pendant hanging from the rear-view mirror and stroked it between his fingers before starting the engine and driving through the streets.

Houses along the way bore the brunt of the carnage, and with the gruesome bodies littering the road, the once quaint seaside village now resembled a war torn domain from the bowels of hell.

Trigger-happy soldiers fired at any straggling Fangtooth. "Do you think that will be the end of it?" Bruce asked Erin.

"I would like to think so, but the sea's a big place. Who knows how many of them are out there."

A horn sounded out at sea, and Bruce turned to see a destroyer sailing past the harbour.

Jen gave directions from the backseat, and when they reached her house, the door stood ajar.

"I'd better go first," Bruce said as he exited the vehicle. He walked up to the door and carefully pushed it open, shocked to see someone he assumed was Jen's dad hanging from a noose tied to the stair banister. Her mother lay slumped at the foot of the stairs, her neck broken.

He tried to close the door on the scene, but Jen had already seen. She screamed and ran into the house where she collapsed onto the ground, her head in her hands. Jack ran in and tried to comfort her.

Bruce recalled something Lillian had said, a hint that her parents already knew about the sacrifices. He didn't know whether that was true, would probably never know. They might have taken their own lives rather than face the Fangtooth. It certainly seemed an easier option than being eaten alive.

"Jen, you can't stay here," Bruce said. "Jack, come on, bring her out."

Jack looked up at his dad and nodded. "Jen. Jen, come on. There's nothing you can do for them. We've got to go."

"I can't just leave them here like this," she said between sniffles.

Jack looked back at his dad, his expression torn between confusion and concern.

241

"Jack, give me a hand," Bruce said as he entered the hallway.

With his son's help, he cut Jen's dad down, then they carried the two bodies into the living room where they laid them down and covered them with blankets.

"That's all we can do for now," Bruce said.

"Thank you," Jen sobbed.

Bruce nodded. "We'd better go now. It's not safe here."

Once back in the car, they made their way back towards the harbour. Once they reached the seafront, Bruce spotted Brad and Jim.

Bruce lowered the window. "Hey," he called. Brad waved and ran across the road.

"Glad to see you both made it," Bruce said.

Brad looked back at Jim. "That remains to be seen. This has affected him badly."

"How about you?"

"I'll manage. Probably have to get a job with my brother now that the boat's wrecked, but at least I came through in one piece, which is more than can be said for some people." He indicated the couple across the road stepping into an ambulance, who Bruce recognised as Albert and Doris.

"Did you see what happened to Zander?" Bruce asked.

Brad nodded. "However you look at it, the Skipper went down with his boat." He shook his head and sighed. "So what are you going to do now?"

Bruce glanced at Jen in the rear-view mirror and then looked at Erin.

"We're getting the hell out of here. If you and Jen want to come, you're welcome."

Erin stared out to sea, her expression unreadable. "I love the sea," she said. "But then I never had anything else in my life worth a damn." She kissed him on the cheek. "Wherever you go, I'll come too."

Bruce grinned and squeezed her hand. "Jen, what about you?"

She wiped tears from her eyes and coughed to clear her throat. "There's nothing left here for me now."

"Jack, that okay with you?"

Jack looked at Jen and Erin and smiled. "Wouldn't have it any other way."

Bruce turned. "You take care, Brad."

Brad nodded. "You too."

Bruce looked across at the fire where Rocky stood with his arm around Sara. He waved. Bruce and Jack waved back.

"Is there anything anyone wants to take?" Bruce asked.

"I just want to get away," Jen said.

Bruce knew how she felt. He put the car in gear and made to drive off when Jack said, "Hold on. There's something I've got to do."

Bruce looked in the rear-view mirror and frowned. Without offering any explanation, Jack jumped out of the car and ran across to the bar. He reappeared a few minutes later with Graham's cat in his arms.

"Don't know what Shazam will think, but I couldn't leave it behind," he said when he reached the car.

Bruce smiled. "Come on, get in."

Jack clambered in and Shazam sniffed at the cat, then licked it on the head. The cat ran its paw over where the dog had licked as though disgusted.

Bruce laughed to himself. They had arrived in the village as a widowed father, an errant teenager and a dog. Now as he threaded his way along the street, careful to avoid the bodies, they were a family.

Outside the village, Bruce stopped the car and turned to stare at the sea. He watched the destroyer sail towards the horizon, and heard the muffled thump of the depth charges she cast into the ocean.

The wedding ring on his finger glinted in the pale morning light. Bruce twisted it off to reveal a white band on his finger that would fade in time. He put the ring in his pocket.

Erin put her hand on top of his and squeezed

He noticed his son staring at him in the rear-view mirror. "Forget Tenerife, remember Mulberry," Jack said.

Bruce stared at the sea–a shroud for the denizens of the deep; then he focused on the road ahead and started driving. "Let's go home."

About the author:

Shaun Jeffrey was brought up in a house in a cemetery, so it was only natural for his prose to stray towards the dark side when he started writing. He has had five novels published, 'The Kult', 'Killers', 'Deadfall', 'Fangtooth' and 'Evilution', and two collections of short stories, 'Voyeurs of Death' and 'The Mutilation Machination'. Among his other writing credits are short stories published in Cemetery Dance, Surreal Magazine, Dark Discoveries and Shadowed Realms. The Kult was filmed by Gharial Productions.

Visit the author's site at: http://www.shaunjeffrey.com

Made in the USA
Lexington, KY
15 December 2014